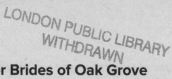
## Mail-Order Brides of Oak Grove

*From runaways to brides!*

When twins Mary and Maggie McCary
are caught selling their family tonic without a permit,
they're forced to agree to become mail-order brides
to stay out of jail! Taking the train to Oak Grove, the
pair are soon separated—but both their adventures
lead to unexpected romance...
and the promise of wedding bells!

Don't miss this delightfully warm and funny duet—
two stories in one volume—from

**Lauri Robinson** and **Kathryn Albright**

Read Mary's story in

*Surprise Bride for the Cowboy*

by Lauri Robinson

and

Maggie's story in

*Taming the Runaway Bride*

by Kathryn Albright

D1405830

A lover of fairy tales and cowboy boots, **Lauri Robinson** can't imagine a better profession than penning happily-ever-after stories about men—and women—who pull on a pair of boots before riding off into the sunset...or kick them off for other reasons. Lauri and her husband raised three sons in their rural Minnesota home, and are now getting their just rewards by spoiling their grandchildren. Visit her at laurirobinson.blogspot.com, Facebook.com/lauri.robinson1 or Twitter.com/laurir.

**Kathryn Albright** writes American-set historical romance for Harlequin. From her first breath she has had a passion for stories that celebrate the goodness in people. She combines her love of history and her love of stories to write novels of inspiration, endurance and hope. Visit her at kathrynalbright.com and on Facebook.

# Mail-Order Brides of Oak Grove

## LAURI ROBINSON
## KATHRYN ALBRIGHT

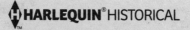

ISBN-13: 978-0-373-29931-7

Mail-Order Brides of Oak Grove

Copyright © 2017 by Harlequin Books S.A.

The publisher acknowledges the copyright holders of the individual works as follows:

Surprise Bride for the Cowboy
Copyright © 2017 by Lauri Robinson

Taming the Runaway Bride
Copyright © 2017 by Kathryn Leigh Albright

Recycling programs for this product may not exist in your area.

Printed in U.S.A.

www.Harlequin.com

# CONTENTS

# Surprise Bride for the Cowboy

**LAURI ROBINSON**

Evelyn Putnam,
thank you for the use of your son's name.
Steve's a great guy, and you have a lot to be proud of!

## Prologue

"We won't go." Mary McCary wrapped her fingers around the bars separating her from Sheriff Willard Freiday and his spit-polished shiny badge. "We simply refuse."

"You can't refuse," he replied.

She squeezed the bars a bit harder as his grin grew as smug as a cat lying in the sun. "Yes, we can. You can't make us become mail-order brides."

He shrugged. "No, I can't, but I do have orders from Mayor Winsted that you two either agree to go to Kansas as mail-order brides or the town will press charges against you."

Mary kept the growl that rumbled in her throat as quiet as possible. She'd figured all the bottles of tonic that Mayor Winsted's wife kept buying would eventually get them in trouble, but not so much they'd be jailed, or exiled. Still, that had happened before. Da had gotten them kicked out of towns all across Ohio and a good portion of Pennsylvania. Or they'd left before they could get kicked out. "We didn't do anything illegal," she insisted.

"You are behind these bars because you don't have a permit to sell those bottles of snake oil your father made.

I'd have thought that stuff was all gone by now. He's been dead going on a year."

Disrespecting her kin was a sure way to get her riled up, but the good sheriff had already done that. "Our father died six month ago, Sheriff, and if anyone is pressing charges, it should be us. That stagecoach ran Da over in broad daylight."

"Your father was drunk off his own concoction and stumbled in the stage's path. There was nothing the driver could do. The judge already told you that."

Her temper made the top of her head burn. "It's a medicinal tonic. McCary's Finest Recipe Tonic, and of course the judge says there was nothing anyone could do. He's the stage driver's brother. Furthermore, I already showed you Da's permit. You have it."

"Which doesn't have your names on it, does it?"

"This town wouldn't give us a permit even if we asked," Maggie piped in.

"My sister is right," Mary pointed out. "This town has never been overly friendly to any of us McCarys."

The sheriff grinned. "All the more reason you should appreciate the efforts the mayor is taking. Oak Grove is a growing community in Kansas and needs women to marry some of the already prosperous men settling in that area."

"Kansas?" Maggie asked. "Where's Kansas?"

"West," Mary answered her twin. Questioning if she was correct, she turned to the sheriff. "It's west of here, right?"

"Yes, Kansas is west of here, and you aren't the only women making the trip. There will be a dozen young ladies from this area. A Pullman car has been reserved for your trip. You'll have beds to sleep in, plenty to eat, and of course you'll be able to explore the sights of many fine cities along the way while the train makes its regular stops."

"You can sweet-talk us all you want, Sheriff," Maggie

said. "My sister and I aren't leaving. We are staying right here. Permit or not."

Mary laid a hand on Maggie's shoulder. Life had never been easy, but they'd gotten used to living in a house this past year. Granted the house was owned by the city and every month the sheriff stopped by to collect the rent, which wasn't always easy to come by. Da had sold enough tonic to cover the bills, but since his death, she and Maggie had had to supplement their income by placing friendly bets they could pick the right card out of the deck or find the rock under the correct cup. It wasn't too hard to collect a few dollars from local men. The McCary sisters' shiny black hair and sky-blue eyes was the reason. They'd inherited that from their mother. At least that was what Da always said. However, those dollars were getting harder to come by considering the sheriff didn't approve of the betting games any more than he did the selling of their tonic. Maybe it was time they moved on.

"I'm not becoming a mail-order bride," Maggie said. "Marrying a man I don't know and then living with him the rest of my life. I'm only nineteen. That could be a long time."

Being twins, they could practically read each other's minds, and that was what Mary took into consideration right now. The town owned the house they rented, and could evict them as easily as they'd been arrested. They'd had to sell their wagon to pay Da's funeral bills, so an eviction would leave them completely homeless.

Lifting a brow, she looked directly into Maggie's eyes. "Marriage is only until death do we part," Mary said. There were plenty of towns between Ohio and Kansas where they could part from the others, and a fresh start might be exactly what they needed.

A smile formed on Maggie's face. Mary's too.

The sheriff cleared his throat, but the way his gaze shot between her and Maggie was enough to make Mary want to giggle.

"You are right, dear sister," Maggie said. "Until death do *we* part."

"You girls—"

"We'll accept your offer, Sheriff," Mary interrupted. "When does the train leave?"

# Chapter One

*Oak Grove, Kansas.*

Steve Putnam flipped the reins of his big gray gelding over the hitching post outside of the Wet Your Whistle Saloon and stepped up on the boardwalk in order to get out of the cloud of dust being swirled up along the main street of town. A parade of wagons, buggies and people on horseback and afoot was the cause. All headed in one direction. The train station. The last place you'd find him today. In his opinion, the entire town had gone loco over this mail-order bride scheme.

Turning about, he headed toward the batwing doors of the saloon. The *"Closed"* sign didn't stop him from pushing the doors apart and letting them swing shut behind him.

The sight of Chris and Danny Sanders dressed in their Sunday best had Steve pushing the brim of his hat up in order to take a second look at the cousins walking toward him.

"Sorry, Steve, we're closed," Danny said. "Didn't you see the sign?"

"Why?" Steve asked, not bothering to say he'd seen the sign.

"The women are arriving today," Chris answered.

Taken aback, Steve shook his head. "You two bought into this hare-brained idea?" The cousins had opened the saloon in Oak Grove with the insurance money they'd received after the one they'd owned in Dodge City had burned down. Their business seemed to be flourishing and he couldn't believe either Chris or Danny was looking for a mail-order bride.

Pointing a thumb at his much taller cousin, Danny said, "Chris here contributed heavily to the cause."

"Why?" Steve directed his question toward Chris.

The cousins didn't look much alike, not even with their blond hair oiled smooth against their heads and matching black suits complete with red vests and gold watch chains hanging from their pockets. They didn't act much alike, either. Danny was shorter and always smiling and joking, while Chris was tall, thin and far more serious, especially when it came to money, and that was what Steve couldn't believe. That Chris would have made a contribution to the Oak Grove Betterment Committee that had been raising money the past year *to bring suitable women of marrying age to their fine community.* He'd seen so many fliers and newspapers articles about the far-fetched idea he knew the sales pitch word for word.

"For the betterment of the community of course," Chris answered.

Steve gave him a glare that said he knew the man was lying.

"Fine," Chris said. "If there's anyone we can trust with the truth, it's you. Danny and I aren't looking for wives, and we don't believe every woman on that train will make a suitable one, either."

Danny's laughter left a sly grin on his face. "But they

just might want to work in a high-end establishment such as the Whistle."

"You're hoping to get a couple of saloon gals out of the deal?" That was as hard to believe as the idea of getting a wife through this scheme.

"Why not?" Danny asked. "Working here would be far better than marrying a few of those men offering up their hands. Can you imagine any woman wanting to take up residence with Wayne Stevens and that creature he calls a dog? It's dang near as big as your horse and I hear tell it sleeps in his bed every night."

Steve had heard the same, and Wayne's dog was big enough to saddle. Still he shook his head. "I just didn't expect you two to participate in this idea."

Chris withdrew his watch and clicked open the cover to check the time. As he poked it back in his pocket, he asked, "If you aren't here to meet the train, why are you in town in the middle of the day?"

"Rex buried an ax in his knee chopping kindling last night," Steve answered. "Doc was out and stitched him up, but said he'd be laid up for at least three weeks. I came to see if I could hire Helen Oswoski to cook for my boys for a month or so. With it being roundup time, I don't have a man to spare."

Danny let out a whistle. "Rex already has a hunk of wood for one leg."

Everyone knew Rex Walton had lost a leg in the war, and Steve was worried the man would end up without both legs if he didn't follow the doctor's orders. "Unfortunately, it was the other leg he buried the ax in."

"Sorry to tell you, but Helen Oswoski got married last month," Chris said. "To Ole Hanson. She's helping him run his stage stop between here and Dodge."

"I hadn't heard that," Steve admitted. He'd made a mental list of people he could hire to cook for his hands, and Helen, being a widow, had been the only viable choice.

"I sure can't think of anyone who might be able to help you out," Danny said. "Maybe you can pick one of the brides off the train."

Frustration made Steve's neck muscles burn. "I don't need a bride, I need a cook."

"Suppose you could ride down to Dodge, might find some options there," Chris suggested.

"I might have to," Steve admitted. "Don't have that kind of time, but might have to make it. Walter cooked breakfast for everyone and the entire lot said they'd quit if that happened again tonight."

Chris slapped Steve's shoulder as the train whistle sounded. "Maybe there're some other newcomers getting off the train in need of work. Won't hurt to check."

The odds were slim, but men working their way west and looking to earn a few dollars had been known to get off the train now and again. For the time it would take, it sure as heck was a better choice than the hundred-mile ride to Dodge City, which could prove just as futile. This time of year, most everyone who wanted to be working had a job.

Steve followed the cousins out of the saloon and up the boardwalk to the train station, which was already packed with people. Of course Josiah Melbourne was in the middle of the crowd, up on a platform that had been decorated with ribbons for the occasion and acting like his pompous self. This entire bride idea had been his. Short and pudgy, he probably knew this might be his only hope of ever acquiring a wife.

As far as Steve was concerned, the mayor could have every bride the town had ordered. He'd seen what this county did to women, and men. There hadn't been a town here fifteen years ago when his family had left Georgia shortly after the war. He hadn't known what his father had promised his mother, but he remembered all the things he'd dreamed about while walking alongside the wagon for months on end. A house far bigger than the one that had been burned down by Union soldiers, a barn full of horses, rivers full of fish to catch and woods full of deer to hunt—things ten-year-old boys dream about.

Their arrival to what everyone now knew as the Circle P Ranch, his ranch, hadn't been what any of them had expected.

Used to growing cotton and tobacco in the fertile soil of Georgia, his father had taken one look at the treeless, dried-up ground and concluded whatever might grow here would never feed a family. But, it would feed critters, so he'd invested the last bits of money they'd had in cattle. His father's investment had paid off—selling cattle to the army posts and later the railroad as tracks were laid west proved lucrative—but it hadn't happened fast enough for his mother.

She hadn't lasted two years out here. Losing an infant son to pneumonia the first winter and a three-year-old daughter to rattlesnake bite the next summer had taken its toll on her. The morning after they'd buried his sister, his mother was gone. His father had found her less than twenty miles away, but it had been too late. A band of Kansa Indians had gotten to her first.

His mother was buried next to his sister and baby brother, and to his father, who after losing his wife had slowly started to die, blaming her death on himself. He'd watched his father drink himself to death for five years. The day his father died, Steve had determined he'd never get married. He'd been seventeen, and in the past eight years he'd never once questioned that vow.

Partly because he hadn't had time to. He'd been too busy

building the Circle P Ranch to one of the largest in the state. He now had a house bigger than the one he'd been born in down in Georgia, a barn full of horses, and more cattle than he could count in a day. What he didn't have was a cook for the men who worked for him. The men who made it possible for him to be the rancher he was today. The men who counted on him for three squares a day.

Ignoring how the mayor was welcoming the crowd and congratulating everyone on the *"betterment of the community,"* Steve worked his way to the front of the crowd, where he could watch the passengers depart and hopefully snag a man who knew the difference between salt and sugar to work for him for a few months.

The door of the passenger car had yet to open, and the windows were too full of soot to see through, but he kept his eyes peeled for a suitable candidate to step off the short metal stairs.

"You here to get wife, no?"

Without turning his head, Steve glanced to his right and then upwards. He was close to six feet tall, but Brett Blackwell, the local blacksmith and owner of the feed store, towered over him. With arms thicker than most men's thighs and an equally thick Swedish accent with touches of the Midwest in it, the blacksmith looked down at him.

"You, Steve Putnam, you here for wife?"

"No," Steve answered. "I'm here for a cook."

"Ya, me, too," Brett answered. "My ma was da best cook. She cooked for all da men." The man inhaled through his nose so loudly it drowned out the mayor's speech. "I still smell her bread. So good. I want a wife like that. Good cook."

"Good luck with that, Brett," Steve said. "I hope you find one. I'm not here for a wife. Just a cook. Rex got hurt. I need someone to fill in for him. I'm hoping they're on this train."

"Ya. Dr. Graham told me. Poor little man, Rex." For a man who could throw hundred-pound feed sacks in a wagon one in each hand, the blacksmith was a sensitive man. "You tell Brett what I can do."

"Haul a cook out to my place," Steve muttered while taking note of how Brett had nodded toward Nelson Graham standing on his other side. Frowning, Steve gave his head a quick, clearing shake. He hadn't expected the doctor to be looking for a wife, either. Had every man in town gone loco? If they all thought a woman was going to make their lives easier, they needed a new line of thinking. While peering around Brett, Steve caught sight of the man standing next to the doctor and clamped his jaw tight.

"Excuse me, Brett," Steve said, while squeezing past the man. After nodding to Dr. Graham, Steve planted himself next to the cowboy who should be rounding up spring calves. "What the hell are you doing here?"

The look in Jess Rader's eyes said he would have run but was squeezed in too tight to move. "I told you this morning I was coming to town, Boss."

"No, you didn't."

"I didn't?"

"No."

"Well, I meant to." Jess glanced left then right, and then must have concluded he still didn't have an escape route. "I ponied up five bucks, Boss. I gotta be here for one of the gals to pick me or I lose my money."

"You lose your money either way," Steve pointed out. "And if you want one of those gals to pick you, you should have taken a bath."

"It ain't the first of the month yet," Jess said. "Besides, with Rex hurt, there's no use taking a bath. Ain't no one to wash my clothes while I'm washing my skin."

Steve huffed out a breath. Besides being able to cook, his new hired hand would need to know how to wash clothes.

"What are you doing here?" Jess asked. "I thought you didn't like this idea of brides."

"I don't," Steve said. "I'm here to hire a cook."

"Good," Jess said. "Did you know Walter put salt instead of sugar in the flapjacks this morning? They were awful."

"Yes, I know. I tasted one." And had tasted the eggs Walter had sprinkled with sugar. The bacon had been burned black, and the coffee had been too full of grounds to swallow.

"Aw, what? Really?" Jess stomped a foot. "If that don't beat all."

Steve glanced around as moans and groans filled the air from the men standing around him. "What?" he asked Jess.

"Didn't you just hear that?"

"What?" Steve repeated.

"Someone just said there are only five. Five women instead of twelve." Jess pointed up and down the men standing on either side of them. "Look at all these fellers; that ain't good odds."

Steve glanced up and down the row. Besides the blacksmith, the doctor, Jess and the saloon-owning cousins, the banker, the gunsmith, a couple of farmers, a couple of ranchers, as well as the hotel owner and few others he didn't know were lined up next to the platform.

"All these men paid up front?" he asked Jess.

"You had to in order to be in the group the gals have to choose from."

Lester Higgums started pounding on his drum, a signal that the train door would soon open, and suddenly Steve didn't want to be in the front row. He didn't want it assumed in any way he was here for one of the girls to pick from. In fact, the idea of finding a cook amongst all this hullabaloo was as far-fetched as the whole bride project.

Other instruments joined Lester's drums; an entire band was playing. The pomp and circumstance the town was putting on for this was laughable. Or disgusting. Either way, he wasn't impressed, and shouldered his way through the crowd.

Shouts and cheers said the conductor must be opening the door, and without a backwards glance, he headed toward the Wet Your Whistle to collect his horse.

Once mounted, he muttered a curse at how the road heading west out of town was blocked by wagons and buggies. He urged his horse eastward in order to cross the tracks behind the train and then he'd head north, back to his ranch, empty-handed.

## Chapter Two

Mary had never been so frazzled. Her hair had never been so dirty or her clothes so dust-covered. And she'd never been so mad at her sister in her life. They were twins. They were supposed to think alike. They were supposed to have gotten off this stupid train miles ago. Days ago.

"We have to go," Mary hissed. "Now. It's our last chance."

"I want a bath," Maggie said. "I want a decent meal. The girls say that the town is supposed to have hotel rooms for us and everything."

"We're not staying in this dusty cow town," Mary insisted yet again.

"Well I want to enjoy it while I can," Maggie spouted back. "Nothing is wrong with a little pampering."

"Pampering!" For being twins there were times they were as different as night and day. "We need to find jobs and I need to find a place to make more tonic."

Maggie raised her chin as if she was some high and mighty princess. "The tonic needs another week before it's ready to bottle. What does it matter whether we are comfortable at the hotel?"

"It matters. We've got to show them right from the start

we aren't going to marry anyone and they can't force us." Mary had to draw a breath to calm her ire. "You know how it is…how it's always been with our business. We need to be ready to leave town if necessary. That's why you need to come with me. We have to stay together."

"We won't make it. That conductor has eyes like an eagle. Besides, I heard the sheriff talk to him in Bridgeport. They won't give us a permit to sell it here anymore than they would in Ohio."

"Then we will just have to be more careful. Anyone who tries the tonic is happy enough with the results. It will only be for a few weeks. By the time the authorities find anything out, we will be gone."

"Where will we go after this town?"

"I don't know," Mary admitted. "Maybe Denver. Somewhere big enough to make a good profit. Somewhere far enough west that selling permits aren't a problem."

"We can talk about it at the hotel," Maggie said before she crossed her arms and spun around.

Mary may have been angry before, now she was furious. Her entire being shook. Ever since they'd boarded the train Maggie had been too busy making friends to care about anything else. Well, maybe it was time for her to discover friends weren't the same as sisters. It would be a rude awakening for her, but if that was what it took, so be it.

As the wheels screeched to a halt and the others, including Maggie, rushed to stare out the windows, where the music played and people shouted, Mary slid into the small latrine. Her anger continued to fester. If Maggie had kept quiet, they could have snuck out without catching the conductor's attention more than once.

Cracking the latrine door open, Mary peered out, waiting for the chance she wouldn't let slip by.

As a portly man stepped aboard, commanding everyone's attention, Mary slipped out of the latrine and out the door before anyone noticed. Taking a deep breath, which caught in her throat because the air was full of smoke from the puffing smoke stack, she grabbed the railing and hoisted herself over the edge and then down the ground. Everyone else was on the other side of the train, and that was just fine with her. She traveled past another car holding animals of some sorts, and then to the one carrying their baggage. It wasn't as if they'd brought a lot with them from Ohio—the sheriff had limited them to a bag and trunk each.

"Pampering," she muttered. "Fairy dust." Mary slid the door open and easily spotted her and Maggie's things. The ruckus on the other side of the train made it so she didn't need to be too quiet, therefore she wasn't. "She's been pampered most of her life, that's what the problem is," Mary muttered as she climbed into the car. Tossing aside various bags and bundles, she collected her tapestry bag and tossed it out the open doorway and then pushed aside other trunks until she could grasp both of the handles on the sides of hers.

They had packed carefully back in Ohio, choosing what they would bring, and she regretted that now. Her tapestry bag only held an additional change of clothing and a few other basic necessities. Everything else was in Maggie's trunk—the one she'd leave behind after she slipped a note inside it for her sister. Her trunk held what she needed to make some money. Fast money that would get her out of town. It held several full bottles, but more important, a brewing batch of McCary's Finest Recipe Tonic. All she required now was a place it could brew for a bit longer and then she could bottle it up.

The trunk was heavy, and the only way to maneuver it to the opening of the rail car was to walk backwards, pulling it across the rough floor. As she gave the trunk a solid tug with each step, Mary's irritation at Maggie continued. Talking about finding a job had been useless. Maggie hadn't worked a day in her life. She'd always had something more important to do than washing or cooking or—

Her step had found nothing but air.

Startled, she let go of the trunk handle and grabbed for it again, but it was too late.

Her fall ended almost as quickly as it started, but her moment of gratitude disappeared almost as soon as it started. She had fallen out of the train car, but hadn't landed on the ground. It had been years since she'd sat on Da's lap, but would never forget what it felt like.

Scrambling and with her heart racing, she tried to get off whoever's lap she was on.

"Hold still."

The unfamiliar male voice had her struggling harder. "Let go of me!"

"I will. Just let me back my horse up otherwise you'll break the neck I just saved you from breaking."

His actions were as quick as her fall had been. Almost before she could blink, he'd backed the horse up, lowered her to the ground, and jumped off himself. Leaving her to look up into a set of eyes so dark brown they could have been black if not for the specks of gold. Horse feathers. If all the men in Kansas looked like this one, she could almost understand why the girls on the train had been so giddy.

"What were you doing?" he asked. "The depot agent will see the baggage car is unloaded."

Snapped out of her stupor, Mary said, "I—I don't want anyone touching my things." Or her person. Sitting on his lap had caused nerve endings to tingle in places she didn't know she had nerve endings.

"You one of the brides?"

"Me? Not on your life." Praying for some kind of believable reason to be unloading her belongings, she glanced at the baggage car. "I—I'm heading west as soon as the train is unloaded. To Denver, and I don't want my belongings mixed up with the ones that will be unloaded here."

His expression—a dark scowl—didn't change. Flustered by the way her heart wouldn't stop trying to beat its way out of her chest, she said, "I'm meeting my husband in Denver and don't want my china broken before I get there." Pointing toward her trunk, she asked, "Would you mind?"

His gaze wandered left and right and then over her from head to toe before he swung around and lifted her trunk out of the car.

"Right there is fine," she said. "I'll wait with it until everything else is unloaded. Thank you for your assistance."

Her heart was still pounding, perhaps because of her lies, but more likely because of him. He was tall and muscular, and could very easily thwart her plan before she ever put it in place. "Good day, sir."

His dark glare once again went from her head to her toes, leaving her quivering, but then he grasped the saddle horn, swung onto his big gray horse with one easy movement, and touched the brim of his black hat with one hand as he turned the horse about.

Relief oozed out of every pore of her body as she watched him ride away. She sighed. Heavily. She'd just seen a true-to-life cowboy. Maggie said this country was full of them. That was what the other girls had said. Mary didn't believe a cowboy was any better than any other man and was glad to see this one riding further and further away from her. A man had never made her entire being tremble before, and she certainly didn't want that to happen again.

As he became little more than a speck on the horizon, she frowned. She had no idea what she'd hoped to see, but this wasn't it.

Town was on the other side of the tracks, but other than a couple houses, this side was barren. "Good Lord, the harder I look, the less I see." Twisting her neck, she scanned the area from her left shoulder to her right. "There's nothing. Not a tree or bush. Nothing."

Well, there was a building. A feed store by the name on the front. There was also a closed sign hanging on the door.

Fearing someone else may round the train at any moment, she picked up her bag and grabbed one trunk handle. Careful to not jostle the trunk too much and fighting the wind the entire way, she dragged the trunk around the backside of the feed store. Spying a lean-to on the side, she dragged the trunk inside it and then sat down on top of it to catch her breath.

Oak Grove sure didn't have any groves. Could there be a more barren land in all of the world? The grass wasn't even real grass. It was barely summer and it was already brown and had crunched beneath her feet as she'd walked. Good thing she had made a batch of tonic mixture before leaving Ohio. Finding a way to burp the crock along the way hadn't been easy, but she'd managed, and soon could bottle it up.

The music had stopped, but she could still hear people talking. Mainly one person. The conductor had said the mayor would provide a welcoming speech, and from how he went on and on, it appeared the mayor liked hearing himself talk.

Oh, well, the mayor wasn't any of her concern—neither was the image of that dark-haired cowboy that kept flashing in the back of her mind. Finding a place for her tonic to finish brewing was what she needed to focus on. She'd been hoping to find a grove of trees on the edge of town to hide it in, but that obviously wasn't going to happen.

A loud cheer echoed against the building behind her, as did the whistle of the train, and a couple of loud blasts that made her nearly jump out of her skin. Gun shots! Good heavens, what kind of place was this?

The cheering that sounded again gave her a touch of relief. She'd heard men did that, fired guns for just the heck of it. Cowboys. Uncouth beings!

The idea of Maggie encountering a man much like the one who'd ridden away on his big gray horse rattled Mary slightly. She couldn't remember being this upset with her sister, at least not for a long time, but she wasn't going to give in. Being the older sister, if only by a few minutes, she was always the one to give in. Not this time.

Perhaps by the time she'd bottled up the tonic and sold it, Maggie would come to her senses and be ready to head out with her. She'd tried to tell herself she couldn't care less if Maggie stayed here and married some uncouth man or not, but that wasn't true. She did care, but Maggie had to learn sometime. And this appeared to be the time. Until that happened—when Maggie discovered the older and wiser sister was always right, Mary figured she'd stay well-hidden. Teach Maggie a lesson she'd never forget.

No longer winded, Mary stood and then crouched down beside the trunk to carefully lift the lid. Happy to see everything still safely packed amongst the straw, she eased the cork toward the top of the crock—just enough to let air out, but none in. When the hissing stopped, she pushed the cork down tight and closed the trunk lid before the bitter scent of fermentation could fill the air.

Now to find a place to hide. Her and the tonic.

Focused on surveying the lean-to, she jumped to her feet when an elongated shadow covered the ground near the wide opening. Fearing the cowboy had returned, she tried to come up with yet another excuse.

As a man appeared, she concluded the shadow hadn't been elongated. He was that tall, and big, and clearly following the marks she'd left in the dirt by dragging her trunk.

Dang it. Why hadn't she thought of that?

A tinge of relief that this wasn't the cowboy had her drawing in a deep breath. She didn't have an excuse for being in the lean-to but did have her wits.

Hurrying forward, she held out her hand. "Hello. I'm Mary, Mary McCary. Goodness, it is so hot I had to find some shade." That wasn't a lie. Sweat trickled down the back of her neck, making her wish she'd pinned her hair up. However the weight of it pinned up often gave her a headache. The same was true for Maggie. "I hope you don't mind," she continued when the man didn't shake her hand. "I'll be on my way shortly. I just needed to rest a moment."

"Vhere you come from?"

"Where did I come from? The train. I just arrived."

"The train? You a bride?"

The cowboy had been tall, but this one was a giant, making her half wish it was the cowboy again. "No, no, I'm— I'm a…" She pointed toward her trunk and said the first thing she could think of. "A cook." That was true. She'd need a place to cook up the syrup to thicken the tonic. "I have all my supplies right there. The trunk is heavy so I dragged it in here, out of the sun." Her insides quivered slightly. She'd never told so many lies in her life. "I'm sorry. I'll leave now."

"No. You stay."

"I can't stay," she shouted over the train whistle. "I— I—I'm looking for—" Her brain wasn't working as fast as she wished it would. Furthermore, the ground was shaking, which said the train was pulling out of the station.

His thick black brows met as he frowned. "The Circle P? You looking for the Circle P Ranch? To cook for Rex?"

"The Circle P Ranch? Rex?" A ranch had to be out in

the country, a place she could mix up her tonic, and hide in case someone started looking for her, which was likely to happen. The conductor had kept a guarded eye on both her and Maggie. Thanks to Sheriff Freiday. Which was another reason she was so upset with Maggie. The way her sister kept feeding the other girls their tonic—in order to calm their nerves—could have easily have made the conductor wonder where it had come from and search her trunk. Thank goodness that hadn't happened. At least not yet. It still could. "Yes. Yes, the Circle P Ranch. To cook for Rex. Is it far? Can you tell me how to get there?"

"Steve Putnam left. I vill take you," he said. "If you don't like it, you come cook for me, ya?"

Focused, she asked, "Right now? You will take me there right now?"

"Ya. I get my wagon."

Mary wanted to jump for joy. She'd never been on a ranch, but surely it would provide a place for her to thicken and bottle the tonic and acquire a ride back to town in order to sell enough bottles to get her and Maggie on a train. An eastbound one. She'd already seen enough brown grass to last a lifetime. Although she hadn't realized it before, there was a lot to be said about the tall green trees and lush rolling hills of Ohio.

The huge man pulled a wagon up to the side of the lean-to in hardly no time and hoisted her trunk into the back of it with no effort whatsoever. Thankful for small miracles, she climbed onto the seat and quickly braided her long hair to keep the wind from blowing it across her face.

As the wagon started rolling away from town, she learned the big man's name was Brett Blackwell and that he was a blacksmith, as well as the feed store owner. The fact he'd moved to Kansas from northern Wisconsin explained his thick brogue, which grew increasingly easier to understand the more he talked. She let him ramble on as they traveled, focusing on her change of luck.

She normally made friends easily—less the train ride where the other three "brides" had irritated her from the get go. They had irritated Maggie at first, too. The two of them had come up with their own names for the others. Miss Know-it-All Rebecca, Miss Quiet-and-Quaint Sadie and Miss Gullible Anna, who all had been over the moon at the idea of finding a husband. Foolish girls. Men only made life more difficult. They'd have to figure that out on their own. She and Maggie had, long ago. They hadn't attempted to transfer Da's permit to sell their tonic because they both knew the men on the Bridgeport town council would never approve it because she and Maggie were women and considered incapable of running a business. Men here wouldn't be any different. It shouldn't take Maggie long to realize that. After all, they were sisters. Maggie should remember that, too.

As Mary's wandering mind snagged something Brett said, she asked, "He what?"

"Rex dang near cut off his other leg."

"His other leg?"

"Lost the first one in the war, and buried an ax in the second one. That's why he needs help." A frown drew his thick brows together as he continued, "I thought Steve hired you to cook. No?"

"Yes. Yes, he did," she flat-out lied—again. "I was just confused there for a moment. Forgot about Rex." She'd have to figure out the being-hired part once she got there.

Brett's frown didn't ease, which sent a shudder up her spine. Reacting to that, she glanced behind them, seeing nothing of Oak Grove but small dots. "So how much farther is it to the ranch?"

"A ways," he answered.

"Meaning half a mile or…" Once again glancing around at the barren land, she continued, "or a couple of miles?"

"Five."

A lump formed in her throat. She and Maggie had never been a mile apart, let alone five. Maybe this wasn't the best idea she could have come up with.

Awhile later, she concluded it wasn't. Not only had that been the longest, roughest five miles she'd ever ridden in a buckboard, she truly was hired as a cook. Well, she was cooking anyway. There hadn't been any real hiring. Yet.

Upon arrival at the Circle P Ranch, which included several obviously planted trees and a large house that was very nice, she'd encountered a man older than Da had been, and who clearly needed to be in bed, trying to mix up a batch of bread dough. Without ado, she'd ordered the man back to bed, taken off her jacket and rolled up her sleeves.

The man, who turned out to be the Rex who had indeed injured his leg severely—the one that wasn't a piece of wood from the knee down—said the men expected a hot meal and he couldn't let them down. Her heart had gone out to Rex while anger built for his boss. A man named Steve Putnam who evidently expected people to work themselves into their graves. Literally. She'd give him a piece of her mind when she met him. For now, she'd cook a meal for the other men who were out rounding up the young ones. That was what Rex had said. Brett had explained Rex meant young calves. It turned out not only the grass was brown in this godforsaken place, the cows were, too.

She'd told Brett the only cows she'd ever seen were black and white. He said those had to have been milk cows. The ones on the Circle P were beef cattle. Whatever that meant. If you asked her, a cow was a cow. You fed it, milked it, and when it was too old for that, you ate it.

Once she got the dough mixed and set to rise, she filled a

bucket with water and gave the kitchen a good scrub down. It needed it. Then, with Brett's help and guidance from Rex, who shouted orders from the bedroom off the kitchen, she found everything she'd need to cook a meal for the six men expecting to be fed—plus Rex and Steve Putnam. And of course Brett whom she promised to feed if he'd stay and help her get things in order. He'd been so excited over that prospect, she'd feared he was going to hug her with those huge arms and had run to the other side of the table.

Stew was what she made, using beef since there was no mutton, and a big pot of potatoes that she'd mash up before serving. Pouring the stew over the potatoes not only made the stew go further, it was how Da had liked it.

Between helping her find things and placating Rex, Brett had carried in her bag and trunk and put them upstairs, in one of the bedrooms. The house had six, and after all the work she was doing, Steve Putnam better not refuse to allow her to use one. While showing her the outdoor ground cellar, Brett had pointed out a long and narrow building that the hired hands slept in—a bunkhouse, he'd called it. From the state of its porch, it needed scrubbing as badly as the kitchen had.

Where all the dirt came from was beyond her. The ground was rock-hard, yet the crazy wind that hadn't stopped blowing since she'd stepped off the train was full of dirt. Luckily she'd found a cloth to put over the bread dough while it was rising. She'd folded another cloth into a triangle to cover the top of her head and tied it beneath her hair at the nape of her neck since her braid had long ago separated. A scarf tied so was how Da had liked her to keep her hair contained. He'd never wanted her or Maggie to cut their hair, so they hadn't, but he'd insisted they keep it contained while cooking, especially over an open fire. Said he didn't want it or them catching fire.

"What are you looking for?" she asked Brett when he started opening cupboard doors. The man's size and rough voice no longer intimidated her.

"Something for Rex. His leg hurts. Steve must have a bottle around here somevhere."

"Let me finish putting this bread in pans so it can rise one last time and I'll get something for him," she said.

"Vhere is it? I'll get it," Brett replied.

"No, I'll get it," she said firmly. "Go tell Rex I'll be in with something that's sure to make him feel better in a few minutes."

## Chapter Three

Steve had stopped at every farm and ranch between his place and Oak Grove, and though his neighbors were willing to give him food out of their larders, not a one was willing to hire on as a cook for his men, or part with an employee to do so. He couldn't blame them. This time of year was busy for everyone. He'd thanked them for their offers just the same and headed for home empty-handed.

His mind kept going back to the woman at the train station, contemplating if he should have asked her if she wanted to earn a few dollars before heading west again. Yet, he knew that would have been a bad idea. A woman that pretty would cause a stir like no tomorrow at the ranch. Furthermore, any man who had a wife that fine would be searching her down when she didn't arrive as scheduled, and that would leave him in the same predicament. Perhaps a worse one.

He'd have to rustle something up for his men to eat on his own tonight, and lacking a better idea, would head to Dodge tomorrow. Or he could take Fred Matthews' advice and send a telegram to the newspaper down there, place a want ad for a cook. Either way, it would be days or even weeks before he'd have the help he needed. He could cook enough to get by, but his men wouldn't like what he made any more than they had Walter's flapjacks this morning.

The sun was dipping low in the sky by the time he arrived at the ranch, and the weight on his shoulders pressed a little harder as he wondered what he could muster up to feed the men who were washing up at the barrels beside the bunkhouse.

As he climbed off his horse, he spun around to take another look. Why were they washing up at the barrels? "What's happened?" he asked as Leroy grasped the reins out of his hands.

"Always said you're the best boss a man could hope for," Leroy said while his long and gangly legs almost tripped over themselves in his rush to lead the horse to the barn.

Confused, Steve stared at the rest of his men. The ones who weren't splashing water on their faces were combing their hair back with their fingers or tucking in their shirts. Normally they didn't even take the time to wipe their feet before stomping into the house to eat.

"You outdid yourself, Boss, and we thank you," Wyatt said, slapping the dust off his pant legs with both hands. "Thank you kindly."

"Outdid myself with what?"

"That new cook you hired," Henry said, using his hat to get the dust off his britches. "She sent us out here to clean up before we eat. But that's all right. We don't mind."

A shiver tickled Steve's spine as he turned to gaze toward the house. "She? What new cook?"

"The one you had Brett drive out," Henry replied. "Can't wait to taste those vittles. If they taste half as good as they smell, I'm gonna think I died and went to heaven."

Still confused, Steve asked, "Brett Blackwell?"

"Yes, sir," Leroy said, slapping him on the back as he

walked past. "And here I was thinking we'd have to eat Walter's salty flapjacks again for supper."

"They weren't that bad," Walter said while smoothing his mustache back in place after his hearty scrubbing.

"Yes, they were," several others answered in unison.

Steve started for the house along with the rest of them, until Jess laid a hand on his shoulder.

"You might want to wash up, Boss," Jess said. "Henry was the only one who made it inside the door. She snapped him with a towel and told him to go wash up before stepping foot in the kitchen again, and that went for the rest of us, too."

Steve had no idea who this woman was, but if she was half the size of the blacksmith, it was no wonder the boys had all washed up. However, it was his house and he didn't take orders from anyone.

His men, trying to get through the opening two at a time, dang near broke the door off its hinges. He followed them over the threshold once the ruckus settled down, and then wasn't exactly sure what stopped him dead in his tracks. Her or the aromas.

The house hadn't smelled this good in so long—actually it had never smelled this good. Cinnamon. And apples. Baked apples. Apple pie maybe? He treated himself to a slice of pie every now and again while in town, but not often enough.

She stood at the stove, with her back to him, and was nowhere near the size of Brett. She was about the size of the gal who'd fallen onto his lap back at the train station, the one he couldn't get out of his mind.

Tiny and slender, with one cloth tied around her waist and another over her hair, she spat, "For heaven's sake, close the door before that wind covers everything with dirt." And, "Hats are not to be worn at the table."

While hats hit the floor all around the table, Steve shut the door, hung his hat on a hook and then took a seat next to Brett. The blacksmith's grin was bigger than his biceps. Steve was about to turn around, to get a good look at the woman, when she barked out another order.

"Start passing the bread around." A second later she set a huge bowl next to him. "Fill your plate with potatoes then pass the bowl on."

As soon as he did, she set down another pot. "Now cover your potatoes with this."

The thick gravy looked more like stew, but he did as ordered, as did everyone else, ladling the stew over the potatoes.

Setting another plate of sliced bread atop the one that was already empty, she said, "Eat up. There's plenty."

Appreciative groans echoed throughout the room, and his could easily have joined the others, but Steve held it in. Not only because the mouthful of potatoes and stew was delicious and the delectable smell of apples still filled his nose, but because he sensed something familiar about her, yet couldn't say what. Other than… It couldn't be her. She was on her way to Denver.

Once again squeezing between him and Brett in order to do so, she set a large baking pan in the center of the table. "Once you've had your fill, there's apple cobbler for dessert."

Steve had a great desire to twist about and get a good look at her, but the appreciative groans from his men had him leaning toward Brett. "I owe you, my friend. Where did you find her?"

"At my place, waiting for a ride," Brett answered.

"Hey," Jess said. "Didn't I see you get off the train with the other women today?"

Steve's spine stiffened as he spun about. As their eyes met, his and her sky-blue ones, he knew she was the woman he'd seen at the train station—she knew he knew, too.

She quickly turned toward Jess and leveled a glare that could have sliced the cowboy in two. "No."

Jess nodded. "Yes, I did. I saw you."

"You couldn't have," she said. "I did not get off the train with the other women."

"I'm sure—"

"That would have been my sister," she said, cutting Jess short. "We look alike." Setting a smaller kettle on the table, she said, "This is caramel sauce for the cobbler. It's best eaten warm."

The men needed no further invite than that, even Jess, and though Steve wanted a piece of that cobbler so bad he could taste it, his mind couldn't get off why she was in his kitchen. Why she'd claimed she was going to Denver. His gaze settled for a second on each one of his men, wondering which one was responsible. Jess had been the only one he'd seen at the station, and was also the only one who'd been remotely taken with the idea of a bride.

"You sure—"

"Eat," Steve told Jess, cutting short whatever the other man had been about to say. He'd get to the bottom of it, but feeding his men came first.

"You want cobbler, no?" Brett asked.

"Yes." Steve took the dish, spooned a large portion onto his plate and then took the smaller pan and poured the thick brown syrup atop the cobbler. It was even better than the meal had been, and that shouldn't have been possible.

Silence other than satisfied moans and groans surrounded the table again—and polite requests for more.

Once they'd all had seconds, and would have taken thirds

if the pan hadn't been empty, Steve nudged Henry and then nodded toward the door. His silent command circled the table. With obvious reluctance, one by one the men stood, thanked the woman generously for the meal and then exited the house, closing the door quietly behind them.

Steve contemplated his words and what might follow carefully before asking, "Why aren't you on your way to Denver?"

She paused stacking the empty plates and met his gaze eye for eye. Hers were bluer than the Kansas summer sky, but they weren't nearly as friendly.

"I—I—uh—"

"You are one of those brides."

The gasp that sounded came from Brett.

"If you don't want her, I'll take her," the blacksmith said. "She cooks like my ma."

"No, I'm not one of those brides," she snapped. "I had no intention of marrying anyone." As she glanced toward Brett her gaze softened slightly. "Still don't."

Steve read around her answer. "But you are from Ohio. You are one of the girls the mayor paid to have sent out here."

"If you don't want her, I'll take her," Brett said again.

Flustered, Steve growled, "I never said I didn't want her." He bit his tongue as soon as the words were out. "As a cook," he clarified. Mainly because her eyes had grown as wide as the plates she'd been about to pick up.

"Oh, Miss McCary!"

The shout was slightly elongated and slurred, but he recognized Rex's voice and a hint of shame stung Steve's gut. He hadn't checked to see how the man was doing. Frowning at how Rex sounded, he pushed away from the table. She was already on her way into the room off the kitchen and Steve paused at the doorway.

"Can I have a little more tonic?" Rex asked, smiling at her.

A smile from Rex was as rare as the rest of the men washing up before eating.

With her cheeks still burning, Mary hurried toward Rex's bed. So much for good luck. Bad luck was the cowboy from the train being Steve Putnam. She'd recognized him the moment he'd walked in the door and her entire being had been shaking—inside and out since that moment. "Of course," she said to Rex. "Is your leg still hurting?"

"No," Rex said. "But I don't want the pain to come back."

"This will help." She picked up the bottle of tonic she'd left next to the bed and carefully poured a spoonful of the thick liquid. Rex had his mouth open like a baby bird waiting for a worm from its momma. That was how it normally was. It truly was a cure-all, just as Da always said. Of course, she'd seen it cure many ailments herself. Everything from gout to gas when administered correctly.

"I think I need two spoonsful," Rex said. "I'm in pretty bad shape still."

He certainly was. She'd changed the bandage on his leg earlier. Now was not the time to be stingy or think of profits, considering how badly Rex needed the tonic, so she filled another spoonful and fed it to him. Then, while replacing the cork in the small bottle, she said, "You can have some more in a little bit, before you go to sleep for the night."

"Can I just suck on the spoon?" Rex asked.

She couldn't help but giggle. The man's face might be wrinkled and his hair gray, but he put her in mind of a little boy the way he was looking up at her. She handed him the spoon. "Of course."

"What are you feeding him?"

Tingles shot up her spine. She'd momentarily forgotten the man who stood in the doorway—the one she'd lied to about going to Denver. The one whose lap she'd fallen into. No matter how hard she tried, that memory wouldn't leave her alone.

"The best tonic I've ever tasted," Rex said.

"Tonic?"

She turned around and held up the bottle as the man walked closer. "Yes. McCary's Finest Recipe Tonic."

Beneath a set of dark brows that were frowning, his brown eyes bore so deeply her hand shook as he took the bottle from her. "McCary? That's your name? You made this?"

"Yes, that is my name. Mary McCary, and yes, I made it."

He pulled out the cork and smelled the contents. His frown increased as he poured a small amount onto the tip of one finger and then stuck it in his mouth.

"Good stuff, isn't it?" Rex asked.

Steve's face filled with something she'd seen before. Disgust. And that turned her stomach hard.

"It's snake oil," he said while sticking the cork back in the bottle.

She snatched the bottle out of his hand. "Only ignorant people call it that."

His hard stare never faltered as he said, "Only ignorant people think alcohol will cure what ails them."

"It sure took away my pain," Rex said. "And tastes a whole lot better than the stuff the doc left."

"Because you're drunk."

"He is not." Mary set the bottle on the table. "This tonic is an old family recipe and has been proven medicinal many times over." Trying to convince men of that was next to impossible. Because doctors refused to prescribe it. That was only because it cured their patients. Her family had been run out of town by more than one doctor over the years. She drew a deep breath and asked, "Are you interested in hiring me as a cook or not?" Nodding toward the doorway behind him, she added, "If not, Brett and I need to head out before the sun sets."

"Ya," Brett said from the doorway.

Steve's jaw twitched but he didn't glance over his shoulder, just kept staring at her.

"I thought you already hired her," Rex said. "I can't cook for the boys, not in my condition."

"I'll hire you," Brett said from the doorway.

This time Steve gave Brett a glare. "You don't need a cook."

"Ya, I do." Brett looked her way. "I'll pay you twenty dollars a month."

Mary bit down on her bottom lip. She'd have to sell an entire batch of tonic to make twenty dollars.

"Cooks don't make twenty dollars a month," Steve said.

"You pay me thirty," Rex said. "Same you pay the cowboys."

The way Steve scowled at Rex tickled Mary's insides. Thirty dollars would be more money than she'd ever made in a month. More than Da had made.

"I can't pay her what I pay the boys," he said.

"Sure you can," Rex answered. "The boys won't mind."

"You're drunk," he snapped.

"I'm not," Brett said. "I'll pay her thirty-five."

Steve threw his arms in the air as he spun around. "This isn't an auction."

So much excitement danced inside her, Mary's toes were tapping inside her shoes. Thirty-five dollars would go a long way in getting her and Maggie westward. It took her a moment to remember Brett had said he'd put money toward bringing the brides to Oak Grove, but had left the train when the girls got off, figuring he'd get to know them later when it wasn't so crowded. But he wanted one. A bride. And she wasn't about to become that.

However, she could take advantage of the situation. Stepping forward, she put herself between Steve and Brett who were in a staredown. At this moment, they looked to be about the same in size and temperament. If push came to shove, either one had a good chance of winning. But this win would be hers.

"No, it's not an auction," she said, "but it is a contest, and I know how we can settle it fair and square."

"How?" all three men in the room asked at the same time.

Keeping her smile well-hidden, she said, "Rex, you get some rest now. You other two follow me."

Once in the kitchen, she cleared a section of the table and then gathered three tin cups of manageable size and the cork from the vanilla bottle she'd used to make the caramel sauce. "Sit down, gentlemen."

Casting each other stern stares, they sat.

Positioning the cups on the table, she said, "Whoever guesses which cup this cork is beneath will be the winner, and that person will agree to pay me forty dollars for a month of cooking."

"Thirty-five," Steve said.

She was about to agree when Brett said, "Forty."

Steve shook his head, and for a moment her breath stalled. She feared she'd gone too far, until he blew out a long sigh.

"Fine," he said, "forty, but that includes laundry and housekeeping."

"All right," she said quickly before Brett could say more. "Forty dollars for cooking, laundry and housekeeping for one month. Now watch the cork." With great show, she put it under one of the cups and then started shuffling them around each other. After switching her hands back and forth over the moving cups several times, she lined them in a row. The odds hit her then. They were much more in her favor when only one person was guessing. She should have thought of that earlier.

It was too late now. Besides, she was fairly confident neither of them would pick the right cup. "Brett, you can pick first," she said.

"Ya, I vill." He stared at the cups while rubbing a hand over his chin.

After an extended length of time, Steve said, "Pick one, will you?"

"I vill," Brett said. "Let me think."

After another length of time, the rancher huffed out a breath, "Oh, for—"

"That one," Brett said.

Having started to worry, Mary let out a sigh and lifted the cup to reveal the empty space.

"Who wins if Steve doesn't pick the right one?" Brett asked.

She really hadn't thought this through. Usually she didn't want the cork found. "I guess we'll try it a second time," Mary said.

"No, we won't. It's under this one."

The rancher picked up the cup, revealing the cork. The glint in his dark eyes had Mary's insides quaking, and she wondered if she'd just won or lost.

# *Chapter Four*

As Steve watched Brett drive away the thrill of winning seeped out of him like a bucket that had sat in the sun too long. Slowly, he turned to face the house. What the hell had he just done? Forty dollars? For cooking and cleaning? His stomach did an odd little flip-flop. It wasn't the money. Feeding his men was worth that. It was her. In his house. She'd made a point of claiming that included room and board. He'd known that was a given, but what that meant hadn't completely struck him until right now.

She'd be living in his house. With him. What was he thinking? He'd already concluded that would start a stir long before he found her in his house.

"It's only for a month," he told himself aloud. "Rex will be up and about by then."

*Or drunk as a skunk on her tonic*, the other logical part of his mind pointed out.

That he'd put a stop to right now. A few other rules wouldn't hurt, either.

Steve entered through the kitchen door, and was amazed to find the room clean. Cleaner than he'd seen it in a long time. She was efficient, he'd give her that.

Snoring from the little room off the kitchen told him

Rex was sleeping. Steve made his way through the front and back parlors, his office and the front entrance way, where he stopped to stare up the staircase. It was a given she'd stake claim on one of the bedrooms, and the notion of her sleeping down the hall from him instilled an agony he'd never experienced. Except for when she'd landed on his lap back at the train station.

Flustered by the entire situation, he started up the steps. She was in the third bedroom, the one that faced east, and staring out the window. Her hair was pulled over one shoulder and she slowly dragged a brush from the crown of her head to the tips of the long strands she held in her opposite hand. If he hadn't seen it, he wouldn't believe how much gumption came out of that short and slender body.

Her shoulders squared at the same time she turned about.

"Do you always sneak up on people?"

Speechless for a moment, he took a second or two before he said, "No."

"You did at the train station and again now."

"I saw you climb into the train car and figured you were up to no good." Her pinched lips had him asking, "Why did you tell me you were going to Denver? To meet your husband?"

Her shoulders heaved as she sighed. "What was I supposed to say?"

"The truth," he suggested. "That you were sneaking off the train to avoid the men waiting for a chance to marry you."

"Posh! I'm not marrying anyone." She flayed her arms in the air. "Fine. If that's what you want to hear. I was sneaking off the train to avoid those men. Can you blame me?"

He couldn't. Nor could he blame himself for admitting she was probably the best-looking woman any train had ever brought to Kansas. Which made no difference to him.

At least it shouldn't. Flustered, he drew in a deep breath. Something caught inside his nose. "Do you have more of that tonic up here?"

A nervous gaze shot to the trunk at the foot of the bed before she asked, "Why? Does Rex need some?"

"No," Steve answered, moving into the room. "He's sleeping off what you already gave him." Upon arriving at the foot of the bed, he reached down to flip open the trunk lid. "China, you said?"

She hurried forward, but he'd already lifted the lid. A large corked crock and several bottles—too many to count—were packed securely in straw. The smell was stronger, and although he hadn't smelled it in years, he clearly recalled what the wine his grandfather used to make back in Georgia smelled like.

She pushed his hand off the lid and gently closed it. "You have no right to go snooping in my things."

"That's a trunk full of wine, and it's in my house, so I'm not snooping."

"Your house or not, the trunk is mine." Planting her hands on her hips, she continued, "And while I'm here, this room is mine and you'll stay out of it."

He held his stare, all the while wanting to shake her. Ask her why she'd ever felt the need to agree to be a mail-order bride. "While you're here, you'll take orders from me. And I order you to dump it out."

"I will not."

"Then pack up your stuff," he said, gesturing to the few things lying on the dresser.

"Why?"

"Because I'm taking you to town." Ignoring the pang that shot across his stomach, he said, "Chris and Danny Sanders will give you a job peddling alcohol at their saloon. You're already good at that."

A flicker of fear crossed her face, but then she crossed her arms. "And who'll cook for your men? You?" The smile that appeared on her lips was full of conceit. "We've made a deal, shook on it. I never go back on my word, and I wouldn't think a man of your stature would, either."

Steve's back teeth clenched. She had him over a barrel, and knew it. He never went back on his word. Her knowing that was enough to infuriate him, but it was another feeling he couldn't ignore. That of how her flushed cheeks and pursed lips made him want to kiss her like he hadn't wanted to kiss anyone in years. Tossing aside that thought took will. Deep will. "My men expect three meals a day, morning, noon and night. Good meals. Their clothes washed once a week, the bunkhouse swept and mopped weekly, and this house kept clean."

"I already agreed to all that."

She was so smug he searched his mind to come up with other chores. When none appeared, he said, "And there will be no more of your tonic. Not for Rex or anyone else."

Mary squeezed her fingers tighter around the brush handle. She should be mad enough to pitch it across the room, but it wasn't anger she fought to control. It was how he'd looked at her. How his eyes had settled on her lips so completely it made them tingle—just like her insides had when she'd fallen onto his lap back at the train station.

With lightning speed, she crossed the room and shut the door. Her heart was pounding so hard she laid a hand against her chest and the other over the flock of butterflies swarming in her stomach.

Why did he make her insides go so crazy? Even while he yelled at her, ordering her to dispose of the tonic, all she could think of was how the other women on the train had been right. That the cowboys in Kansas were a handsome lot.

"Aw, fairy dust," she muttered. How could someone in her predicament have such thoughts? Perhaps because despite his handsomeness and her other cauldron of silly thoughts, this was rather a perfect solution for her situation. Not only would she gain finances, she could stock up on her supply of tonic while here. There had been honey and jam in the larder downstairs, which meant there must be more where they came from. Rather than train tickets for her and Maggie, maybe she'd buy another horse and wagon like Da. They'd traveled all over Ohio and Pennsylvania with Buck pulling their wagon.

She and Maggie could do that again. Travel about, selling tonic until they found a suitable place to settle. Perhaps a place with cowboys as handsome as Steve Putnam.

Telling herself that was a marvelous plan, she changed into her nightdress and climbed into the bed that had to be one of the softest and largest she'd even lain in.

Sleep came as quickly as the sunrise. She'd chosen this room just for that purpose, so the first rays of the rising sun would wake her. Although she didn't like how he turned her inside out—for no one had ever done that to her before—she would not let Steve find fault in anything she did. It would be a challenge, she couldn't deny that. The only people she'd cooked for were her family. Da had always been in such a hurry, off here or there, he'd rarely said if what he'd eaten was good or not, and as long as Maggie hadn't had to prepare it, she hadn't cared what she ate.

A wave of sadness washed over Mary as she folded back the covers and flipped her legs over the edge of the bed. That had been the first night she'd slept without Maggie nearby. Even on the train, while mad at each other, they'd settled down next to each other come nightfall.

Rising, she walked to the window and hoped that wherever Maggie was she was safe and knew they'd soon be together. Despite their differences, they were sisters, twins, and always would be.

Watching the rays of sunlight growing brighter, Mary decided she'd find a way to get a message to Maggie, just to assure her sister all would be well soon. But first, she had a bunch of men to feed. The task wasn't all that daunting, though. Between Steve's outdoor root cellar and the kitchen pantry, there was more food than she'd seen in some shops.

She dressed and covered her hair with the same cloth she'd used yesterday, tying it beneath her hair, and then quietly snuck out of her room and headed downstairs. After building a fire in the stove, she made a pot of coffee and then set about making a batch of biscuits. Once they were in the oven, she poured Rex a cup of coffee and pushed the pot to the back of the stove top to stay warm.

After a brief discussion with Rex, who was feeling better this morning, she ventured into the cellar for a large slab of bacon, and then went outside to gather eggs from the fenced-in chicken coop.

That task was easy—gathering eggs, it was the one she'd have to do next that had her a bit nervous. They—her family—had never owned a cow. Rex had said his morning chores included gathering eggs and milking the cow. She knew what to do with the milk once it was in the bucket—how to skim off the cream and make butter, buttermilk, even a soft cheese, but how to get the milk in the bucket was a different story.

She didn't want to fall short of her duties. That—the fear of falling short in his eyes—must be why Steve affected her so. She'd concluded that this morning, while being as quiet as possible to not wake him.

"Morning, ma'am," one of the cowboys said as he

stopped near the door of the chicken pen. "Is there anything I can do to help you this morning?"

Problem solved. "A matter of fact there is. I have biscuits in the oven, and wouldn't want them to burn. Would you mind milking the cow?"

"Consider it done," he said with a grin. "Name's Walter, Walter Reinhold. You can just call me Walter. Everyone goes by first names around here."

"In that case, you can call me Mary, and thank you, Walter, I appreciate the help."

"Not a problem at all, ma'am. I'm glad to be of assistance."

More than satisfied, she went back into the house to resume preparing a meal Steve would not find any fault in.

All the while she'd cooked, she hadn't heard any movement upstairs, so was a bit surprised when Steve walked through the kitchen door with the rest of the men. She was a bit flustered, too, at the way her heart picked up an extra beat.

He didn't say a word, and neither did she. Not to him. The rest of the men were very appreciative of her efforts this morning, and weren't shy about saying so. She replied to their generous compliments, offered second and third helpings, and considering they were a curious bunch, answered their questions, which were mainly about what she would serve for their next meal.

Other than the cowboy with shaggy brown hair— she recalled his name was Jess Rader—who was curious about other things. "So, what's your sister's name?" he asked, spooning eggs into his mouth.

"Maggie." Hoping to get the subject away from the whole bride scenario—mainly because it had Steve's brown eyes focused on her, she added, "Actually, it's Margaret Mary, and my name is Mary Margaret."

Several frowns formed as all their eyes landed on her.

"Couldn't your folks think up any other names?" the tall and thin cowboy named Leroy asked.

"Mary Margaret was the name my mother had chosen, not knowing she was carrying two babies. She died shortly after my sister and I were born, so, since I was born first, my father named me Mary Margaret, and my sister Margaret Mary."

"Don't that beat all," one of them said, she hadn't caught exactly who because the very thoughtful expression on Steve's face held her attention.

"How do you know that?" he asked.

"Because my father told me," she answered the obvious.

"If you're twins, identical, maybe he mixed the two of you up." Looking at her over the rim of his coffee cup, he continued, "Maybe she's Mary and you're Maggie."

Confident that had never happened, she smiled. "No, he didn't. I'm Mary. Mary McCary."

"How can you be so sure?"

She could tell him the truth. Show him the birthmark on the back of her neck that proved she was exactly who she said she was, or tell him about it and why she and Maggie always wore their hair down, so people were never sure which sister was which. Maggie had no such birthmark, and more than a time or two they'd used their likenesses to their own advantages. She then wondered if he'd be able to tell her and Maggie apart without knowing their secret. There was something about him, his intuition, maybe, that said he might be able to.

Still smiling, she met his gaze eye for eye. "Why are you so suspicious of people? Or is it just me?"

The nervous silence that settled around the table told her what she already knew. Few people questioned Steve Putnam. She didn't mind being one that did. As crazy as it seemed, she didn't mind getting under his skin—most likely because he got under hers so thoroughly.

He never looked away while saying, "Saddle up, boys."

As they all gathered their hats and stood, he added, "Lunch will be at noon, Miss McCary."

"Yes, it will be, Mr. Putnam," she replied.

He waited until the rest of the men exited, and then while standing in the open doorway, he said, "Walter won't be milking any cows tomorrow morning. That's your job."

She should have known he'd discover that. "So be it." As he pulled the door shut, she started gathering dishes off the table and muttered, "Insufferable beast."

The door opened again and he poked his head through the opening. "I heard that."

Hoisting the pile of dirty dishes off the table, she merely repeated, "So be it." She'd learn to milk a snake just to spite him. Of course snakes couldn't be milked, at least she assumed they couldn't. She couldn't be sure about the snakes in this country, though. They had to be different from the ones she'd ever seen. Just as different as the cows. Men, however, were the same everywhere. Insufferable beasts.

Not a single man had ever appealed to her in any shape or form, and Steve Putnam had to be the least appealing of all. At least he should be. The way he antagonized her with nothing more than a look was reason enough. Sure he might be more handsome than all the others, but some dogs were better-looking than other ones, too, and that sure didn't make them better dogs.

"Mary?"

She let the smile that wanted to appear at the sound of Rex's voice form and after setting the dishes on the counter, walked into his room. "Yes?"

"Is there something I can help you with this morning?

I'm sure I could sit at the table and peel potatoes or something."

Maybe she was a bit wrong. Rex wasn't unlikeable or insufferable. A matter of fact, she'd already grown a bit fond of him. Why couldn't Steve be more like him? She gave her head a quick shake. What was she thinking? She didn't want to become fond of Steve.

Crossing the room, she said, "I'm sure you could, but I'm not going to let you. You need to stay in bed so that leg heals." That needed to happen as much for him as for her. She couldn't stay here any longer than necessary. "However," she continued, noting the frustration in Rex's green eyes. "I am hoping you'll be up to churning butter later today. And…"

He frowned slightly. "And?"

"Telling me how to milk a cow."

## Chapter Five

Steve led the group of cowboys toward the house at full speed. It was a half hour or so before noon, but that was how he wanted it. Showing up early and frazzling Mary's composure a bit would suit him just fine. He couldn't say why. Normally he was easygoing. He loved his ranch and wanted everyone who worked here to love it, too. It not only made for a happier group, it got more done. Men who liked their work accomplished more than those who didn't. He should consider that when it came to her, but couldn't. There was something about her that got to him.

As did the way the men behind him were shouting at each other, guessing what they'd have for lunch and betting it would be one of the best meals they'd ever eaten. They could very well be right. In fact, they better be right. At the fortune it was costing him to feed them, they better enjoy every morsel.

On that thought, Steve reined in his horse, slowing the pace for everyone. Mary wasn't costing him that much more than he'd paid Rex to cook and clean, and considering the quality of the meals last night and this morning, the extra money was worth it.

They rode into the homestead around the back of the

barn, which was where Steve caught sight of the two horses
tied up outside the bunkhouse, and the two men sitting in
the shade under the awning.

"What are they doing here?" Walter asked, drawing his
horse to a stop.

"I don't know," Steve said. "But I have a good idea."

"What?"

"She's cooking our lunch." Steve dismounted and
handed the reins to Leroy before he crossed the yard to
the bunkhouse.

"Sheriff, Mayor," he greeted as the men stood. "Hot day
to be sitting out here."

Pulling his britches up over his pudgy waistline, Josiah
Melbourne puffed out his chest. "You tell that woman to
get out here right now."

"I'm assuming you're talking about my new cook."

"Of course I am," the mayor said. "You can't hire her
as a cook. You never contributed to the Betterment Committee, therefore she can't be here."

Tom Baniff stepped forward. He'd been the sheriff for
the past two years and was doing a dang good job of it. He
always got straight to the point, and did so now.

"Mary McCary is one of the brides," Tom said. "And
Brett Blackwell confirmed he brought her out here right
after the train arrived."

"Brett did," Steve agreed, "but Miss McCary claims she
had no intention of becoming a bride."

"She doesn't have a choice," Josiah barked. "She knew
the rules before she left Ohio."

"Could you have her unlock the door so we can talk to
her?" Tom asked. "We've been here long enough."

Steve started for the house, and as the sheriff stepped
up beside him, he asked, "How long have you been here?"

"Left town at eight this morning."

"And you've been sitting here the entire time?"

"Yes. Josiah refused to leave, and I didn't want to have to ride out again because she shot him or something."

"There's a town full of men expecting—"

Interrupting the mayor, Steve asked the sheriff, "She pulled a gun on you?"

Tom shook his head. "Not that I saw, but she said she had one and would use it if needed. Josiah wanted me to kick the door in. I said we'd wait for you."

Steve walked up the back steps and tried the door knob. It turned easily. After pushing the door open, he waved for the sheriff and mayor to enter while holding his other hand up to his men, telling them to wait outside.

The table was set, the room smelled wondrous and Mary stood near the doorway to the parlor, as puffed up as a grouse guarding her nest. Steve had to keep his grin hidden, but couldn't deny he felt a fair amount of respect for this little woman and her gumption. "These men would like to speak with you, Miss McCary."

"I'm aware of that," she answered. "I didn't think it was appropriate until you were present to vouch for the agreement we've made."

"There can be no agreement between you two," Josiah shouted. "I already told you that. Now, get your belongings. You are coming to town with us."

The man was crossing the room as he shouted. Steve crossed the room, too, and planted himself between the mayor and Mary. "She's not going anywhere. I hired her as my cook for the next month."

"She isn't available for hire," Josiah bellowed. "Especially not by someone who wouldn't even contribute to the cause!"

That was a sore spot for the mayor. He'd been out to the ranch several times asking for contributions, and had been upset that *"the most prominent citizen of Oak Grove"* wouldn't participate. Steve didn't care how prominent others proclaimed him to be, he thought it was a stupid idea from the start, and wasn't going to put his hard-earned money behind it.

"I'll contribute to your committee," Rex shouted from the bedroom. "How much do you want?"

Obviously listening from the back porch, Walter stuck his head through an open window. "All of us out here will contribute, too. How much will it take to keep her?"

Steve smothered a growl. They'd all been on his side until they'd met her. Actually, he no longer had a side. If it came to keeping her, he had no choice but to pony up. "How much?"

"I got twenty-five dollars ready to hand over," Rex shouted from the bedroom.

"It's too late for that," Josiah said. "You had to make your contributions before the brides arrived."

Steve glanced past the mayor, to the table where a plate of cornbread sat and whatever was in the oven, ham he'd guess, had the house smelling as good as it had yesterday. Settling his gaze on the mayor, he said, "I'll give you fifty bucks. That should more than cover her travel costs. Once she's done working for me, she can marry any one of the other contributors."

"I'm not—"

The glare he cast over his shoulder stopped her protest.

"Take the money," the sheriff said to Josiah. "We have to get back to town. The party will be starting soon and you're to give the opening speech."

The mayor shook his head. "That won't—"

"Seventy-five," Steve interrupted.

\* \* \*

Mary gulped. No one had that kind of money just lying around. Leastwise not anyone she'd ever known, nor would they have been willing to donate it to a committee of any sort. The air in her lungs started to burn, but she didn't dare let it out. Didn't dare make a peep. Not even to say no one needed to cover her traveling expenses. She'd traded Buck, their horse, for her and Maggie's train tickets, but she doubted anyone wanted to hear that. The mayor was so red it looked like his head was about to burst off his shoulders, and the sheriff's gaze was wary as he looked from Steve to the mayor and back again.

"I said seventy-five dollars, Melbourne," Steve said. "Take it or leave it. Either way, you will be leaving without Miss McCary."

"It's time we leave, Josiah," the sheriff said.

Mary let her breath out then. The sandy-haired sheriff appeared to be a much more intelligent man than the mayor—who was still red-faced and glaring at Steve.

"Fine," the mayor said. "I'll take your money, Mr. Putnam, but Miss McCary will be expected to fulfill the terms of the agreement she signed at the end of her employment with you."

Mary wanted to protest, but pinched her lips together instead. There was no sense arguing a moot point. She'd be hightailing it out of Kansas at the end of her employment. A twinge of what she could only describe as guilt fluttered through her midsection. Steve—who had spun around and left the room—was laying out an enormous amount of money in order for her to cook for his men for the next month. The forty dollars he was paying her and the seventy-five he'd agreed to give the mayor was more money than she'd ever seen at one time. She'd fulfill her commitment to him. The McCarys had honor and never had been indebted to anyone. Which was what she'd told Sheriff Freiday back in Ohio upon trading Buck for their train tickets.

Steve returned and handed the mayor several bills. As the sheriff led the mayor toward the door, Steve said to her. "The men are hungry, Miss McCary."

Her thudding heart told her she should say thank-you, but her commonsense said not within hearing distance of the mayor, therefore she nodded and walked toward the stove. "Lunch is ready, Mr. Putnam. Please tell the men to come in and eat."

The two large kettles of boiled dinner she'd made of ham, potatoes, carrots, onions and cabbage, as well as the cornbread disappeared in no time, as did the spice cake she'd baked for dessert, making her glad she'd carried Rex in a plate before the others had started to eat.

Relatively quiet while they ate, the men thanked her boisterously once they'd finished. Gathering their hats off the floor, they filed out the door. Steve followed, collecting his hat from a hook by the door. He paused, though, to glance back at her.

"Thank you, for—" Shrugging, she simply said, "Everything." She hadn't meant to whisper, but her voice didn't want to work.

His expression softened as he said, "I expect supper on the table by six."

"It will be."

He nodded and pulled the door closed, and she pinched her lips as a grin formed. She would be eternally grateful that he hadn't sent her back to town. At this moment, there was no place else she'd rather be than here.

Organized by nature, she had always liked being busy, and with the generous supply of food stuff, cooking for the men was not overly taxing. Most of her life she'd had to scrounge for the ingredients to put together every meal, which had taken far more time and effort.

After cleaning the kitchen and providing Rex with a couple spoonsful of tonic in order for him to rest for a bit, she went upstairs to burp the tonic. The fact Steve had told her to get rid of the tonic jiggled and mixed with her other thoughts. He was paying her well for being here, and she should obey some of his orders. Not this one of course—the tonic was her and Maggie's future—but she could pretend to. Easing the cork back into the crock, she stood and crossed the room to look out the window. There had to be someplace she could hide it. Close enough to be tended to regularly, but hidden well enough that no one would notice.

After contemplating the underground cellar and spring-house and deciding they would be too cool, she settled her gaze on the woodshed. This time of year, the only wood needed was for the cook stove, and therefore she'd be the only one visiting it regularly. The jug could easily be hidden there, and no one would question her venturing out to get wood.

As she removed the jug, the jar of yeast starter she'd brought from Ohio shifted. She quickly caught it before it had a chance to tumble. The lid could never be tightened completely or the yeast would go bad. Noting the contents had more than tripled in size, she set it on the floor along with the jug of tonic. The yeast could be used for many things besides making tonic.

After she had the tonic jug hidden in the wood pile, she returned to the bedroom and using the straw from the trunk, carefully packed the bottles of tonic into two small crates she'd found in the pantry. The bottles would be easier to spot in the woodshed, so she stored them under her bed. Then she went to the kitchen where she'd left the jar of yeast starter on the table. There was more than enough yeast to make several batches of iron muffins.

Her heart tumbled inside her chest. Maggie loved iron muffins. Mary however, was not overly fond of them, probably because whenever their larder had been low, that was what she'd made, knowing Maggie loved the muffins so much no other food was necessary. She'd never told Maggie that. Letting her sister believe they were a treat had been more comforting than telling her it was their way to stave off hunger.

As she separated the starter, setting aside enough to feed over the next few days until it would be ready to rest and ferment into more, she wondered how Maggie was faring. Steve's abundant supply of food had guilt twisting her stomach into knots. Being separated from Maggie, wondering if she was getting enough to eat, had a place to sleep, if people were being kind to her, was a constant worry. One she wasn't taking lightly.

The idea she couldn't do anything about it for the next thirty days weighed heavily. A few days were one thing. Being separated from Maggie for an entire month was entirely different. She would have to find a way to get a message to her sister. Perhaps she could convince Steve she needed help. He wouldn't have to pay Maggie. What he was already paying her would be more than enough for both of them.

Her mind was as busy as her hands as she mixed up a batch of dough and set it to rest while mixing up a second batch. Surely he would agree to the idea. He would be getting twice the help for the same amount of money. That wasn't true. As much as she loved her sister, Maggie had never been fond of work—that had been part of their argument on the train. Selling tonic was the only task Maggie had willingly taken on—and that wasn't really work. The tonic sold itself.

Thinking of the tonic made Mary's mind return to Steve. And she grinned. This time because of how he pretended he wasn't pleased to have her here. At least that was what he wanted her to believe. To believe he was a tyrant. That wasn't true. If he was, he'd have sent her to town with the mayor and the sheriff. Or with Brett last night.

A tyrant wouldn't have put out that kind of money just to have his employees fed. A tyrant would have told his men to fend for themselves.

Which would have not worked in her favor. Not at all.

An odd sensation rolled inside her. It was almost as if she was glad Maggie wasn't here, which made no sense. Flustered, she put all her focus into the muffins. By the time the first batch was ready to roll out, she had four other batches resting. She had to pull out every frying pan in the cupboards and when she was done grilling the muffins, there were enough to feed the men nothing but the spongy-on-the-inside-crisp-on-the-outside griddle cakes.

That of course wouldn't do, but she grinned, hoping Steve liked the muffins as much as Maggie did.

## Chapter Six

Steve couldn't remember a time he'd been so flat-out angry. At least not at himself. Like he was right now. The idea he'd given the mayor seventy-five dollars had eaten at him all afternoon. Was he daft? No cook—no woman—was worth the kind of money Mary was costing him. How tasty her food was didn't matter. Men ate for the substance not the taste.

At least that was the way it had always been. In less than a day, Mary had his men talking more about their next meal than the work they were doing. Other than Jess. Rather than talking about her cooking, he was talking about her. As in how she'd be marrying some lucky fellow next month.

Steve didn't consider any man getting married lucky, and considering how much she'd already cost him, the man marrying Mary McCary would be the unluckiest one ever. He couldn't wait for the month to be over and bid her good riddance. Hopefully he'd still have two nickels to rub together by then.

More eager than ever, the men put up their mounts, washed their hands and faces and all but knocked him down in their rush to get in the house, which only added to the fury fueling inside him.

The wondrous smells filling the kitchen didn't help his mood whatsoever. Neither did how every bite he took seemed tastier than the last. Those little round pieces of honeycomb bread that when slathered with the butter she'd mixed with honey were downright addicting. Every man at the table ate four or more, including him. The two platters that had been piled high when they'd entered the house now held nothing but crumbs. He wasn't sure what she'd done to the pork, either. Usually this time of year, having been smoked last fall, it was tougher than old leather, but what he'd just eaten hadn't been. It had been as soft and easy to chew as the beans she'd also served.

"That was the best bread I've ever eaten," Jess said, licking his lips. "What's it called?"

Steve had purposefully kept his gaze off Mary since entering the house. The anger that had built in him all afternoon hadn't only come from the money he'd laid out, or her cooking. It was the way she'd smiled and said thank-you to him earlier. At that moment, he'd known he'd never seen a more beautiful woman. With everything else, it would have been more fair if she'd been as homely as a half-plucked chicken. Beady eyes and all.

However, her eyes were far from beady. They were sparkling now, and twinkled brighter than stars in a midnight sky when she started to sing.

*"Do you know the muffin man, the muffin man, the muffin man? Do you know the muffin man, who lives in Drury Lane? Oh, yes, I know the muffin man, the muffin man, the muffin man. Yes, I know the muffin man who lives in Drury Lane."*

The men all clapped as she finished her little tune, which had been sung with a pitch-perfect cadence and a hint of an Irish accent that had put smiles on everyone's faces.

She curtsied. "Thank you. To answer your question, they are called muffins, and are my sister's favorite. A woman in Pennsylvania taught me how to make them several years ago."

It couldn't have been that many years ago. She wasn't that old. That thought brought upon another and Steve asked, "Pennsylvania? I thought you lived in Ohio."

"We did," she answered. "But we also lived in Pennsylvania."

"Well you can make those Pennsylvania muffins any time you want," Jess said.

Her giggle tickled something inside Steve. Or maybe it was the way she was smiling at Jess.

"They are called iron muffins because you grill them on top of the stove, like flapjacks," she said.

"We all like flapjacks," Jess said. His gaze then settled on Walter. "When made right."

"Perhaps I'll make some for breakfast then," she said while opening the door.

"Where are you going?" Steve asked.

"To get the clothes hanging on the line out back while you all finish eating."

Steve glanced at the table that didn't hold enough food to satisfy a ground squirrel. He would have told her that, but she'd already slipped out the door. He pushed his chair away from the table and grabbed his hat on the way out the door. However, once he found her at the clothesline, he had no idea why he'd followed.

"Did you need something, Mr. Putnam?" she asked while plucking off the pins with one hand and gathering the dried laundry with the other. "Was the meal not satisfactory?"

"The meal was fine." Still trying to come up with a reason to have followed her, he asked, "When did you live in Pennsylvania?"

Without looking his way, she asked, "Why?"

"Because—because I like to know a bit about the people who work for me." That was true. He usually interviewed any person he hired. Asked about their past, such as where they used to live.

"Actually, I lived in Pennsylvania several times. My father was a traveling man. Ohio just happened to be where he died."

"How? When?"

"Last winter. He was run over by an out-of-control stage."

The sadness of her tone had him wanting to touch her, to comfort her in some way. He settled for saying, "I'm sorry."

Sincerity filled her eyes as she said, "Thank you, but you didn't have anything to do with it." She dropped the handful of clothes into the basket near her feet. "However, this seems like the perfect time to mention something."

A shiver rippled over his shoulders. "What?"

"Rex." She started taking more clothes off the line. "I'm wondering if he should see the doctor again. When I changed his bandage today, there was still blood in it. I understand it's a deep wound, but would have thought it should be done bleeding by now."

Guilt shot up inside him. Once again he hadn't checked on Rex upon entering the house. That wasn't like him. He'd always prided himself on taking care of the men in his employ. "I'll send one of the men to town."

"It's not an emergency," she said. "Perhaps I could go tomorrow after lunch. I'd be back in plenty of time to have supper ready. If you'd loan me a horse."

"No, I'll send someone now." The men were filing out

of the house and he waved Jess over. For some reason, he didn't mind keeping Jess away from Mary.

Mary bit the inside of her cheek to keep from speaking. Rex didn't need a doctor. His wound was healing just fine—due to her tonic. She'd been attempting to finagle a way to see Maggie. That clearly wasn't going to happen. Jess was already on his way to the barn, more than happy for the chance to go to town. As she watched him disappear into the big building, she questioned the possibility of sending a message with him for Maggie.

"He'll be back shortly. I'll go see to Rex."

Mary spun around. "No." Catching how quickly she'd spoken, she added, "He's sleeping and shouldn't be disturbed right now." She gathered the last of the clothes. "I'll let you know when he's awake. Right now I need to get these clothes put away, the kitchen cleaned and then the cow milked."

Her conscience was kicking in again. Using Rex's injury hadn't been right. She'd seen the concern that had flashed in Steve's eyes, and knew she'd been unfair. Something he hadn't been at all.

Laying a hand on his arm, she said, "I'm sure Rex is fine. I just haven't had much experience in doctoring people."

He took a step backwards, pulling his arm out from under her hand. "You aren't expected to be a doctor. Just a cook."

That made her feel worse. As did the way he walked away. Sighing, she gathered the basket off the ground and carried it to the house. To her surprise, the dishes were stacked on the counter and the table wiped clean. A heavy bout of remorse struck her. The men, all of them, were more helpful than they needed to be, and here she was trying to find a way to shuck her duties in order to see Maggie, when in truth, there wasn't much she'd be able to do for her sister. Knowing Maggie—and she did know her sister well—she was probably having the time of her life. She certainly had been while they'd been on the train.

"Aw, fairy dust," Mary muttered. It was her curse. That's what Da had always said. No matter how they were treated, the oldest always felt responsible for everyone else. That certainly was true for her. She'd felt responsible for Maggie for as long as she could remember. Still did.

After folding the laundry, mainly her extra dress and underthings, and the few items of Steve's and Rex's that had needed to be washed—Rex had said Saturday was his normal washing day but she couldn't wait for tomorrow—she set into doing the dishes.

She was still elbow deep in sudsy water when Steve walked in and set a bucket on the counter.

"What's that?" she asked.

"I had other chores to see to, so I went ahead and milked the cow."

She closed her eyes against another good bout of shame. "Thank you, but that wasn't necessary."

"You might be needed when the doctor gets here."

"What's that sawbones coming back out here for?" Rex shouted. "Who got hurt?"

"He's awake," Steve said.

Mary merely nodded while not looking his way. Nor did she follow him into Rex's room. There was no need to be in attendance when he discovered Rex was healing fine. Other than in case he decided to fire her.

If that was her fate, so be it.

That thought sent a fiery sting up her spine. No. She couldn't be fired. She had to stay here long enough to bottle up her tonic. More than that, she needed to fulfill her part of their bargain. Steve deserved that much. Grabbing a towel, she dried her hands while walking to Rex's room.

"Will you tell him I don't need no doctor?" Rex asked as she entered the room. "With you nursing me, I'll be dancing a jig in a day or two."

"I'm sure you will be." Smiling as she crossed the room in order to fluff the pillow behind him, she said, "But there is no harm in the doctor confirming that, now is there?"

Rex glanced to the spoon he insisted upon keeping on the table by his side. They'd agreed to keep the tonic hidden, and that he could only have small amounts at a time—with no one but the two of them knowing about it. "I suspect not," he said. "But if he starts poking and prodding, I'm gonna tell him to leave. Same goes for the medicine he left behind. That stuff's as bitter as unripe chokecherries."

Her mind once again shot to her tonic, and had her asking, "Are there chokecherry trees around here?"

"Sure are," Rex answered. "Several line the creek that runs through the springhouse."

They would be perfect, but, unfortunately, they wouldn't be ripe yet, not for another couple of months.

"Why?"

Feeling Steve's eyes on her, she said, "Because their drupes make very good jam."

"Mmm…" Rex said. "I bet that would be tasty on those muffins you made."

"Yes, it would be," she answered. Chokecherry syrup would also be perfect for sweetening the tonic. She wouldn't still be here when the berries would be ripe, so it was a good thing any type of fruit would work. When in a pinch, Da had just used sugar water. Of course that lacked flavor, but loyal customers had still bought the tonic. It had been her job to harvest whatever berries they could find and make syrup in order to sweeten the tonic batches throughout the winter. Unfortunately, she hadn't been able to collect enough berries last fall and still needed something to add to the batch brewing in the wood pile. If unable to find anything else, she'd already concluded she'd use some of the dried apple chips in the pantry. Made out of just honey, water and yeast, the tonic was too bitter to be taken without sweetener. It was too potent, too. Da claimed that without the sweetener watering it down it would get a man drunk faster than a sailor sucking on a rum pot.

Once again, it was the sense of being watched that drew her mind back to the present. She turned to meet Steve's frowning stare, and her stomach bubbled. The only other person who had ever known her thoughts was Maggie, yet, her instincts said Steve knew exactly what she was thinking about. Darting for the door, she said, "I—I'll go finish the dishes."

After the cream was separated from the milk and the kitchen put to order, with the tonic still front and center in her mind, she carried the milk and cream to the springhouse and then stopped at the woodshed to burp the crock. Satisfied it was well-hidden and safe, she gathered an armload of wood and returned to the house. Once it was neatly stacked in the box by the stove, she collected the clothes off the table.

She was putting her things in the dresser when Steve appeared in the doorway of her bedroom. She sensed rather than saw him. Her insides were extremely good at letting her know when he was near. Drawing a deep breath to calm the butterflies taking flight in her stomach, she said, "I set your things on your bed. If you have anything else to be washed, please set it in the hallway tomorrow morning."

"Did you get rid of it?"

She not only knew exactly what he referred to, she had

proof he'd read her mind downstairs. With a wave towards her trunk, she said, "Go ahead and see for yourself."

"I'm not going to rummage through your things, Miss McCary. A simple yes or no is all I need."

Neither yes nor no was simple. Both would be a lie. The crock was gone, but there were two crates of bottles under the bed.

A knock on the door downstairs saved her from answering. Walking past him, she said, "That must be the doctor."

It was, and his arrival hadn't saved her from anything. Brushing past Steve upstairs had made her heart miss several beats. Perhaps because now he'd know Rex was healing just fine. She certainly was making a pickle out of things.

"Doc, thanks for coming out so quickly," Steve said as he welcomed the doctor through the front door. "Jess must have had his horse at a run all the way to town."

"No, he caught me as I was leaving the Matthews place," the doctor answered. "One of Fred's cowboys had a run-in with a rattler. They're thick on the ground this year. Tell your boys to keep an eye out."

"I will," Steve said, closing the door. "I hope Fred's cowboy's all right."

"He will be," the doctor answered. "It happened near the house and Mrs. Matthews instantly put an onion poultice on it to draw out the poison. Wasn't much I could do except recommend some whiskey." He was looking at her while talking, and with a shake of his head, said, "You and your sister are identical. If not for your dress, I'd believe I just saw you in town, singing an Irish ballad with Otis Taylor." He held out one hand. "I'm Dr. Nelson Graham."

Mary managed to smile and shake his hand while the contents of her stomach curdled. Maggie *was* having the time of her life. Singing songs with strange men it appeared. Mary should be happy her sister was faring so well, but couldn't find much to be happy about—knowing Maggie was having fun while she was working her fingers to the bones. Actually, that wasn't any different. The fact Maggie didn't seem to be concerned about her at all was what bothered her. Just as it had bothered her on the train. When Maggie had been too busy with her new friends to fulfill their plan of getting off the train.

"Rex is this way," Steve said. "In his room. Miss McCary said there was fresh blood in the bandage she changed today."

"Let's have a look-see," the doctor said. "Oh, and by the way, Jess told me to tell you he went on into town to check out the party they're having for the brides."

Mary watched the two walk through the front parlor. Both were tall with black hair, but while the doctor had a shiny black mustache, Steve's face was clean-shaven. She wouldn't call the doctor homely, but Steve was far more handsome. What an odd thing for her to consider right now. Perhaps her thoughts went in that direction because Maggie was still on her mind. Her sister had always been the first to point out a handsome man and was most likely dancing with every one she saw at that party right now.

"Miss McCary?"

She hurried forward, "Coming."

"The doctor asked when you'd changed Rex's bandage," Steve said as she stopped in the doorway to Rex's room.

She glanced from Steve to the doctor and back again, taking note the butterflies only appeared while looking at Steve. Or standing next to him. Or thinking about him. For a brief moment, she wondered if Maggie ever experienced these types of butterflies. With a quick vow to stop thinking of such things, she said, "This morning."

"I told him that," Rex said. "And that I'm healing faster than an egg fries. Ain't that right?"

"How much blood was there?" the doctor asked her.

"None," Rex answered.

"Some," she added, purposefully not looking at Steve. "Not a lot, but some."

The doctor finished removing the bandage around Rex's shin. "Hmmm," he mumbled, turning the leg to look at both sides. "The stitches are holding, it's even starting to scab. Perhaps that's what happened, a scab let loose during the bandage change. It looks to be healing nicely." Glancing toward Rex, he asked, "How's it feel?"

Rex had his arms crossed over his chest and a rather pouty expression on his face. "Fine. Which is exactly what I told Steve there. Don't need no one doctoring me except Mary there, she's doing a right fine job."

"I can see that," Dr. Graham said. "But I'd planned on stopping out here as soon as I was done at Fred's, just to check on you."

Steve's jaw went tight. Not because of what Nelson had said. He believed the doctor would have planned on stopping out to see Rex considering he'd been so close, it was how Nelson had winked at Mary that didn't set well. He glanced her way. "Miss McCary, would you put on some coffee for the doctor before he makes his leave?"

"Yes, of course," she said, turning about.

Steve waited until she was out of the room before he lowered his voice to ask, "Did you donate to the committee for a wife?"

"Yes," Nelson answered. "But I'm actually hoping to find a nurse. I could use the help. One that doubles as a wife…" With a shrug the doctor turned his attention back to Rex's leg.

"Mary ain't up for grabs," Rex said. "Steve hired her to cook for the boys."

"I heard as much," Nelson said while winding the bandage around the wound. "I heard he also donated to the committee."

"He sure enough did," Rex replied. "A very fine donation to keep her right here with us."

"Plan on marrying her?"

Nelson was looking at him now and the hair on Steve's neck stood on end. "No."

"How is she going to make her choice then?" Nelson asked.

"What choice?"

"Which man she'll marry," Nelson answered.

"She doesn't plan on marrying any of them," Rex said.

Steve shot a glare at the old coot. When had everyone started butting into his conversations? That never used to happen.

"Well," Nelson said, dropping the sheet back over Rex's leg. "She has to marry one of us. One of those who donated."

"Why?" Steve asked. "If she doesn't want to, she doesn't have to."

"She doesn't have a choice," Nelson said. "She signed a contract that says by the end of thirty days, she'll marry one of the participating men."

"She did?"

Nelson nodded. "Josiah, as the town's only lawyer, wrote up the contracts, and the women signed them as they stepped on the train. Of course, in pure Josiah fashion, the clause about marrying one of the men by the end of thirty days was in fine print at the very bottom of the page."

"You can't force someone to marry if they don't want to," Steve said.

"In this case, I'm sure they'll each want to," Nelson said.

"Why?"

"From what the train conductor said, none of them had much of a life back in Ohio, and it appears, for the McCary sisters, it was jail or Kansas. I doubt either of them wants to go back to jail, so they'll marry someone."

# Chapter Seven

Steve gestured for Nelson to take a seat at the table. Even though he'd eaten his fill just a short time ago, the sight of a plate of muffins made his mouth water.

"Would you care for a muffin, Dr. Graham?" Mary asked. "Rex was afraid the others would eat them all and asked me to hide a few."

"No wonder he's so keen on having no one else doctor him," Nelson said, taking a muffin and coating it with the butter she'd mixed with honey. "I doubt he's ever been so pampered."

Steve sat down when Mary put a cup of coffee in front of him and reached over to take a muffin. The way the doctor was devouring the one he'd taken, there soon wouldn't be any left.

"These are delicious," Nelson said. "I've never tasted anything like them."

"Thank you," Mary said, putting a muffin on a plate. "Please excuse me, I'm going to take Rex some coffee and a muffin."

Nelson took a second muffin and as he spread the butter over it, he said, "I'll stop to see Rex regularly. Don't want infection setting in that leg."

Steve didn't tell the doctor that wasn't necessary, but he wanted to. Sincerely wanted to. More than an hour later, when it appeared Nelson might never leave, Steve told Nelson, "I had Walt saddle your horse. It'll be dark soon and Miss McCary needs to be up early to have breakfast ready."

"I hadn't realized so much time had passed," Nelson said, making no move to push away from the table where he'd sat and eaten a plate full of muffins and drunk a pot of coffee, all the while conversing with Mary after she'd returned from serving Rex. He'd started out by telling her how to care for Rex's leg, but that had only taken five minutes.

The next hour the two of them had talked and laughed, and laughed and talked. Steve had known Nelson since the man had first traveled through while working for the railroad, healing those injured during the building of the line. Nelson had returned to Oak Grove because the mayor had promised it would be a growing community in great need of a doctor. In all that time, the doctor had never irritated him once, but tonight, Nelson had Steve's nerves grinding against each other.

"Thank you for the visit, Dr. Graham," Mary said as the man stood. "Though I've never visited the cities in Pennsylvania that you have, I enjoyed conversing about them. I sincerely miss the countryside." She side heavily. "The lush green grass and tall trees."

"Please, you must call me Nelson, and it was a delight to visit with you, Mary." Nelson gave a slight bow as he smiled. "Perhaps we can do it again soon."

*Not in his kitchen.* Steve didn't say that aloud, but he would make sure it didn't happen. "Thanks for stopping out, Doc." He opened the back door. "Your horse is right there."

While he held the door open for Nelson's exit, Mary disappeared into Rex's room, and shouted for the doctor within seconds. Steve left the door to hurry across the room, almost running into her as she exited the bedroom.

"Doctor Graham," she shouted around him. "You forgot your bag!"

"Oh, thank you, Mary," Nelson said, planting an elbow in Steve's side. "I would have remembered before I arrived in town and then would have had to return."

Right then Steve knew full well the doctor had left the bag behind on purpose, and that irritated him more than a pack of coyotes. He'd never been a jealous man, but Mary was his. His cook anyway. He took the bag from her, handed it to Nelson, and all but dragged the man to his horse. There he growled, "You best set your sights on one of those other gals, Doc."

"You said you weren't interested in marrying her," Nelson said as he climbed into his saddle.

"I'm not," Steve agreed, "but I hired her as my cook and that means she's not available to anyone else, for any other reason."

"For the next month," Nelson said, swinging his horse around. "Which is exactly when she'll be getting married. It's only fair she gets to know the men who are her options."

Steve's back teeth clenched together so hard his jaw stung. Without a word, he spun around and marched back into the house. Mary was once again walking out of Rex's bedroom, carrying a plate and cup. Too irritated to say much, Steve walked past her, but as he passed Rex's door, he said, "You better hurry up and heal old man."

Mary turned about to watch as Steve stormed out of the room, and a moment later, heard the front door slam.

"What's gotten into him?" Rex asked from the bedroom.

"I'm not sure," Mary answered. Yet the sinking feeling she had told her what was bothering Steve. Her. He'd been grumpy the entire time she'd been visiting with the doctor. She hadn't enjoyed Nelson Graham's company as much as she let on. She simply hadn't wanted either Steve or Rex to mention her tonic. The doctor could cause trouble for her and Maggie. After she washed up and put away the few dishes, she bade good-night to Rex and hurried upstairs to prepare for bed before Steve came back in the house.

She must have been sound asleep when he walked past her bedroom door, for she certainly hadn't heard any footsteps. Not last night or this morning. The sun had awakened her bright and early, and she already had a stack of flapjacks staying warm in the oven when the men made their way into the kitchen.

Jess crossed the room with a shy smile. "I could milk for you this morning if it's helpful."

"Thank you," she answered. "But it's already taken care of. I knew it would take a lot of flapjacks to feed you all."

"I figured the same thing," Jess said. "I tried to talk to your sister last night, tell her you were out here, but she kept disappearing on me."

"Disappearing?"

"Yep, dancing from one man to the next, then she just up and disappeared from the party. I thought I saw her over by Jackson Miller's place, but it wasn't her." He shrugged. "Sorry."

"Thank you for trying, Jess, that was kind of you." Glancing around the room again, and still not seeing Steve, she said, "Next time you go to town, would you mind taking a message to Maggie for me?"

"Not at all," he said. "Just say the word." He winked at her as he started for the table. "It'll be just between the three of us."

Steve walked in then and Mary's insides jolted so hard

she almost spilled the pancake batter. She thought twice then about involving Jess. Steve expected loyalty from his men.

She should provide that same loyalty and respect. Maybe that was why she was so out of sorts.

"It sure smells good out there," Rex shouted from the bedroom.

"I'll have a plate for you in a minute," she responded.

"I'll fix one for him."

Steve's voice was so close behind her she jumped. Planting her feet firmly on the floor, she scooped several flapjacks out of the pans and set them on a plate she'd set near the stove for Rex. "Thank you. There's a tray with syrup and butter on the other side of the sink for him."

"I know," he said. "Expected it to have a vase filled with flowers."

The snide remark said he wasn't in any better of a mood than he had been last night, but she chose to ignore it. She'd dealt with ornery people her entire life. Very few had ever been kind to her or her family. That, however, had not influenced her behavior in return—less a few people, namely the sheriff back in Ohio. She'd tried being nice to Sheriff Freiday many times but because of his attitude an eye for an eye had come to play.

Her stomach sank at the idea of that happening here.

Steve returned while she was setting two steaming plates of flapjacks on the table. "Eat up," she told the men. "I'll keep cooking flapjacks as long as you keep eating them."

"Don't say that around Leroy," Henry said. "We'll be here all day."

Leroy was gangly and thin, but she'd already seen him eat twice as much as everyone else. Laughing along with the others, she said, "Well, then, I may have to go gather more eggs at some point."

It wasn't until their laughter died down because they'd started forking flapjacks dripping with syrup into their mouths that she realized she'd started to like these men. They were each good people in their own right, and treated her with more respect than she'd ever had.

She then concluded that could be why she wasn't dreading the next few weeks. Cooking for Steve wasn't nearly the chore it could have been.

He was eating along with the others, but while they were grinning and enjoying their meal, a scowl that was now becoming familiar sat upon his face. She knew it was because of her, and that made her feel sad in a way she never had before.

She'd already learned that when his plate became empty, the others took that as a sign to quickly finish theirs. By the time he set his fork down, the men were already reaching for the hats they'd set on the floor.

One by one they thanked her as they made their way to the door. He was always the last one out, and this morning, she spoke before he had a chance to. "Lunch will be done by noon."

On impulse, she met the dull glare he sent her way with a smile, and held it on her face until he'd shut the door. Then she slumped against the counter. "Horse feathers," she muttered. Why did she let him get to her so deeply? Sure he was paying her, had laid out an extraordinary amount of money for her to be able to remain here, but that wasn't her fault. And yes, she'd shown up out here uninvited, but he had needed a cook and she fit that bill. She'd even hauled her brewing batch of tonic outside just to please him. Well, partially please him. Which she also needed to go see to. In this heat it needed to be burped more than once a day or it would blow the cork clear out of the cask.

She set into clearing the table and told herself to just

stop worrying about Steve Putnam. There was nothing she could do about him so there was no use wasting time on it one way or the other.

Hours later she'd just completed layering onion slices amongst several slabs of beef she'd cook for the noon meal when she heard the thud of horse hooves along with the jangle of harnesses. Curious, she made her way through the parlor and to the front door. Joy filled her so fully she rushed onto the front porch and then down the steps.

As soon as Maggie hit the ground, lifted out of the wagon by a tall man, she ran to the porch, arms open wide.

"I'm sorry about the train," Maggie said as she rushed up the steps.

Mary wrapped her arms around Maggie and held her tight. "'Tis forgotten," she whispered, holding back stinging tears. "We both have our tempers."

"I couldn't wait another day to make sure you were all right."

"It's good you came," Mary said. "I've been so worried about you."

Maggie sniffled against her shoulder before saying, "You smell of onions! You really are working, aren't you?"

Mary chuckled. She'd always worked, but Maggie had never considered all she'd done as work. Not willing to go into that now, she looked over Maggie's shoulder. "I see you brought Anna." Mary's stomach fluttered at seeing Steve walk out of the barn that Anna was pointing toward while talking to the man who'd driven the wagon.

"She's making eyes at Mr. Miller," Maggie said. "I don't know who was chaperoning who on our drive out here."

Mary felt more than heard something in Maggie's tone, and as her gaze settled on Steve, who stood near the barn door staring back at her, she knew what it was. Jealousy. It dawned on her then, that she'd had these feelings once before. On the train. She'd been jealous of Maggie paying so much attention to her new friends.

Maggie had taken a step back, and Mary took her hand. "Looks like she's following him to the corral. Come inside and we will catch up." It would do her mind and her heart good to visit with her sister privately.

In the front parlor, she asked, "Would you care for something to drink? I have some fresh buttermilk."

"Goodness, you sound like I'm a guest rather than your sister," Maggie said.

"You are both," Mary said, glancing out the front window at where Steve stood with the other two guests. She couldn't be jealous of him. Just couldn't. "One I'm extremely happy to see."

"I had to make sure you were all right," Maggie said.

"I am," Mary said, turning away from the window. "Jess tried to tell you that, but you kept disappearing on him."

Maggie's eyes widened. "Jess Rader. You know him?"

"Yes, he works here. Steve had sent him to town last night to fetch Dr. Graham."

"I had no idea," Maggie said. "I thought he was after me for another reason."

"A dance mayhap? Or to join him in song?"

Maggie frowned slightly. "No."

Mary bit her lip. She wasn't that upset over her sister enjoying the party. She just wasn't herself. "Come into the kitchen. I need to put the beef in the oven."

"So you really are cooking meals for people?"

"Yes, that's what a cook does, and what I've done for years. Cooking for ten isn't that much different than cooking for two or three."

"Ten?"

Mary grinned. "Some of the men eat enough for two,

and unlike you and Da, they are all very appreciative of my skills."

Maggie frowned. "Da and I were never unappreciative of your cooking." She shook her head, and her voice grew small as she said, "We both knew neither of us would have had anything to eat if not for you."

A touch of chagrin made her stomach bubble. "I'm sorry," Mary said. "I was teasing you. I just wanted you to know I'm appreciated here, and well, enjoying it. However," she whispered since they were near Rex's doorway and she'd have to introduce Maggie within moments. "I have a plan. This is the perfect place to bottle up the tonic, and to make a second batch. Steve has an entire crock of honey in the root cellar. By the time I'm done working here, we'll have more than enough money to leave town with enough tonic to sell in order to get us wherever we chose to go."

## Chapter Eight

The young woman's squeaky voice made Steve's spine quiver. Whatever she was talking about, something to do with the buggy ride to the ranch, was so jumbled he looked at Jackson Miller, hoping the man would interrupt. Instead, Jackson shook his head and rubbed one temple.

As soon as the woman took a breath, Steve asked, "Wouldn't you like to join the women in the house?"

"No," the woman said. "I told Maggie I'd stay out here so she and her sister can visit in private."

"Isn't that kind of you," he muttered.

"Yes, it is," she said.

Over the top of her head, Steve met Jackson's apologetic gaze and his shrug. As the woman started talking again, and while Jackson rubbed at his other temple, Steve sent up a silent prayer concerning how thankful he was that Mary was nothing like this woman. If that had been the case, he couldn't have endured her for an hour let alone thirty days. That also made him concede he'd have to put up with this woman for a bit longer. Mary deserved a few minutes alone with her sister.

Less than an hour later, he concluded the sisters had had all the alone time they were going to get. Both he and Jackson were squeezing their temples, and it didn't help. The shrill-voiced woman didn't shut up, which made him sincerely regret not riding out with the other men this morning. He'd chosen to stay close to the house because of last night and when he'd heard a wagon rolling in, he'd been ninety percent sure it would be Nelson Graham.

Then he'd been ready to tell the man to leave.

Now he wished it had been Nelson.

"Let's get some coffee," he said when the woman took another breath.

"Sounds good to me," Jackson said.

Steve led the others through the back door, but found no reprieve when he saw the kitchen was empty. "Wait here," he said, hurrying across the room. He paused at Rex's doorway.

Rex pointed to the ceiling.

Steve nodded and hurried to the base of the stairway. "Miss McCary?"

"Coming," she shouted. "Be right there."

When she appeared at the top of the steps, he'd never been so glad to see someone.

She frowned slightly as she stared down the steps. "Is something wrong?"

"Why?"

Eyeing him closely, she said, "Because you're smiling."

"Because I'm happy to see you," he said, and then caught her arm as she stumbled forward having missed a step. He grabbed her other arm to stop her wobbles and then lifted her down the last two steps.

Her eyes were wide and startled. "You're happy to see me?"

"Yes," he whispered honestly. "That Anna woman is driving me batty. She doesn't shut up. I can't take it any longer."

She took a step back, her feet now on the floor, but he didn't release her arms, afraid she might run back up the steps.

"I'm serious. I can't—" He shook his head, not sure how to explain how annoyed his nerves were. "I just can't."

She giggled slightly. "I know what you mean. I was stuck on a train with her."

"I'm sorry," he said, meaning it.

The twinkle in her eyes made him smile again. She smiled, too. "I have coffee and cookies ready. That will help."

"Thank you." Suddenly remembering why he'd been stuck with Anna, he asked, "Where's your sister?"

"She'll be down in a minute," Mary said. "Come, I'll make a tray for you to take outside."

Steve had a sudden urge to hug her. Instead he said, "I knew I could count on you."

True to her word, within minutes, she shooed him and Jackson outside with cups full of coffee and a tray of ginger cookies. Once they'd eaten a few cookies and emptied their coffee cups, they headed for the barn. He needed a couple of cabinets built for the tack room, and having Jackson here was a great opportunity to have the area measured and to explain exactly what he wanted.

They were still there when the women appeared. Mary introduced him to her sister, who did look a lot like her, but different at the same time. He couldn't put his finger on it, for their features were virtually identical, including their long wavy black hair and glistening blue eyes, but… That was it. It was the eyes. Mary's were brighter, bolder and prettier. Much prettier.

"Mr. Miller," the sister, Maggie, said, "I believe it's time for us to return to town."

Jackson nodded. "Whenever you're ready."

The squeaky-voiced Anna pronounced she was ready to leave, too, claiming she'd seen enough cows. Steve hoped she'd seen enough for a lifetime. Every ounce of his body thanked the heavens above that he didn't have to ride in that buggy all the way back to town, but at the same time, he noticed how sadness clouded Mary's eyes. He stepped closer to her side. "You're welcome to visit any time, Maggie."

"Thank you, Mr. Putnam, I will be back, and in the meantime I do expect you to take very good care of my sister."

He grinned. They were alike in many ways besides looks. "I promise I will." He then slapped Jackson on the back. "I'll help you hitch up the horse."

Once the buggy was ready, he talked to Jackson about his order for a moment longer while the sisters embraced. When they parted, he helped Anna into her seat, Jackson assisted Maggie onto the bench next to her and Steve moved to stand next to Mary again. Noting the moisture on her lashes, he couldn't stop his arm from wrapping around her shoulder.

"She can visit any time," he said.

"I know," Mary whispered while slightly leaning against him. "I just miss her. We've never been parted before."

He held his breath at how right it felt to have his arm around her. Then, while questioning that, he asked, "Do you want to go with her?"

"To Oak Grove?" Mary asked.

"Yes."

"What for?"

"To live. So you aren't parted."

She tilted her head upwards. "Who would cook for the men?"

He shrugged. "Me."

She laughed. Then slapped his chest playfully and laughed harder.

"I can cook," he said.

Lifting a hand, she waved at her sister as the buggy started down the road. "Probably about as well as I can milk a cow," she said dryly.

He couldn't stop a chuckle. Or the silent acknowledgment of how much he'd come to like this woman. "Probably."

As she turned and glanced at the house, a serene smile covered her face before she looked at him. "Thank you, though, for offering. I appreciate that."

Meeting her gaze, eye for eye, smile for smile, he concluded how lucky he was that she'd come along when she had. "Thank you for staying," he said. "I appreciate that."

"Then we're even," she said.

"I guess we are."

"Good." She frowned slightly. "That is good, isn't it?"

"I hope so, because we're stuck with each other for a few weeks yet."

She turned slightly, looking toward the buggy that was growing smaller. "It could be worse."

A shiver rippled his shoulders at the memory of Anna's voice. "You don't have to tell me that."


Mary wasn't exactly sure what made her so happy. It could have been Maggie's visit, but the warmth filling her hadn't appeared until Steve had put his arm around her. That wasn't completely true. It had started when she'd seen him at the bottom of the staircase, staring up at her and smiling. For a man, he was very likeable when he wanted to be. Extremely handsome, too. Even Maggie, and of course Anna, had said so.

Actually, after the men had gone out to the barn, Anna had barely stopped talking. As ususal. She'd even had the nerve to suggest it wasn't proper for Mary to be staying out here, living with so many men all by herself. Anna had claimed Rebecca would say it was highly improper. That there should be a chaperone out here. Mary had pointed out that Oak Grove didn't have enough women for the men to marry, let alone act as chaperones, hence the reason they'd all been shipped out here, and that she was far more chaperoned with all the men living here than any of them in town were.

Anna didn't have a response to that, or if she had, Mary simply hadn't listened. She hadn't cared what the girl had to say on the train, and certainly didn't now.

"Well," she said, "I have potatoes to peel. The boys will be in to eat soon."

"Do you need any help?"

Holding in a giggle, she shook her head. From what Rex had said, Steve's cooking skills were worse than Walter's. "No, but Rex is awfully bored. Do you think we could fashion a crutch so he can get out of bed and join the rest of you at the table for meals?"

"I'm not the carpenter that Jackson Miller is, but I probably could come up with something."

"That would be wonderful," she said. "I know he'd like that."

"And you would, too."

The shine in his eyes made her heart skip. "Yes, I would."

"Then consider it done. I'll have it ready by the time you have the potatoes cooked."

As they parted, Mary released a sigh. A heartfelt one. She'd told Maggie that landing in Steve's lap—no she hadn't mentioned that specifically, but had said acquiring a job at Steve's ranch—had been the luckiest thing that had ever happened to her. And it was.

## Chapter Nine

Mary couldn't put her finger on exactly what or why, but ever since Maggie's visit, something had changed between her and Steve. Something that made her feel, well, content. Happy. Working for him hadn't been difficult before, and now with a new crutch, Rex was helping out more and more, which gave her spare time. She wasn't used to that. Scrounging for money and food took up far more time and effort than working for Steve ever would. The past few days she'd almost resorted to twiddling her thumbs. She hadn't, of course. The house, despite being neat and tidy on the surface, had needed a deep cleaning and a bit of organization. It was by far the most beautiful home she'd ever lived in, and she liked making it shine and sparkle.

Her efforts had unearthed a treasure. Another full pot of honey and a crock perfect for mixing up a second batch of tonic. The first batch wasn't quite ready to bottle up, but the next time Jess went to town, she planned on sending a message with him asking Maggie how the bottles she'd taken to town were being received. With two further batches to sell, she and Maggie would be practically rich by the time they left Oak Grove.

The honey she'd found had separated from sitting in the

cellar for so long, but that hadn't mattered since she had to heat it up to make the tonic, and she'd covered up what she was doing by making several batches of honey taffy. Her arms had ached that night from pulling the taffy and the tedious work of wrapping each piece in buttered paper, but the cowboys had appreciated her labor. Every day they each had pocketed a few pieces to tide them between meals.

Even Steve.

A tinge of heat tickled her cheeks at the thought of him. She ignored it as she stuck the hoe in the ground again, but couldn't ignore how other parts of her body reacted to thinking about him. Somewhere along the way, she'd started to like him. A lot. It may be because Maggie's visit had given her a glimpse of what she'd be dealing with back in town. She'd have gone crazy having to live with all the other girls. Although she missed Maggie tremendously, she was enjoying the peacefulness of living on the ranch. Crowds, people in general, got on her nerves at times.

No matter where they'd lived, she'd always enjoyed the times when both Da and Maggie were off selling the tonic or doing some other task. It gave her time to think and she most certainly got more done without interruptions.

An inner sense had her lifting her head, peering into the vastness of the wide open space. Little more than a dark silhouette of a rider could be seen, but the skip of her heart told her who it was. Lunch had only been an hour ago, so there was no reason she could think of for Steve to return so soon. Rex had said the roundup and branding would continue for several weeks yet.

She carried the hoe to the garden gate. After stepping through the opening, she leaned the hoe against the fence while hooking the gate closed. The sight of him made her smile. He was not only handsome, he was kind and, well, fun. At the end of the working day, he'd taken to inviting her to sit on the porch with him and tell her about something funny that had happened that day.

"Forget something?" she asked as he brought his horse to a stop.

"No. Found something." He climbed off the horse, holding the kerchief he usually wore around his neck in one hand.

Curious, she stepped closer. "What is it?"

He folded back one corner of the kerchief and the cutest little faces she'd ever seen appeared.

"Oh, my. Two baby raccoons."

"Careful," Steve warned as she reached a hand out to stroke the little heads. Normally he'd have left the coons alone. Walter had been the one to find them, and the one who suggested bringing them home to Mary. Said that all women liked babies and that she'd enjoy seeing these two. Steve wasn't completely convinced bringing the coons home was a good idea, but the shine in her eyes said Walter had been right about her joy in seeing them.

"Where's their mother? They'll die without her," she said sadly.

"A coyote got her. I thought you might like to feed these two for the next few days."

Her eyes shone brighter than stars as she looked up at him. "Really?"

"Yes, really." Even with his insides beaming over her joy, he felt inclined to warn, "Only for a short time. They are wild animals."

"Oh, I know," she said, gently taking the kerchief. "I know coons can be a menace, but these two won't be. I promise."

Satisfied she understood, and pleased she liked his surprise, he nodded. "There's an old crate in the barn. I'll put some straw in it for them."

Cradling the coons in the crook of one arm while stroking their heads with her other hand, she walked beside him toward the barn. "Could they stay in the house, just for today? I have bread to bake and don't want them to feel abandoned again so soon."

The pleading in her eyes made saying no impossible. "I expect so."

She gave a little squeal of delight. "Thank you, Steve. I've never had a pet before." Quickly, she continued, "Not that these two will be pets. I understand that. They are just so adorable."

"My granddad had a pet skunk," he said as they walked. "It lived under the outhouse."

"He did?"

As her gaze wandered toward the outhouse between the house and the woodshed, he chuckled. "Not here. Back in Georgia."

"Weren't you afraid of getting sprayed?"

"I was too little to remember, but my father talked about it, and how afraid my mother was to go to the outhouse by herself."

"I don't blame her."

They entered the barn, and as he opened the door to the tack room, she asked, "Was it hard for you to move out here? Leaving your family behind?"

"Didn't have much family to leave behind. Just a few cousins. Most of the rest had been killed during the war, and I was excited to move West." He wasn't one to talk much about his life, but he'd found her easy to talk to, and had started to share more than usual with her.

"Has it been all you dreamed it would be?"

He paused momentarily, remembering the hardships and

losses, but then nodded. "Yes, it has been. Not at first, but nothing is in the beginning."

"That's an interesting way to look at things."

He carried the crate out the doorway and toward a pile of straw. "What is?"

"Well, it seems to me that people expect the most in the beginning."

"I suspect that is why most people are disappointed, then, isn't it?"

Her gaze was thoughtful as she glanced down to the baby raccoons.

A twinge of guilt at stealing away her excitement had him saying, "You don't have to take care of them. I'm sure one of the boys—"

"No. I want to take care of them." She shrugged. "I was just thinking about what you said, about being disappointed because things didn't work out in the beginning."

"Are you referring to leaving Ohio?"

She shrugged.

"Why did you agree to leave if you never intended on becoming a bride?"

She looked around the barn and then at the raccoons again before saying, "Because there was nothing there for us. No family. No friends."

Her despondent tone had him wanting to squeeze her hand, or her shoulder, or all of her. Give her a big solid hug. He couldn't do any of those things, so he held up the crate now full of straw. "Put those little guys in here and I'll carry them into the house for you."

She gently set the coons still wrapped in his kerchief in the crate. "Thank you."

"You're welcome." As she fell in step beside him, he said, "I'm sure these critters will be as happy as my cowboys that you didn't get off that train before it arrived in Oak Grove."

The smile that appeared on her face was accompanied by a shine on her cheeks. "Only because they were, and always are, hungry."

"And they like clean clothes," he teased.

She smiled again, but said nothing more while opening the door to the house. He wanted to ask if she liked being here, but, in truth, was afraid she might say no. It wasn't as if she'd had a lot of options. Nor had he. Which didn't goad him like it once had. Neither did the money he'd put out. The house was so clean it gleamed, there wasn't a hole or loose button on any of his clothing, and the meals always on the table were beyond any he'd eaten in the past. All of that, and her, had given cause for the pride he felt over his ranch to increase even more.

"I'll put the crate in the far corner," he said, walking past Rex's closed bedroom door. Without her, Rex may have lost his other leg. The old man would have insisted on feeding the men, and that wouldn't have given him time to heal.

"Thank you. I'm going to soak some bread crust in milk, see if they'll eat that."

She was at the counter, already taking a dish out of the cupboard. He set the box down and unfolded the kerchief so the critters could move about. Curious by nature, the raccoons started sniffing and scratching at the hay and kerchief with their little front paws. He hadn't thought much about her arrival, but now figured she had to have been about as nervous as the raccoons when she'd first entered his kitchen. Guilt once again filtered through his system. He was being more kind to these baby critters than he had been to her. Yet, without her, life around here would have been a fiasco.

He stood, and before he lost the courage, crossed the

room and set both hands on her shoulders. As he turned her
about, his heart stopped midbeat. So did his mind. Looking upon her adorable face, all he could think about was
kissing her.

Her gaze skimmed over his face, his lips, making him
wonder if she could read his mind. He let go of her shoulders. "I—I'm also glad you didn't get off that train before
Oak Grove."

She frowned slightly, as if not sure she believed him.
Then a smile formed. One that dang near knocked the
breath right out of him. She was pretty, remarkably so, but
up close, seeing how those blue eyes shone, he couldn't say
he'd ever seen a more beautiful woman.

Shifting slightly, she opened the cupboard door again
and took something out. "Here," she said, holding out her
hand. "I saved some. Just for you."

Two of the little candies she'd made out of honey sat in
her palm. They were excellent, and he did have a taste for
them, but he liked the fact she'd saved some just for him
even more. Before he could consider his actions, he took
the candies, pocketed them and planted a kiss square on
her lips.

## *Chapter Ten*

The lips beneath his were so soft and kissable Steve didn't want to pull away, but the sound coming through the open door made him. When she stumbled slightly he held her arms for another moment, before saying, "I have to see who that is."

He waited until she nodded before stepping away, and glanced back to make sure she was all right before heading to the door. She appeared so, but he may not be. Kissing her had ignited something deep inside him.

The buggy rolling into the yard irritated him in more ways than one. He'd figured the doc would be out again, and not just to check on Rex.

"I didn't expect to see you around in the middle of the day," Nelson said as he stopped the buggy.

"It's my house," Steve said.

"So it is."

He'd already told Nelson Mary was off limits and shouldn't have to repeat himself.

"Here to check on Rex," Nelson said, climbing out of the buggy.

Steve folded his arms across his chest.

"Is he in the house?"

Steve turned to glance at the sound of the footsteps on the porch, and his heart skipped a beat at how flushed Mary's cheeks were when their eyes met. Yet, with dignity, she turned to the doctor.

"Yes, but he's napping."

"I'm in no hurry," Nelson said. "It's nice to see you again, Mary."

"Hello, Dr. Graham."

"Come now, I said you must call me Nelson."

For the briefest of moments, Steve had the urge to trip the doctor as he walked past on his way to the porch. As his gaze once again met Mary's, he had to grin. There were times when it was as if he could read her mind, and at this moment, the hidden smile on her face made him wonder if she'd just read his.

Spinning about, he beat the doctor to the steps and took Mary's arm, guiding her to his side while opening the door. "Come on in, Nelson. We can have a cup of coffee while you're waiting for Rex to wake up."

Mary glanced up at him, frowning slightly.

Once the doctor had entered the house, Steve whispered, "I'll keep him company so you can see to the raccoons."

Her face glowed. "Thank you, but will it keep you from your work?"

"No. Everything about the ranch is my work. Including Rex's health."

"Of course," she said, stepping into the house. "It'll only take me a moment to make fresh coffee and warm up the cinnamon rolls leftover from lunch."

That was one more thing he liked. How she always had leftovers or sweet treats readily available. Taking a seat at the table, he asked Nelson of any news happening in town, and wanted to bite off his tongue when the doctor started talking about the brides and the events the town was hosting on their behalf. Parties and dances and picnics.

He kept glancing at Mary, as did Nelson. Steve couldn't help but wonder if she was sorry to be missing the affairs.

"Your sister seems to be enjoying herself, Mary," Nelson said. "I'd gladly escort you into town to visit her, or to attend one of the events. There will be—"

"I'm far too busy with my duties here to run off visiting," she said, cutting Nelson short as she set two cups of coffee on the table along with two plates and then a platter of cinnamons rolls. "Now, please excuse me, but I have things to see to."

Steve made no comment. He was too busy biting the inside of his cheek at how she'd declined Nelson's invite. As she picked up the crate and carried it out of the kitchen, Rex's bedroom door opened.

"I thought I smelled cinnamon," Rex said. Then with a frown, he asked, "What are you doing out here again, Doc?"

Although put out by the visit, once the cinnamon rolls were consumed, Rex agreed to an examination by the doctor.

"Told you Mary's taking excellent care of me," Rex said once the poking and prodding was done.

Closing his medical bag, which he hadn't needed, Nelson said, "I can see that. I'll need to speak to her now."

Holding his stance in the doorway, Steve asked, "Why?"

Nelson's expression grew stern as he approached the doorway. "It's a private matter."

Steve made no effort to move, other than to let his stare tell the doctor if it was a challenge he wanted, it was a challenge he'd get. "She's busy doing the things I pay her to do."

Nelson's eyes narrowed.

Neither of them had guns drawn, but it was a showdown just the same.

"Perhaps we should step outside," Nelson said.

"By all means," Steve agreed.

As they headed for the door, the click-clack of Rex's crutch hitting the floor said the other man wasn't about to miss the action. Steve waited until Nelson had crossed the threshold before he spun around. "Stay inside," he told Rex. "And make sure Mary does, too."

Rex growled, but then nodded as Steve pulled the door shut.

"I didn't come out here to fight you," Nelson said. "But you're being unreasonable."

Steve rolled up his sleeves while walking down the porch steps. "I don't believe I'm being unreasonable about anything."

"Aren't you being unfair to Mary?" Nelson gestured toward the house. "In three weeks, she has to decide who she'll marry. You've claimed it won't be you, and it's unfair of you to not let her get to know her choices."

"She doesn't want to marry any of them."

"She doesn't have a choice. Three weeks from tomorrow all five women will be wed in a ceremony at the church."

Steve shook his head. "No one can force—"

"I told you about the fine print on the contract. Mary either marries someone in three weeks, or she's sent back to Ohio to serve out her jail sentence." Glancing toward the house again, Nelson continued, "You know Josiah isn't going to let any of the women out of that contract. He not only has the law on his side, he has the entire community. Now, considering you won't need her once Rex is healed, I'm asking you as a friend to step aside so she and I can get to know each other. So she's comfortable with my proposal."

Tension was tightening every muscle Steve had. Not only at Nelson's request, but at the fact that what the man said was true. The entire town had backed the mail-order bride scheme, and no one would stand aside and watch it fail.

"Trust me, once the other women make their choices, you're going to have a steady stream of suitors pounding on your door. Everyone knows this is where Mary's at. Letting it be known she's chosen me will lesson your problems tenfold."

"I don't have any problems," Steve insisted. But he did. Not only was Nelson a good friend, he was also telling the truth. Every man who had made a donation to the Betterment Committee could start pounding on his door.

Mary couldn't hear what Steve and the doctor were saying, but their stances said neither of them was happy.

"What you gonna name them?" Rex asked.

He was the reason she couldn't hear Steve and Nelson. Not only had Rex shut the window before planting himself on a chair next to the crate, he'd talked nonstop since she'd carried the raccoons into the kitchen upon hearing the door shut.

"I'm not sure," she said, leaning to peer around him and out the glass on the other side of the room.

"I think you should call them Spit and Spat," Rex said. "That's what it sounds like they are doing."

"They are sucking the milk out of the bread," she said.

"That was a good idea," Rex said. "How'd you think of it?"

Her mind wasn't on the coons, or how she'd come up with the idea of how to feed them. It was on the conversation happening outside. Which had nothing to do with Rex, and plenty to do with her. Her stomach, the way it was rolling, told her that. Every time the doctor appeared, she worried he'd learn about the tonic.

Rex was still talking, but she was no longer answering.

Her mind had now gone to her sister, and how the doctor had said Maggie was enjoying herself. Maggie had always enjoyed social affairs, but should realize she shouldn't be participating in them—not as one of the brides. That could ruin everything. It would be expected that Maggie marry one of them, and where would that leave her? She couldn't leave town without Maggie, but she couldn't stay here, either. She'd rather return to Ohio and face Sheriff Freiday than marry one of the men in Oak Grove.

No she wouldn't. She had no desire to return to Ohio, nor could she live that far away from Maggie.

Spying the doctor walking toward his buggy, she took the baby raccoon out of Rex's hands and set it amongst the hay. "I think they're tired," she said. "And I have bread to bake and the rest of the garden to hoe."

Rex glanced out the window before he said, "I'll see to the bread while you do the hoeing."

"Thank you." Mary hurried out the door, hoping to catch Steve, but was sorely disappointed to see him riding his horse alongside the doctor's buggy. The two soon separated, the buggy continuing along the road while Steve rode his horse across the grass in the direction he'd approached from earlier. With a sigh, she headed toward the garden.

Once she started digging in the dirt, she let her mind consider some possibilities. Such as figuring out a way to get to town, or an excuse for Jess to take a message to Maggie, telling her to stop acting like a potential bride.

That thought made something else shoot across her mind, and she closed her eyes at how her lips started to tingle. She had never been kissed, and Steve's lips pressed against hers had not only taken her by surprise, it had filled her with something she'd never experienced. An excitement that still lingered inside her. One that made her wish Steve had been looking for a wife instead of a cook.

## *Chapter Eleven*

The sun had long ago set, leaving the sky black except for some faraway stars, and the only sound, other than the wind, was that of a cricket calling for a mate. Steve pushed one foot against the front porch floor to make the chair rock again. He should be in bed. Tomorrow would be another demanding day, but his mind was too busy to let him sleep. Had been too busy ever since Nelson had driven away two days ago. He'd made a mental list of options and outcomes, but not a one was up to his liking.

Josiah Melbourne wouldn't let his betterment scheme fail, had gotten the entire town to back his plan right from the beginning and therefore there was no way Mary would escape being married off to someone. More than once, even before kissing her, Steve had considered being that someone, but couldn't grasp onto the idea. Or refused to. For her sake more than his. This country was tough on women, and he didn't want Mary's life to be tough.

Watching her with Spit and Spat proved how gentle she was, how deeply she cared about things. Actually, there were moments he wished he hadn't brought her those two little raccoons. The way she coddled them showed him how attached she'd already become to them, and letting them go was going to be hard for her.

He didn't want her to suffer any hardships. He didn't want her to marry Nelson, either. Or any of the other men who may have contributed to the Betterment Committee.

The cricket started chirping again, and the sound made him feel lonesome—something he hadn't felt in a very long time. There was no reason to. A short distance away the bunkhouse was full of men he considered to be not only some of the best cowboys in these parts, but his friends, too. He had other friends as well. Folks in town, farmers, ranchers. He had this ranch, in addition. Had worked hard to get it to where it was today. All that should be more than enough.

A yawn pulled at his jaw, and hoping that signaled his mind was tired enough to let him get some sleep, Steve stood and made his way into the house. He climbed the stairs and started down the hall, but a rustle made him pause near Mary's bedroom. The door was open, as were all the others, and all of the windows in order for the wind to make the summer heat more bearable for sleeping.

The moon cast enough light into her room for him to watch both raccoons tumble out the top of the crate and make a beeline for her bed. Using the bedding hanging over the edge, they quickly climbed onto the bed. He started forward, intent upon catching them before they woke her, but the coons were faster. They quickly scampered across the sheet and then snuggled up to her side.

"It's about time you came up to bed."

Steve froze.

"I'm talking to you, not the coons," she whispered.

"I didn't mean to wake you."

"You didn't."

"I—I was sitting on the porch."

"I know. I love sitting in the rocking chairs out there," she said. "It's so peaceful and relaxing."

He nodded. Then realizing she probably couldn't see that, said, "You could have joined me. It's cooler out there."

"I didn't want to intrude. I did think about going down to the parlor and sleeping on the sofa, but this bed is too comfortable."

"I'm glad you like it." He was glad she enjoyed the rocking chairs on the front porch, too, and he wanted to tell her she wouldn't have intruded. But she would have. Other nights he had invited her to sit outside with him, but tonight, he'd wanted time to think. The last two days, every time he looked at her, he remembered kissing her, and wanted to do it again. Wanted to do more than kiss her. Having her mention the bed didn't help those thoughts at all. "Jackson Miller made all my furniture. Once I got the house built, I asked him to make whatever he figured I needed."

"He did a fine job." Shifting slightly, enough to look his way without disturbing the coons, she asked, "This wasn't your parents' house?"

"No. I didn't build it until a few years ago. The cabin my father built is now the bunkhouse. I added on to it to make room for all the cowboys."

"I bet you miss your parents, wish they could have seen all this. All you've accomplished."

He leaned against the door frame. "Sometimes."

"I miss my da, too. I know death is a part of life, and that we have to go on without those who are gone, but that doesn't stop us from missing them." She shifted again, just her head and sighed. "They'd be proud of you. Your parents. My father would never believe I was living in a house this fine."

"Why? What was your house in Ohio like?"

"Four walls and a roof. Not much more. But we had real beds. Hadn't had that in a long time."

"Why?"

"I told you Da was a traveling man. The tonic business… well…it's not always respected by lawmen. Hard to stay in one place too long. A person can get themselves caught up like that. We lived out of our wagon most of the time. Usually, come winter, he'd find a house to rent. One year it was a chicken coop."

"A chicken coop?"

"Yes. Maggie and I were small, so there was plenty of room."

From anyone else, he'd think they were lying, but knew Mary wouldn't lie about that. About anything. "You miss her, don't you? Maggie."

"Yes, I do. Mainly because I worry about her. That's the thing about family, you love them, but at the same time they can worry you to death."

"You wouldn't trade your sister for the peace of mind, though," he answered softly.

"True enough."

Then, because his mind was starting up all over again, he said, "I better get some sleep. Good night."

"Good night."

Steve made his way down the hall and into his bedroom, and long after he'd lain down, his mind was still going in several directions. By the time the sun rose, he wasn't sure if he'd slept or not, and was wondering if he should let Nelson court her. If she married the doctor, at least she'd live in town, near her sister.

Each day that passed brought Mary no closer to a solution, but it did bring about the time for the first batch of tonic to be sweetened and bottled. Jess had taken the other crate to Maggie a few days ago when running an errand for Steve. The guilt at keeping it hidden under her bed had made her feel terrible about defying Steve.

Bottling this batch did, too, but she had no choice. It was her and Maggie's future. She decided to use the dried apples out of the pantry for the syrup, and planned on making several apple pies so no one would question the smell of apples cooking. Her bottling plan was somewhat thwarted when a rainstorm appeared out of nowhere while the men were still eating breakfast.

"Looks like it could be an all-dayer," Rex said while peering out the window.

"We sure need the moisture," Steve said.

"And a day to get a few other things done," Leroy said. "Every bit of my tack needs a good oiling and my saddle needs a new leather strap."

Others agreed and started discussing what they could do during a rainy day. With all of them around the house, Mary couldn't bottle the tonic, but she could at least make the syrup and pies.

As soon as the men departed and the breakfast dishes were done, she started on the pies. Rex's suggestion that if she didn't need him he'd venture into the parlor to work on rope he was braiding lessened the worry of him questioning the syrup, for he was the only one she felt might notice.

By the time the pies were done baking, the syrup was bottled and hidden in the back of the pantry. She cut two slices of warm pie and carried one into the parlor for Rex and the other into the office where Steve had been working all morning. He smiled as she set the tray on the corner of his desk, and her heart skipped a beat.

"I thought I smelled apples," he said.

"Apple pie." She handed him a plate and fork and then a cup of coffee.

"My favorite." After taking a bite, he said, "I don't think I pay you enough."

A bout of shame had her admitting, "I think you pay me too much."

"Says the woman who insisted upon forty when I offered thirty-five a month."

"Only because I knew Brett would pay it."

He set the fork down. "You wouldn't have to work so much at his place."

She bent down and scooped up Spit and Spat, who'd followed her out of the kitchen. In truth, they followed every step she took, which she loved. "But I wouldn't have these two."

He patted the head of each coon. "They've grown a lot in a week."

"Yes, they have." The day would come when he'd say Spit and Spat needed to move to the barn, and not wanting that to be today, she changed the subject. "What are you working on?"

He took another bite of pie before saying, "Ranch records. I keep track of all the stock, the feed we buy and grow, wages, supplies, that sort of thing."

"It must be expensive owning a ranch."

"It is, but it's profitable, too."

"And a lot of work."

He shrugged. "It's not really work if you love what you do."

It was strange how he could say something in a way she'd never thought of before. "That's true. I love cooking and—Oh!" Spit for whatever reason leaped out of her arms and bounded across his desk. A split second later, Spat followed, and in her rush to capture them, her coordination failed. The inkwell flew in one direction and the cup of coffee toppled in the other. Steve reached for the coffee at the same time she reached for the ink, and their hands collided. Somehow they managed to splatter ink and coffee over each other, and themselves.

"Oh, I'm so—" Her breath stalled. His laughter was the reason. She hadn't heard him laugh before, not like this, and it made her laugh too, and then say, "Sorry. You have coffee on your face."

"You have ink on yours."

"Oh, those little rascals," she said, examining her ink-splattered hands.

"I think we are the one that spilled everything, not them." Standing next to her, he reached down and lifted the hem of the cloth she used as an apron. Using the corner, he wiped her cheek, then grimaced. "Oops."

"Oops what?" she asked.

He wiped her cheek again. "All I did was smear the ink. It looks a bit like war paint now."

"Really?"

Not doing a very good job at holding back a grin, he nodded.

Knowing what would happen, she used an ink-covered fingertip to wipe at a drop of coffee on his chin. "Oops, now it looks like you have war paint on, too."

"Well, you little imp," he said, while swiping a finger over her other cheek.

"Imp you say," she challenged while smearing ink on the end of his nose.

The battle was on then, with both of them smearing ink across the other, dipping their fingers in the inkwell when needed, and laughing. Laughing like she hadn't in so long she'd forgotten how good it felt.

His face was practically covered with ink when he captured both of her wrists.

"Enough."

He was still laughing, and so was she. And happier than she'd been in years.

Nodding, she said, "Yes, that's enough. You're a sight."

He pulled her closer. "So are you."

The pressure of his chest against her breasts sent her heart pounding, and the look in his eyes made her breath catch. In that one unbelievable split second when her brain registered what he was about to do, a shiver of delight spread throughout her body, and the moment his lips touched hers, it was as if she became weightless. Boneless.

His lips were warm and firm and she grasped his shoulders as her useless knees threatened to buckle. He released her wrists and his arms encircled her, pulling her closer as the firmness of his lips increased. She stretched onto her toes to match the pressure, and stretched again when the tip of his tongue floated along the seam of her lips.

Following some silent but natural suggestion to part her lips, she squeezed his shoulders when his tongue entered her mouth. With one fascinating swish, the kiss became as fun, as fast and enjoyable as their ink-smearing contest.

When something intruded upon her enjoyment, she tried to ignore it, but couldn't ignore how Steve's lips left hers and his hands once again grasped her wrists.

"Yes, we're fine," he said.

She opened her eyes and took a step back at the same time the door swung open.

"I heard all sorts of commotion and then silence," Rex said, entering the room.

"The coons spilled the inkwell," Steve said.

"On your faces?"

Steve still held her wrists, and as she glanced from Rex to Steve, her eyes were drawn to the blue ink on his shoulders. The handprints, her handprints, couldn't be missed on the white shirt.

"Yes, on our faces," Steve said, releasing one of her wrists and tugging her to walk beside him by pulling on the other. "We're going to the kitchen to get cleaned up. Catch Spit and Spat."

"No need to," Rex said, moving aside so they could exit the room. "They're following you." His laughter boomed in the room. "They probably need to get cleaned up, too."

## Chapter Twelve

If any of the cowboys noticed how hers and Steve's hands and faces were tinted blue, none of them asked, and thankfully, Rex didn't inform them of what had happened. Perhaps because she claimed to have baked one entire pie just for him. By the time lunch was over, so was the rain, and Steve suggested they ride out to check for flash flooding.

Shortly after the dishes were done, Rex claimed fish always bit after a rain. Leroy, who had stayed behind to finish working on his tack, hitched up a wagon for him and Rex to take to the river.

Which meant she was completely alone. Bottling the tonic wasn't as enjoyable as she imagined it would be. Not with Steve's kiss still mingling in her mind. Looking at the second jug made a lump form in her throat.

She considered dumping it out, but couldn't. It was her and Maggie's livelihood. The only way they'd have to make money once she left the ranch.

The idea of leaving the ranch made the lump grow so big she could barely swallow around it. There wasn't a whole lot she could do about any of it. Not the tonic, leaving, or the kiss, so she kept pouring the now thickened tonic into small bottles, corking them, and hiding them amongst the logs. There was more tonic than she had bottles, so she borrowed a couple empty canning jars out of the pantry, telling herself she'd make sure Steve got them back.

Rex had explained that Steve purchased the canned and dried foods, as well as the pots of honey, from neighboring farmers each fall, and always returned the pots and jars to them when he bought more the next year.

Sanitizing and washing the bottles had reduced the stains on her hands, and upon returning to the house, she added some baking soda to lard and washed her face. It did the trick, but she was also a bit disappointed. The ink stains had been proof of the fun she'd had. That was a silly notion, but true nonetheless.

The milk she'd set their clothes to soak in as soon as they'd changed had done the trick too, so she heated wash water and had the clothes hanging on the line by the time the men started returning to the house.

Rex and Leroy had caught enough fish for everyone, and after supper she mixed up more lard and baking soda for Steve to wash with. No one else may have noticed, but she could see the faint ink stains on his face.

"I wondered how you got it off your face," he said as he took the bowl.

She shrugged. "I thought it was worth a try and it worked." Standing this close to him had her insides fluttering. "I—I got the ink off your desk too, but I'm afraid some of your papers got splattered."

"It doesn't matter. I'm the only one who sees them." Eyeing her critically, he asked, "Are you doing all right?"

She had an inkling he was referring to their kiss, but knew she couldn't admit that each time he kissed her, which had only been twice, caused her to wish she wouldn't ever have to leave. "Of course. Why wouldn't I be?"

"No reason."

She nodded. "You?"

"Yes, I'm fine."

"Good." An awkwardness had overcome her. "I—I think I'll go on up to bed then."

"So soon?" he asked. "I was going to sit on the front porch. You could join me."

As badly as she'd have liked to do that, she shook her head. "No, I think I should go up to my room and… Um… I'll ask Rex to help me make a place for Spit and Spat in the barn tomorrow."

"Why? What happened wasn't their fault."

"No, it wasn't. It was mine for letting them stay in the house."

"Mary—"

"Good night," she said quickly, all but running from the room. She'd never had this need before. This *I gotta run* feeling. Not ever. Not even when Da had said they had to hit the road. But she'd never wanted someone to kiss her again so badly, either. Never had wanted someone to kiss her at all.

Watching Mary scoop up the coons and hurry out of the room left Steve feeling lower than a snake's belly. No wonder. It was his fault. He hadn't meant for it to happen, but it had, and just like the first time, kissing her had been like getting hit by a bolt of lightning. He'd kissed plenty of women over the years and not one had affected him the way Mary's had. Did. Practically all he could think about was kissing her again. And again.

He was a fool. That's what he was. She'd said she didn't want to get married. Not that a kiss would lead to marriage, but in her mind, she might think it could. He'd have to set her straight on that. Tell her he'd kissed other women and never intended on marrying any of them.

While smearing the lard and soda on his face, he re-thought that thought, determining that might not be a good thing to tell her. He had no idea what might be, either.

After what seemed like an hour of scrubbing, he walked to the bottom of the stairs and shouted, "Mary, how the hell did you get this lard off your face? I'm greasier than an axel!"

She appeared at the top of the stairs. "You have to use hot water, and soap."

"I did."

"Did you heat up the water that I left on the stove?"

"No, it was still warm."

"Not warm enough," she said, walking down the steps.

"You want me to scald my face? I'd rather have ink on it."

"Oh, good heavens." Reaching the bottom, she grabbed his arm. "How did you manage before me?"

"I don't know, but I never had to scald myself. Never got ink all over my face, either."

She shot him a glare, but he saw the smile there too, and gave her a wink.

To his delight, once he was grease-free, and fortunately, not scalded, Mary agreed to join him on the front porch. Along with Spit and Spat and all of the cowboys including Rex. A day of light work didn't have any of them falling into their beds as soon as their stomachs were full. After a bout of storytelling, mostly by the cowboys and about him, which had Mary laughing so hard she had tiny tear drop-lets falling from the corners of her eyes, Walt pulled out his harmonica. In no time, Henry ran to retrieve his banjo and Leroy to fetch a couple of spoons out of the kitchen.

Soon, the lively music had Rex tapping his peg leg on the floor.

Noting Mary's toe tapping, too, Steve stood and grasped her hand. "Let's dance."

"Here?"

"No," he said, pulling her to her feet. "Down there. The porch isn't big enough."

"All right." With a giggle, she agreed, and ran down the steps beside him.

They danced to a few songs, before, knowing he had to be fair, he let the other men have a turn at twirling her around. However, when the boys started playing a slow ballad, he stepped up to claim her again.

She curtsied, he bowed, and then as they started slowly sashaying around the lawn, she began singing. It was in Irish, he knew that much, but had no idea what the words were. Her voice was mesmerizing, though, as were her eyes that never left his.

When the music ended and her singing quietly faded on the wind, they stood alone together for a moment, still holding onto each other, and Steve knew he'd never been more content, that life had never felt more right.

Rex proclaimed it was time for bed, and as the boys moseyed toward the bunkhouse, Steve escorted her up the steps.

"The dancing tuckered these two out," Rex said, handing her two sleeping coons.

"I know how they feel." She gently tucked the coons in the crook of her arm. "I've never danced so much." Glancing toward Steve, she added, "Or had so much fun. This may have been the best day of my life."

"Mine, too," Steve admitted.

"Well, good night," she said, including Rex in her nod.

"Night," he and Rex said at the same time.

Steve started to follow her, but Rex took a hold of his arm.

"Sit down."

"Why?" Steve asked.

"So I can say my piece."

Steve didn't sit. "What piece?"

Using the crutch, Rex pulled himself up out of his chair. "You best do right by her."

He'd known Rex for as long as he could remember, all the way back to his early years in Georgia, before the war, before Rex had lost one leg, and respected him far more than Rex probably knew, yet Steve shook his head. "I don't need advice—"

"I'm not giving you advice," Rex said. "It's a warning. You break that girl's heart and you'll answer to me, boy."

Mary heard the front door open and close as she entered her bedroom, and held her breath in order to hear footsteps on the stairs. When none sounded, she released the air and closed her door. A skeleton key was tied to the knob with a piece of string, and she questioned using it. Not for safety, but sanity. She might very well bolt out the door when Steve walked by.

"Oh, fairy dust," she muttered. "Of all the silly ideas."

Leaving the key hanging, she carried Spit and Spat to the bed and then crossed the room to retrieve her nightdress. The moon was bright enough she didn't need to light a lamp, or to see her own reflection in the mirror above the dresser. "You're smitten, Mary McCary," she whispered to the reflection. "And you best figure out a way to get unsmitten real quick. If Steve Putnam had wanted someone to be smitten over him, he'd have paid the money to have a chance at one of the brides. He hadn't. A fact he made perfectly clear."

A soft coo had her turning toward the bed, where two sets of tiny eyes stared at her. Walking to the bed, she sat down and waited until both coons were on her lap. "I'm sorry," she whispered. "I didn't mean to wake you. I'm just used to having my sister to talk to. Oh, Maggie, where are you when I need you?"

Sighing, she shook her head. "What am I saying? Maggie is the one likely to become smitten. Not me. She's in town attending parties and dancing and singing and..." A tingle crept up her spine so slowly she quivered. "Oh, goodness. What if that happened? What would I do if Maggie becomes smitten by some fellow?"

## Chapter Thirteen

Becoming un-smitten, if there was such a thing, was much harder than becoming smitten. Especially when the man one was smitten by was Steve. He hadn't done anything different, or changed in any way. Yet ever since the night they'd danced—more than a week ago now—every time Mary looked at him, an intense warmth pooled in the lowest region of her torso, and whenever he touched her, just an accidental brush to her arm, a strong desire had her wanting to be held by him. Kissed by him—again and again and again.

She tried ignoring him, but that was difficult living in the same house. Still it shouldn't be this hard. She'd ignored Maggie and the other women on the train rather easily, and that space had been much smaller. Furthermore, he was gone most of the day—which filled her with longing.

Mary sighed and turned away from the window. Spying Spit trying to climb up a chair made her shake her head.

That was the other thing that had become extremely hard. Attempting to make Spit and Spat live in the barn. They escaped every type of enclosure she put them in, and as soon as one of the house doors opened, they shot inside. Steve told her she might as well give up until they became a bit older. At some point they'd realize she isn't their mother and want to be set free.

She wasn't overly fond of that idea. Of them wanting to be set free. That was bound to happen—sooner than later. She'd started to hate bedtime, only because it meant another day was over. Soon the thirty days Steve had hired her to cook would be over and she'd have to leave. It would be better for Spit and Spat to be gradually separated from her than for her to just be gone one day.

"I put the wire up you asked me to," Rex said as he entered the back door. "But it's not going to keep those two in. I agree with Steve. You should just let them think you're their momma for a bit longer."

"They are twice as big as they were when we got them," she pointed out. "And twice as hard to contain. I can't have them jumping on the counters."

"Then smack their noses," Rex said.

"I will not."

"That's how their momma teaches them."

"Well, I'm not their momma," she said, holding Spit in one hand while chasing Spat around the chair. Finally catching him, she carried them both to the door. Upon opening it, she muttered, "Oh, fairy dust."

"What's wrong?"

"I hope that isn't Dr. Graham walking up the driveway. He just left less than an hour ago." The doctor was nice enough, but she still worried he'd learn about the tonic. He hadn't made mention of it, so she hoped that meant he hadn't discovered Maggie had any, either.

"That's not Dr. Graham," Rex said. "Stay here. I'll see who it is."

The man turned out to be William Stockholm. His wagon had lost a wheel a few miles away, and upon hearing he'd left his wife and children there, Mary, with Rex's help, hitched up a wagon. She also filled a basket with molasses cookies and buttermilk.

By the time they arrived at the wagon, Steve and Walter were there, having seen the billowing canvas of the covered wagon while rounding up cattle.

Steve suggested she should take William's wife, Loraine, and the two children, three-year-old Stella and five-year-old Emil, to the house. Said the rest of them would follow once they got the wheel fixed well enough to make it that far. Rex offered to drive them back, but Mary said she'd manage. She'd been driving a wagon since she was old enough to handle the reins. Plus she could tell Rex wanted to stay with the men. She'd seen that more and more from him. He may have been Steve's cook, but it wasn't what he liked doing. Especially now that he no longer had to use the crutch.

With the children in the back, munching on cookies and drinking buttermilk, she and Loraine chatted as they made their way along the roadway. Mary was thankful for that. It kept her mind off how Steve had held onto her sides longer than necessary after lifting her out of the wagon when she and Rex had arrived. It had been as if he hadn't wanted to let her go.

"Oh, my goodness," Loraine said as they pulled into the ranch. "Your home is beautiful."

"Yes, it is," Mary answered honestly. "I love it."

"I would, too."

Mary parked the wagon and unhitched the horse before inviting the others inside. She warned them about Spit and Spat, just so no one would be afraid when the coons met them at the door as they did anyone walking into the house.

"They've never bitten anyone," Mary added, "but they have very sharp teeth and have never been around children so please be careful."

The children nodded and were soon giggling while watching Spit and Spat chase after the rag balls she'd made for them to play with.

"Goodness, it's been so long since I was inside a house and sat at a real table, I don't know what to say," Loraine said.

"You've been traveling a long time?" Mary asked while setting a pot of coffee on the stove.

"It feels like forever," Loraine said. "We've settled a few places since we left Missouri two years ago, but never for long. Luck hasn't been with us. No water, too much water, Indians, someone else's land. It's always been something. William's sister lives up in Nebraska. We're headed there now."

Loraine's words made Mary pause while taking cups out of the cupboard and close her eyes for a moment. She'd been in Loraine's shoes. That was how it had been with Da. There had always been a reason for them to move on. She and Maggie had probably looked a lot like Stella and Emil. Dirty with ragged clothes, and in awe of some of the houses they'd stopped to seek help from just like the Stockholms were doing right now.

Some folks had been kind, others not so much. Back then, she used to imagine she'd have a fine house someday, and would help others whenever they needed it. That had come true today, and being able to help felt as wonderful as she'd imagined it would, all those years ago. Knowing Steve had already offered to provide them with whatever they needed filled her with pride she'd never known.

"Well," she said upon opening her eyes and taking down the cups. "Staying here for a few days will do you all some good. While the men get your wagon fixed properly, we'll get your laundry caught up and your food baskets packed full again. Then you can start your journey north fresh and ready to go."

She turned to carry the cups to the table, and the tears streaming down Loraine's face had her blinking back a few of her own.

"Thank you," Loraine whispered. "Just thank you."

The Stockholm family spent three days at the ranch, and though Steve assured them there was plenty of room in the house, they insisted upon sleeping in their wagon, saying he was already providing them with far more than they could ever repay. Pride at how kind and generous he was filled Mary continuously. Her heart seemed to double in size every time she looked at him.

On the morning they were set to leave, with the wagon fixed, clothes and bedding washed and their food baskets overstuffed, Mary stood next to Steve as William helped Loraine climb onto the seat and then climbed up himself.

"Remember," Steve said, "if Nebraska doesn't work out, there's a job here if you want it."

"I'll remember," William said. "If my sister wasn't expecting us…" He shook his head. "Thank you for everything. You've been a true blessing to us."

"It was our pleasure," Steve said.

Mary blinked against the sting in her eyes as she once again said goodbye. Steve wrapped an arm around her shoulders and pulled her to his side as the wagon wheels started to roll. Mary waved, but didn't trust her voice not to crack. Especially with Steve's arm around her.

"They'll be fine," he said, rubbing her arm.

She nodded.

"Really, they'll be fine."

"I know," she said as the wagon rounded the barn and started up the road. "I just remember what it's like to be them." She turned to look at the house. "I'd forgotten, or maybe I didn't want to remember, but I do now, and it's hard. Very hard."

Steve folded his arms around her and held her, hugged her, which was comforting and heartbreaking at the same time. She didn't want to live like that ever again, yet it could very well become her life again within a few short days.

"Thank you," she whispered. "Thank you for being so kind to them. So generous."

"You're welcome, but I would have done it for any family traveling past and in need."

"I know you would have," she said, lifting her head to look at him. The urge that overcame her was too strong to fight, so she gave in to it. Stretching on her toes, she kissed him. Not on the cheek, but the lips, and then whispered again, "I know you would have."

Steve had to dig his heels into the packed ground. The desire to kiss her that lived inside him had grown considerably the past few days, especially when it came to watching her with the Stockholm children. At times, he'd found himself imagining them having children. Her and him.

But he couldn't kiss her. Not again. This time he might not be able to stop. Clearing his throat, he said, "William left his sister's name. I'll send a telegram in a month, make sure they made it."

She nodded, and the sadness in her eyes reminded him she may not be here in a month. Might very well be married to someone else, maybe Nelson Graham, who had stopped by again yesterday and proclaimed Rex's leg was completely healed.

There was less than a week left of her stay here, and Steve had no idea what he could do about it. Should do about it.

He had half a mind to ask her to marry him right now, but therein lay the problem. Only half his mind was working. It was only thinking about what he wanted. Not what she wanted, or what was best for her. Practically every time he'd come across her and Loraine talking, Mary was saying something about her sister Maggie. How she hadn't seen her in weeks and missed her terribly. That was how it always would be. There were times he didn't go into Oak Grove for a couple months or more.

Furthermore, the graves not far away were a constant reminder of what living out here did to women and children. Families as a whole.

She stepped out of his arms and clapped her hands. "Well, we both have work to do, and standing here isn't getting it done." Stepping around him, she added, "I'll see you for the noon meal."

## Chapter Fourteen

Steve did see her for the noon meal that day, and the evening, and breakfast the next morning. And the next... He was counting down those meals like a captured outlaw counts the days before the hangman arrives. The cowboys all knew her thirty days were almost up, too. No one asked what he was going to do about it, but they shared their opinions of not looking forward to Rex cooking for them again.

He could have told them Rex's meals weren't that bad, but a man got used to what he had and until he had something to compare it with, never really knew if what he had was good or bad.

Rex's cooking had been dismal compared to Mary's, and whether he wanted to admit or not, Steve couldn't deny his life before Mary didn't hold a candle to what it had been since she arrived.

His heart thudded as he glanced toward the house while stopping his horse near the barn, where he'd fetch a new rope. The one looped around his saddle horn could have sufficed for the rest of the day, but knowing her days here were nearly done, he found any excuse he could to ride to the homestead at different points throughout the day.

About to push open the barn door, Steve stopped, turned around and then started walking toward the house, following a sound. The caterwauling was Rex, but it was more off tune than normal.

Steve rounded the house and then the corner of the woodshed that had a back wall and roof, leaving the other three sides open. Rex, sitting upon the short front row of logs, took a long swig off a jar and then started singing again.

"Me's gonna marry a lass named Mary in the merry month of May. Yes, me's gonna—"

"What the—?" Steve grabbed the half-empty jar out of Rex's hand.

Grinning as his head wobbled to the tune he continued humming, Rex waved. "Hi, Steve. Try it." After a hiccup, he added, "It tastes like you're drinking apple pie."

The jar smelled of apples and cinnamon, and alcohol. "You're drunk," Steve needlessly pointed out.

"Maybe."

"Where did you get this?"

Rex gestured toward the back wall of the shed. "There's more if you want some."

Having seen Steve ride in the yard, Mary had hurried to put on a pot of coffee and then gone outside to let him know it would be ready soon. She cherished his afternoon visits, where the two of them sat and talked.

Her excitement waned and then completely disappeared as she saw him pulling jars and bottles out from behind the stacks of wood.

Rex, sitting atop the first row of wood, waved at her, and then started singing, "Me's gonna marry a lass named Mary—"

"Shut up," Steve barked.

Flinching at his shout, or possibly his glare as he pulled out two crocks, one empty, the other full, Mary considered heading back to the house. She'd wished more than once that she hadn't mixed up that second batch, but not as strongly as she did right now.

"I thought you got rid of this," Steve said.

"I—I got rid of it in the bedroom," she answered.

"You—"

Suddenly, her guilt turned to anger. "What? It's better than that bottle of whiskey in the kitchen cupboard."

"There are times that's needed." He held out both crocks. "But this is nothing but snake oil and not good for anything except getting a man drunk."

"It's not snake oil," she insisted. "It's medicinal tonic." Stepping forward, she grabbed a couple of bottles off the ground. "It helped Rex—"

"It helped him get drunk!" Steve shouted. "That's exactly what can't happen on a ranch, especially during roundup. Men have to have all their senses about them, day in and day out. Dump that out!"

"No." She set the bottles she'd gathered a few feet away from him and went back to move more. Dumping it out couldn't happen. She and Maggie wouldn't have any to sell. "I need it," she said.

"Why?"

"If you must know, I'm going to sell it."

"Sell—"

"Steve—"

"Shut up, Rex," Steve said, before continuing, "Selling it is why you went to jail in Ohio!"

"Mary—"

Ignoring Rex, she said, "No, I went to jail because I didn't have a *permit* to sell it."

"One of you!"

"What?" both she and Steve shouted to Rex at the same time.

"There's a rattler!"

Mary's eyes shot to the ground near Steve's boots, where the snake, coiled and shaking its pointed tail, was lifting its head. Without thought of the contents of the canning jar in her hand, she pitched it at the snake, then spun to grab the ax from the chopping block. As the jar hit its target, knocking the snake to the ground, she swung the ax over her shoulder and down toward the snake.

The shot that sounded made her scream, but the ax still met her target.

The ax handle was still in her hands when Steve grabbed her waist and pulled her backwards. She let go of the ax, but watched the snake, making sure it was only its body that was twisting and coiling. The head was motionless, unlike her. The idea that Steve had been so close to being bitten had her trembling, and the gunshot echoing in her ears had her shaking her head.

"Are you all right?" Steve asked as he spun her around.

"Of course I'm all right. You were the one about to get bit." She pressed a hand to one ear, and due to the ringing shouted, "Why'd you shoot your gun?"

"I shot the snake."

"Why? I was already chopping its head off."

"That was a rattlesnake."

"I know what kind of snake it was." They were both yelling. "Did you want to get bit?"

"No! That's why I shot it!" Tightening his hold on her arms, he said, "And could have shot you!"

The ringing in her ears had stopped and she let out a sigh, "Oh, for—"

"She wasted a whole jar of apple pie making sure you

didn't get bit." Rex sounded forlorn, even with his words slurred and hiccupping.

Mary felt forlorn, too, not because of the wasted tonic, but because she'd disappointed Steve and angered him. Two things she hadn't wanted to do.

"Get a shovel and bury that snake," Steve said to Rex. As Rex climbed off the wood pile—albeit a bit wobbly—Steve turned to her. "Are you sure you're all right?"

The concern in his eyes made her bow her head. "I'm fine."

"Why? Why is this stuff so important to you?"

Mary glanced to the crocks, both broken now. The hopelessness inside her grew a bit deeper. "It's all I've ever known," she whispered. "The only way I've ever known to make money."

"You? The best cook in the nation?" He shook his head. "You could get a job anywhere, at any time."

She'd never considered that idea. Of cooking to make money. It was what she'd been doing, but what would Maggie do then?

"I'm serious, Mary," Steve said. "Peddling that snake oil is only going to keep getting you in trouble."

Although a part of her knew that was true, another deeply embedded sore spot had her saying, "It's not—"

"Fine. Tonic." He sighed heavily. "I'm sorry. It's all the same to me. After my mother died, my father drank it all. Whatever it was labeled, as long as it made him not feel, not think about the pain inside him, he drank it. Drank it until it killed him."

Mary's heart tumbled and she laid a hand on his arm. She knew his entire family had died years ago, from different causes and incidents, but not that his father had died in that way. "I didn't know," she whispered.

"Because I didn't tell you," he said. "I didn't tell anyone."

"I'm sorry. I should never have hid it from you."

"It's not your fault, it's mine. I should have just been honest. Told you why I didn't want it around."

Glancing toward the bottles she'd set aside, she sighed. She hadn't wanted to believe it, but the sheriff in Ohio had been right. The tonic had been why Da died. "I'll get rid of the rest."

Steve grasped her waist to prevent her from moving. "No. You don't have to. But I was honest when I said you don't have to keep selling it."

She laid a hand on his cheek. "That's kind of you to say, but I—I'm not a cook. Not a real one. Not one people would hire me for."

"Yes, you are. I hired you."

The sincerity on his face made her insides warm. She'd come to know him so well the past few weeks—knew he'd give the shirt off his back to someone. Unable to continue looking at him, she bowed her head. "You hired me because there were no other options."

He placed a finger beneath her chin, forcing her to look up at him again. "Maybe that first day, but I kept you here because your cooking is the best I've ever tasted."

This time the look in his eyes made her insides melt faster than butter in a pan. Her heart started racing too, as he tilted her chin higher. He was going to kiss her, something she wanted more than anything else in the world.

"What's all the commotion? I heard a gunshot."

Nelson Graham's voice was the last sound she wanted to hear right now.

"What do you want, Nelson?" Steve asked, sounding as unfriendly as she felt.

"I have something for Mary," he said, holding up an envelope as he stepped closer. His gaze took in the bottles and jars, broken crocks and the dead snake. "That's a rattler. Anyone get bit?"

"No," Steve answered.

As she took the envelope the doctor held out, he glanced toward the ground again. "What's in those bottles? Is this where your sister—"

"Nothing that concerns you," Steve interrupted.

"I need to speak with you as soon as you've read that, Mary," Nelson said. "Privately."

Mary made no promise as she pulled a single sheet of paper out of the envelope. Seeing Maggie's handwriting, her heart skipped a beat. Then fear, dread and a splattering of disappointment rose inside her as she read the note. "Oh, fairy dust and horse shit," she muttered.

As Steve grasped her arm she realized she'd cursed aloud, but this was a curse-aloud situation.

"What is it?" he asked.

"Maggie's been arrested," she said.

"For what?"

She glanced to the bottles, the full ones, still sitting on the ground.

# Chapter Fifteen

The note didn't say much more than what Mary had said. She'd handed it to him and Steve had read it word for word. Maggie was in the Oak Grove Jail for selling their tonic. He could have told Mary that had been bound to happen, but she didn't need to hear that.

"If we could speak privately now, Mary," Nelson said.

Knowing full well that Nelson had read the note, Steve asked, "Why? You going to offer to get her sister out of jail?"

Nelson's face puckered. "As a matter of fact, yes, that is exactly what I can do."

"How?" Steve challenged.

Puffing out his chest, Nelson said, "Once we are married, Mary will be the doctor's wife and—"

"Once you are married? Are you daft? How many times do you have to hear she doesn't want to get married?"

"Perhaps we should let Mary speak for herself," Nelson said.

Steve's temper had boiled at finding Rex drunk, but Nelson's attitude was enough to explode the top of his scalp right off his head. Tightening his hold on Mary's arm, he said, "Come. I'll hitch up the wagon and we'll go get your sister."

Nelson stepped in front of them. "That's only half the issue. As soon as Mary steps foot in town, they'll want to know who she is marrying. The weddings are set for this Saturday."

"I'm not marrying anyone," Mary said.

"I'm afraid you have no choice," Nelson said. "You signed a contract. It clearly stated the town will pay for your trip West and—"

"The town didn't pay for my trip West," she said. "I did."

"You did?" Steve asked.

"Yes." She grimaced slightly. "Not in cash. We sold what we could, but no one was interested in buying our horse, so I traded him to the sheriff in exchange for the tickets."

"According to the mayor, you either marry someone on Saturday or the sheriff will see you are escorted back to Ohio to serve your jail time," Nelson said.

Shock appeared on her face. "Jail time?"

"Do you have a receipt from the sheriff?" Steve asked.

"No, but…"

The way she looked up at him made Steve cringe. She knew she'd been duped and so did he.

She shook her head. "The contract never said they could force me to marry someone."

"There was fine print on the bottom of the contract stating exactly that," Nelson said.

Steve had never wanted to punch someone as badly as he did Nelson Graham right now. Mainly because the doctor was right. Blowing out a breath, he nodded, "Nelson's right. Melbourne will make you marry someone."

"But…"

The quiver of her bottom lip was Steve's undoing. He grasped her arm and started toward the house.

"Where are you taking her?" Nelson asked.

"To speak to her privately," Steve answered, still moving them both forward.

"You can't—"

"Yes, I can." He didn't stop until they were in the house, alone. Then he twisted her so they stood face to face. There wasn't another solution. He'd known that for weeks. Furthermore, it was what he wanted. Looking her straight in the eye, he asked, "Will you marry me?"

She gasped so hard she coughed. And again. He released her to fetch a glass of water. He was still pouring it when she said, "You don't want to get married."

"Neither do you." He carried the glass to her. "We might as well not want to together."

She took a sip and then set the glass on the table. "That's no reason to get married."

The reason was because he loved her. Because he didn't want her to leave, not ever, but wasn't sure how to tell her that. Not in a way she'd believe, so he pointed to the two sets of eyes peeking over the top of the crate. "Then marry me because Spit and Spat are going to think you abandoned them, or because my cowboys are going to quit if they have to start eating Rex's cooking again."

She put both hands on her hips. "Raccoons and cowboys? That's the best you can come up with?"

The stars in her eyes told him more than she was saying. The love he'd been afraid to admit filled him completely as he gently grasped her shoulders. "You could marry me because you want to."

She bit her bottom lip as a smile started to form. "Why would I want to marry you?"

He ran his hands down her arms and then around her waist. "For the same reason I want to marry you."

"You—" She pinched her lips together as she settled both hands on his chest. "And what reason would that be?"

"Love."

Mary's heart was beating so hard she could barely breathe. She wanted to shout yes and jump into his arms, but couldn't. Not until he understood a few things. "I didn't come here to become a bride. I honestly traded Buck, our horse, for the train tickets."

"I believe you." He pulled her a bit closer. "I didn't make that contribution to the Betterment Committee in order to pick out a bride, but I'd have paid ten times that amount if I'd known you were one of them. Still would."

It was growing harder and harder not to smile. Not to shout for joy. Not to beg him to kiss her. "I'm not a weak person," she said, perhaps for her own justification. She wanted him to know she wasn't like those other women that had come out here to be brides. "I don't scare easily and I'm not afraid of hard work."

"I've already witnessed that." His gaze became soft and tender. "If there ever was a woman who made me believe they could live out here, it's you, Mary. But if things do get too tough for you, we'll move to town."

His words, though they were meant to offer comfort, hit her with a realization she'd never had before. She shook her head. "Not this time."

He frowned slightly. "Not this time what?"

"I'm done moving. Done running. That's what my family's always done. When things got tough, we left. But you didn't. You've never run from anything. And that's what I want." Tears stung her eyes as she glanced around the kitchen. "Because of you, the life you've created by not giving up, by not running…" Sniffling, she looked into his eyes. "I have never felt so safe as I have while living here. I've never had food so plentiful, such stability. Nor have I ever seen such kindness and generosity, determination and love. You love your life out here, and I'd be honored to share it with you for the rest of my life. Live, right here, with you, forever, but only if it is what you truly want."

His lips were soft as they pressed against her forehead. "It is what I truly want," he said. "My life has never been so wonderful, so full, since your arrival. I'll buy you a buggy and you can go to town as often as you'd like. Every day if need be. And you can make all the tonic you want."

She grasped his face with both hands. "There will be no more tonic."

"No?"

"No." Smiling, for she'd never been so happy, she shrugged. "I won't need it for anything. Not when I have you."

He pulled her forward so fast their bodies literally collided as their lips connected. The kiss was wonderful, and filled her so completely she wrapped both arms around his neck, hoping it would never stop.

When their lips parted, it was only so they could catch a breath of air before kissing again. That happened several times, and each kiss made her happier—if that was possible.

Her entire body was alive and so full of joy that when Steve did end the kiss, she laughed. So did he. And they kissed again before he grasped her hand and tugged her toward the door.

"Come on."

"Where are we going?" she asked.

"To town. To get your sister out of jail."

Mary slapped a hand over her mouth. Removing it, she said, "Fairy dust, for a moment I forgot all about Maggie."

"Don't worry," Steve said. "As the potential wife of the most prominent citizen in Oak Grove, your sister will be released immediately."

She had no doubt he was telling the truth, and loved him all the more for it. They hurried out the door. Upon seeing Dr. Graham standing near his buggy, she asked, "Should we tell him that things often don't work out like you thought they would in the beginning?"

Steve gave her a wink. "He's a doctor. If he hasn't figured that out, we're all in trouble."

As they walked past Nelson, she said, "I'll be getting married on Saturday, just as the contact says."

"Thank goodness," the doctor said. "I was starting to worry you two wouldn't figure out you're perfect for each other."

As her eyes met Steve's, they both laughed.

"You always were a smart one, Doc," Steve said. Then as they arrived at the barn, he asked her, "Saddle horse or wagon?"

"Saddle horse," Mary answered, her joy momentarily slipping. "Maggie's probably fit to be tied. She believes we paid our own way, too."

He pulled her into another hug. "Don't worry. We'll get it all worked out."

With his arms around her, she couldn't believe otherwise and stretched on her toes to plant a brief kiss on his lips. "I do love you, Steve Putnam."

"And I do love you, Mary McCary," he whispered before he turned her brief kiss into a far more exciting one. When it ended, he added, "And I can't wait for Saturday."

She couldn't, either.

\* \* \* \* \*

*If you enjoyed this story, you won't want to miss
these great full-length reads from
Lauri Robinson:*

*THE FORGOTTEN DAUGHTER
SAVING MARINA
HER CHEYENNE WARRIOR
UNWRAPPING THE RANCHER'S SECRET
THE COWBOY'S ORPHAN BRIDE*

# Taming the
# Runaway Bride

**KATHRYN ALBRIGHT**

Dedicated to my friend Cheryl,
who is every bit as fun as Maggie McCary.

## Chapter One

The steam engine's large wheels emitted an ear-grating squeal as the brakes locked down hard to slow the train. Maggie McCary clamped her hands over her ears. She should be used to the loud noises associated with pulling into a station. How many had she experienced over the past three days?

She looked out the window, hoping against hope that she would see something resembling a town. A bush would be nice. Perhaps a tree. Anything but the empty prairie that had surrounded them for the past three hundred miles.

"I won! You owe me a penny!" Anna cried out delightedly, sitting opposite her.

Maggie dropped her gaze to the makeshift board balancing on her lap. "Why so you did!"

She couldn't begrudge her new friend the win, considering that during her travels she had gathered a small collection of spoils from the other passengers. Anna had made the trip fun. She always had a story to tell or was willing to play a game to pass the time.

"Would you look at that?" Anna said, focusing out the opposite window. A half second later, she rushed over to stand beside Sadie and Rebecca.

"Pssst! Maggie!"

Maggie blew out a breath, recognizing her sister's voice behind her. Mary probably wanted to argue. Again. Just because her twin was a few minutes older she thought she knew everything. She blamed Maggie that they missed their last chance to get off the train in Salina, saying that Maggie had been too busy gossiping and playing games. Well, maybe she was, but that just meant they had to figure out another plan. Things always had a way of working out when they put their minds together. Mary didn't give her enough credit.

Maggie twisted around on the bench seat and stared at blue eyes that matched hers for all the irritation in them. "What?"

"We have to go. Now. It's our last chance."

"I want a bath. I want a decent meal. The girls say that the town is supposed to have hotel rooms for us and everything."

Mary frowned. "We're not staying in this dusty cow town."

"Well I want to enjoy it while I can. Nothing is wrong with a little pampering."

The glare in Mary's eyes could have sparked a fire. "Pampering! We need to find jobs and I need to find a place to make more tonic."

Maggie raised her chin. She wasn't about to let Mary bully her into seeing things her way. "The tonic needs another week before it's ready to bottle. What does it matter whether we are comfortable at the hotel?"

"It matters. We've got to show them right from the start we aren't going to marry anyone and they can't force us. You know how it is…how it's always been with our business. We need to be ready to leave town if necessary. That's why you need to come with me. We have to stay together."

"We won't make it. That conductor has eyes like an eagle. Besides, I heard the sheriff talk to him in Bridgeport. They won't give us a permit to sell it here anymore than they would in Ohio."

"Then we will just have to be more careful. Anyone who tries the tonic is happy enough with the results. It will only be for a few weeks. By the time the authorities find anything out, we will be gone."

Maggie frowned. "Where will we go after this town?"

"I don't know. Maybe Denver. Somewhere big enough to make a good profit. Somewhere far enough west that selling permits aren't a problem."

Maggie didn't want to hear it. She was tired of Mary's bossing, tired of thinking about the tonic and tired of traveling. She wanted a bath. And a meal. And a soft bed. In that order. Mary said they had to stick together. Well, then she could stick right here. With her. For once, her sister could just listen to her. "We can talk about it at the hotel."

She crossed her arms over her chest and pointedly turned away.

The worst of the screeching subsided as the engine shuddered, and then slowed to a turtle's crawl.

Her three companions created a fair wall with their noses pressed to the glass. Maggie could only see bits and pieces of the town moving by through the spaces between the three. She couldn't understand why they were excited about a new beginning and gaining a husband along with it. She certainly wasn't. That's all her life had been for as long as she could remember—always a new city, a new town, a new horizon. A seed didn't have time to flower, nor dust to settle, the way her family lived. And she sure didn't plan to get yoked to a man. A man would only complicate things between her and her sister. He might even separate them.

But while she was here, she would like to see a real cowboy. One with boots and a Stetson. Or one of those ten-gallon hats that the other girls had been giggling about. Did cowboys always wear spurs? These were things a girl should know.

She stored the deck of cards in her satchel. It wouldn't do to lose them. She might have need of a little spending money or even a little "get out of town" money.

She stepped behind Anna to peer over her shoulder. From this position all she saw was a small sea of dusty and dirty cowboy hats and bowlers. A few men waved faded flags—bleached by the sun and whipped by the prairie wind.

She swallowed. Men. All men. At least thirty of them. She rose to her tiptoes in order to see better.

Some were really young, but most looked middling to old. A few appeared weathered. One thing was obvious—no two of the men staring back from the station platform were the same. They were all shapes and sizes. And whether they wore big grins or not as they vied for the front row, they all looked curious to see who would be stepping off the train. Some, she noticed uncomfortably, appeared eager—a bit too eager.

With that thought she shrank back and looked in the seat behind her for her sister. Where had she disappeared to so fast? This bride contract had been her idea from the start. She should be here.

"Oh! I see the one I want!" Anna squealed, her voice blending with the last screech of the brakes.

The train shuddered horrendously to a complete stop. With it, a band started up. A band? A trumpet played "Oh! Susanna" and was joined by the beat of a drum and the trill of a fife.

Panic seized Maggie. She wasn't ready for this! "I have

to find Mary," she croaked out. Swaying slightly, she headed toward the back end of the railcar. She wanted to be with her sister when she faced the men gathered outside—not with these women she'd known only a handful of days.

The door before her swung open.

"Well now, Miss McCary," the conductor said, raising his bushy brows. "A bit anxious I'd say."

She glared at him. He was in league with the sheriff back in Bridgeport—that scoundrel.

Behind him, a man from the platform climbed the steps, pausing when he arrived at the top as if the exertion winded him. He was dressed in his Sunday best, right down to the gold watch fob and chain dangling from his black satin vest. The suit appeared a bit small at the neck—and other places. Probably cutting off his breath judging by the redness of his face. He peered first at her and then at the other women behind her as he blotted a trace of sweat on his forehead.

"Welcome to Oak Grove, ladies. I'm Mayor Melbourne." He paused, looking over the four of them. The welcoming mien dissolved and he turned to the conductor. "Where are the rest?"

The man fumbled in his pocket, withdrew a sealed envelope and handed it to the mayor.

Mayor Melbourne pressed his lips together. He slipped his wire glasses from his vest pocket and settled them on the bridge of his nose, bending the wires over his ears. Then he broke the wax seal on the envelope and quickly read the contents. If possible his face reddened further.

"Not coming!" he sputtered. "Not coming! I asked for twelve and all that answered the call are these four?"

"Actually, Mayor, that would be five," Rebecca said from over Maggie's left shoulder. "Mary McCary is also with us…somewhere."

"Five, you say? The committee sent enough money for twelve. My brother has some answering to do." He read the letter again, the perturbed look on his face slowly settling into resignation as he folded the paper and stuffed it in his pocket. "Very well. Ladies? Welcome. Please come meet your town."

She sensed Anna, Sadie and Rebecca gathering in force behind her. "What about our things?" she asked quickly, hoping to stall a few minutes longer.

"Plenty of men here to see to them," the mayor said. "Please follow me. As you can see, they are anxious to have a look at…I mean…meet you."

Behind her, the others pressed forward, prodding her out the door and onto the steps. A blast of warm Kansas wind swirled around her and picked up her skirt.

"Whoo-ee!" a man in front called out. "Got a looker right off!"

Her cheeks heated as she struggled to subdue the billowing purple cotton, and then she focused on the gawker, raising her chin defiantly and fixing him with a bold glare. She would make sure never to find herself alone with him.

He grinned. "Got spirit too! She's mine. Might as well just check her off your list, men. She's mine! Whoo-ee!"

"Not unless you take a bath and wash off that cow smell, Rader," someone yelled back. A round of chuckles from a few of the others followed.

Behind her, Sadie, Rebecca and Anna must have crowded into view for a cheer went up from the men. "Hip hip hooray!" Several even threw their hats into the air and the small band played louder at a furious pace.

Four strong-looking men stepped forward, and with a great deal more enthusiasm than the situation called for, took hold of her upper arms and whisked her—her body floating through the air—down the last two steps to the platform.

She wasn't ready for this! Where in heaven's name was Mary?

The train whistle blew, announcing the arrival of the Kansas Pacific just as Jackson Miller pounded the last nail into Angus O'Leary's coffin.

*Fit for a king.* O'Leary should be satisfied now. It was the second box the old coot had ordered for himself.

Jackson smoothed his hand over the edges of the box, making sure there were no rough spots. He tested the seams for sturdiness. Building this coffin had been a welcome change—if one could say that about a coffin. The wood transported to Oak Grove was usually pine for constructing buildings, not something as elegant or hard as this cherrywood.

The sounds of a drum and bugle started up from the direction of the train station. Across the street, the door to the Austin Hotel and Eatery slammed open with a bang and Austin's two youngsters flew out, making a beeline to the station. Rollie Austin rushed after his sons, smoothing down his thick beard, and then swiping the few longer strands of hair he possessed on his head over his scalp before plopping on his hat. Between caring for those rambunctious boys and running his establishment it seemed that every day he grew older and gruffer. Jackson wished him well at catching a new wife.

He woke that morning intent on staying clear of the hoopla of the arriving bride train. He hadn't wanted anything to do with the mayor's scheme. He'd learned his lesson the hard way not to put any trust in a woman. Marrying wasn't in his future. His work was all that mattered. Since the women would be staying at the hotel, that meant leav-

ing the work on the hotel's entrance and staircase for another day. And with the church nearly finished, his promise
to his brother would be fulfilled. Then he'd take stock of
what he would do next.

Gunshot sounded. Twice.

He opened the door to his shop and stepped out on the
boardwalk. Whooping and hollering filtered back to him
along with the band taking up a spare version of "Oh!
Susanna." The shots must have been men just blowing off
steam. He listened to the hoopla for a moment, remembering the last time he'd been excited about anything—the
day before Christine had called off their engagement and
run off with his best friend. That had soured him on getting worked up about anything anymore. A man couldn't
trust the feeling.

The shouting and cheering grew louder, coming his way.

The partiers appeared, rounding the corner at the livery
and heading down the main street, making so much noise
that the horses tied in front of the saloon whinnied nervously and shied away from the boisterous group. Probably
not used to the skirts. Men surrounded each woman—four
or five to each gal. Only four women? Where were the rest?

Austin and the mayor led the way flanking the tallest—
a pretty blonde. She walked with a careful air and grace,
her chin high, with two of her fingers holding up the hem
of her blue dress to keep it from the road as though she
were afraid to get any part of herself dirty. In her other
hand, she gripped an open parasol. He imagined that was
for show at the moment. Her large hat, with the long white
feather plume fluttering in the breeze, made the rest of her
look small.

Next came a gal with red hair, her bun halfway off
her head along with her small felt bonnet as if she'd been
hugged too vigorously by one of the cowpokes. Even though

the day had warmed up, she clutched the edges of her coat together at her throat as if deathly cold. Beside her, Danny Sanders talked nonstop—likely already trying to interest her in a tour of his saloon. Didn't look like she was interested. Her eyes were wide and focused—a bit desperately—on the doors of the hotel.

A few steps behind her, a brown-haired gal walked comfortably along swinging her handbag and talking with the four—make that five—cowboys that surrounded her and laughing along with them. She wore a pretty yellow travel dress and a large-brimmed straw hat with a ribbon that fluttered down her back. If he was a betting man, he'd bet that she or the blonde would be the first with a ring on their finger.

The last woman, bringing up the rear, was a dark-haired slip of a girl who hadn't even bothered to pin up her hair. Or if she had, it had come loose completely and fell helter-skelter, wavy and black as a waterfall at night, down to her waist. A plum-colored dress accentuated her pale skin and the finely etched brows that at the moment were scrunched up as she listened to the oldest Austin boy. It was amusing the way all the men who had doled out money to the Oak Grove Betterment Committee for a chance at a bride hovered around her, and yet it was ten-year-old Kade who had maneuvered his way in for the first word.

An overanxious cowboy slipped his hands under the boy's armpits and swung him out of the way, stepping in to sidle up next to the woman. She snapped out a word that left the man frozen with the boy dangling a foot off the ground. He set Kade right back next to her, pulled his hat down to his ears and strode ahead to the brown-haired gal. Looked like that last one could take care of herself despite her size.

A flatbed wagon carrying several large carpetbags and three trunks followed the entourage.

At the hotel, the men grabbed the luggage and would have accompanied the women right on inside, but for Sheriff Baniff's sizable form barricading the way. With a tip of his hat, he allowed the women to pass, and then moved back to block the doorway.

"Give the ladies a chance to settle in and freshen up, men. They've had a long trip. Drop off those trunks in their rooms and hightail it right back down the stairs without dallying. Tomorrow's shindig starts at four. Come back then."

A collective groan went up along with a few choice words from the gathered men. Then someone imitated the sound of a rooster.

Jackson leaned against his doorpost and watched the small crowd disperse. Maybe, like the mayor said, the town could use the softening influence of the women. More men had turned out than he expected. Although he wasn't interested in a bride, it might be amusing to see who ended up with the women after all.

Poor saps—they didn't know what they were in for.

## Chapter Two

Maggie stared out the open window for the umpteenth time. Still no sign of Mary. The sun rested on the horizon and already the brown of the town was changing to gray shadows. She hoped her sister was all right.

She flipped her hair over her shoulder—it was finally dry after her long soak in the tub—and then she stretched. Oh, my, but she felt gloriously clean for the first time in weeks. The wet washcloth and pan she had used since Bridgeport did little more than move the dirt from one part of her body to another. Her first request of Mr. Austin had been to have a bath—with soap! If only Mary could have enjoyed one too. It would have gone far to improving her sister's attitude and making Maggie's point that they both relax until the tonic was ready.

She knelt at her trunk and searched through her things, looking for the bottles of tonic tucked within her clothing. With all the jostling and jarring from the train station to this room, she wanted to make sure they hadn't broken. They were her insurance, her way out.

She unearthed two bottles, finding them intact. A folded piece of paper had been wrapped around the neck of the third bottle. She didn't remember doing that. Unwrapping it, she stared at familiar feminine handwriting.

> *I tried to tell you but you wouldn't listen. I can't stay.*
> *Gonna find a job. Will let you know where I am once*
> *I get settled.*
> *M. M.*

Mary had left her? She had to face the town on her own? Her chest tightened. When she got hold of her sister she would… She would…

Tears burned in her eyes. Mary should be with her. They'd never been separated—not in all their nineteen years. She blew out a breath, refusing to let even one teardrop fall. It was anger she felt. Anger and perhaps a sliver of remorse. Now things were all a mess.

"So that's what happened," Rebecca said, peering over Maggie's shoulder.

Quickly Maggie folded the note and tucked it away. "I thought you were napping."

"Just dozing."

"I'll thank you to keep things to yourself concerning this note."

Rebecca picked through the pile of clothes that she had deposited on her bed, talking as she looked for something to wear for supper. "Why would I tell anyone? One less McCary means I have a larger selection between the men."

Maggie frowned. Rebecca always looked to her own advantage. Why she had insisted Maggie share a room with her was a mystery. Anna would have been much more fun. Maggie shoved the note back into her trunk and closed the lid.

"Your sister is a coward."

Maggie gasped. "What did you say?"

Rebecca didn't repeat herself, instead attending to her bustle. She adjusted it at her waist and tied it in place.

Maggie really, really wanted to punch her. It was tempting. "She is not! She's the bravest person I know!"

"That doesn't sound brave." Rebecca pointed to the trunk, indicating the note. "It sounds foolish." She turned and slipped the dress—a pink gingham frock—over her head. She turned her back to Maggie, then peered over her shoulder and waited for Maggie to help with the buttons.

Is that why she had chosen Maggie to share her room? She expected Maggie to be her private maid? Rebecca Simpson was from a different world—a world that Maggie had only glimpsed through beveled, leaded windows. A world where she had always been warm and fed and wanted for nothing—right up until four months ago when her life had abruptly changed.

Grudgingly, Maggie walked over and helped her finish dressing. "You don't have a sister, so I'll have to allow for your ignorance."

Rebecca sucked in her breath.

Good. Let her suck on a lemon. Maggie wasn't going to let her malign her sister. "Family sticks together. No matter what."

"But she didn't. She left."

"It's only temporary." She met Rebecca's gaze with as much bravado as she could muster.

Maggie turned away and pulled some clean clothes from her trunk. She'd wear her favorite dress tonight—a sky-blue summer dress trimmed in white eyelet. As the last gift from her father, she always felt her father's love protecting her when she wore it.

"I saw Mayor Melbourne take you aside," Rebecca said. "Did he ask you about Mary?"

Maggie dressed as she answered. "He has men searching

for her, but if Mary doesn't want to be found, she won't be."
She rolled her thick hair back high up on her head, stabbing the mess rather savagely with her whalebone stick. She added another to secure the knot completely.

"You McCarys," Rebecca said with a measure of disdain in her voice. She checked her appearance in the standing mirror, smoothing her dress and turning first this way and then that. Satisfied, she slipped her white lace shawl over her shoulders and faced Maggie. "It's nearly seven o'clock and I'm starving. Are you ready?"

And just like that she'd put the incident behind her. Maggie bit her tongue to keep from saying anything more. Rebecca only cared for herself. For now, Maggie would try to get along with Miss Perfect. It was only for a few weeks. With the money from the tonic, she and Mary could take the train on to Denver. After seeing the small, dusty town, Maggie was sure that Mary would be even more anxious to be on her way.

She checked to make sure her short collar stood up at her neckline and that her top button was properly in place, then she followed Rebecca down the stairway, through the open foyer and to the restaurant section of the hotel.

Two large glowing candle chandeliers lit the room even though light spilled through the windows from the setting sun. Anna and Sadie were already seated at a table in the center of the room and appeared relieved to see Maggie and Rebecca approach. Nothing like being put on display. Maggie looked around the room filled with men who, by the scarcity of food in front of them, obviously were only waiting to see the women. Tonight must be quite a boon for business. Mr. Austin had even put his two boys to work clearing tables.

Mayor Melbourne waited beside the table, holding his bowler hat to his chest. "You ladies are a vision in this dusty town. I trust you are recovered from your journey." He helped Rebecca with her chair while Mr. Austin helped Maggie.

"Much recovered," Rebecca said, bestowing her prettiest smile on him. "And looking forward to the festivities tomorrow."

He grinned back and cleared his throat self-consciously. "I've asked the men to hold off until then for introductions, although I can't very well stop them from looking." He said the last and his gaze drew back to Rebecca.

Anna giggled, and then quickly covered her mouth with her hand.

The cook looked a bit harried as she served them a dinner of fried chicken, potatoes and green beans. "Not real fancy but it'll stick. There'll be apple cobbler comin' too."

Maggie had never had such a feast. Her mouth watered at the heavenly aromas.

Mayor Melbourne excused himself. Men at the other tables glanced furtively over at Maggie and the other women as they ate. She felt as though she was in a courtroom again, the way they were all staring at her. When Sadie dropped her napkin, no less than three men came close to blows trying to be the one to pick it up for her. And when the four of them rose to return to their rooms, wood screeched on wood as at least ten men jumped from their seats and rushed in to pull back their chairs.

It all felt strange.

She followed the other three brides to the lobby, feeling the stares of the men on her back. As she started up the stairs, something tugged at her skirt. She stopped.

"Miss?" A man who had just entered the lobby from the street whipped off his flat cap. Quickly he strode toward her. "Wait."

From the third stair, she looked down into the most

arresting eyes she had ever seen. They were the color of moss with a dark lash fringe, and gave him a quiet, self-possessed appearance. Rich brown hair that had not recently benefited from barber shears, a straight nose and a strong chin came together in a remarkably pleasing countenance.

"Aren't you forgetting the rules that the mayor stipulated?" She meant to say it smartly, but only managed to sound amused. Considering that she usually ignored boundaries placed on her it *was* amusing to her. A bit like the pot calling the kettle black.

Then she noticed his attire. He wore work clothes—brown trousers with suspenders and a coarse cotton shirt. She frowned. Not exactly his Sunday best for trying to make a good first impression. "I thought all cowboys wore Stetsons."

He rubbed the short whiskers that shadowed his chin, obviously unperturbed at the criticism. "You're caught up."

"Caught up?" she echoed.

He pointed to her hem. "Your dress."

She twisted slightly. Her skirt had brushed against a rung on the unfinished staircase and caught on a protruding sliver of wood. "Oh, fairy dust and flapjacks!" she mumbled under her breath. So he hadn't been trying to flirt with her. He'd only been trying to help. She gave the skirt an ever so gentle tug. It remained stuck fast.

"I'll get it." He crouched on the stairs and set to work, trying to extricate the material.

Heat crept up her face as she waited. She studied the back of his head, the waves in his hair that swept his collar, the broad shoulders set off even more by the crisscross of his suspenders. Inadvertently, he bumped against her, his broad shoulder pressing against her thigh. Her leg tingled at the point of contact. Disturbed, she inched away.

This was embarrassing—him kneeling at her feet. She

glanced up to see the rest of the men watching from the dining room with interest. This was not how she envisioned being the center of attention.

Sadie, Rebecca and Anna waited for her at the top of the stairs. By Rebecca's exasperated expression, it appeared she suspected Maggie had maneuvered this delay on purpose.

Maggie pursed her lips. Would he not hurry up? "It's all right. Please don't bother anymore. I'll take care of it."

She twisted farther, trying to see better what he was doing, and heard a loud rip.

His shoulders tensed.

"Oh, no!" Of all three of her dresses, not this one!

He rose to his full height—which since he stood a step below her put him at eye level. "Looks like you're free now."

She examined her hem. Six inches of tattered petticoat and blue material now dragged the floor. "Just look at my skirt!" She could have done a better job herself. "The least you could do is apologize."

He tilted his head slightly. "Apologize?" He drew out the word.

She placed her hands on her hips, her temper simmering. Sultry eyes or not, he could at least try to act the gentleman instead of standing much too close and challenging her with his attitude.

"Ah, Miss McCary. Margaret McCary?"

At the deep voice, she glanced over to the entry. A man with a tarnished brass badge on his chest stood there.

"Sheriff Baniff, miss."

She swallowed. What could he want? She hadn't been here long enough to cause any rift with the law. She mustered up her most gracious smile. "It's Maggie McCary, Sheriff. How nice to meet you."

At her pointed look, the green-eyed man moved out of the way and let her pass. He followed her to the lobby.

The two men standing there together were the same height—like bookends—one sandy blond and the other dark. Did Oak Grove grow only tall men? The sheriff, although handsome, couldn't hold a candle to the moody-looking man at his side.

"Mayor Melbourne asked me to look into your sister's whereabouts. I'm sorry to report that I haven't found her. I'm tempted to think she continued west on the train."

"She wouldn't do that. She wouldn't leave me."

"Town's not that big that she could just disappear, yet no one admits to seeing her. And the only thing that suggests she got off the train are those marks where something was dragged in the dirt. It's not much to go on."

She had expected as much. Her sister was a master at hiding. Maggie hadn't been more than five when Mary taught her to fend for herself and how to slip in and out of shadows. "Thank you for trying, Sheriff."

"It's too dark to see anything now. I'll search again in the morning. I don't suppose you have any idea why she ran off?"

*Because she refuses to lose her independence.*

"You will have to ask her that when you find her."

"I intend to."

She turned away from his penetrating gaze and gathered up her torn skirt. "If you'll excuse me." A few steps up the stairs and the back of her neck tingled. She gripped the banister and stopped.

It made no sense to look back. No sense at all, but those green eyes drew her.

The sheriff was heading into the restaurant. Amid a low hum of conversation and the clinking of forks on plates, the men there had returned to their meals. Yet the man who had freed her skirt stood in the same place near the door. He stared at her, seeming to scrutinize her very existence. What was he thinking to look at her that way?

A low thrumming sensation started in her chest—the same sensation as when he'd brushed up against her leg.

Quickly she turned and hurried up the stairs to her room.

## Chapter Three

Late the next morning while they were each putting the finishing touches on their pies for that afternoon's party, Rebecca received a box of candy from the mayor and a book of sonnets from the banker. Men were already lining up for a chance to court her. Maggie wouldn't be surprised if Anna and Sadie had to settle for Rebecca's leftovers—a situation that irked Maggie no small amount. At least she didn't have to concern herself with deciding on a husband.

Now, with only minutes to go until the party started, she laced up her shoe, trying hard not to compare her clothes to Rebecca's. Where her roommate wore a pretty cream-colored dress with dark pink edging and yards of ruffles descending from her bustle, Maggie wore the same dress she'd had on yesterday—the sky-blue one with the torn piece of hem secured by a small straight pin. She hadn't the needle or thread to repair it.

A small flutter of trepidation formed in her gut. It was time to meet the men of this town and figure out which ones she could count on in a pinch and which ones—besides that Rader cowboy—to stay away from. As annoyed as Rebecca made her, she was glad to have her nearby at this moment. Anna and Sadie too. *"Better to go to a hulla-*

*balloo together,"* Da would say when he had to face a judge or jury. He'd drag her and Mary right along with him. Like then, Mary should be with her now.

Inside, her heart hardened a wee bit toward her sibling. She and Mary had made a pact. They would look out for each other—no matter what. But Mary wasn't here.

She gave herself a cursory once-over in the mirror as she adjusted the bow over her small bustle. Then she pinched her cheeks to add a little color, grabbed her shawl and followed Miss Perfect out the door.

Rebecca stopped down the hall at Anna and Sadie's room and knocked. The door cracked open and Sadie peeked out timidly. When she realized it was Maggie and Rebecca her shoulders relaxed and she stepped into the hall. She wore a green-and-white-striped dress with a wide white collar. It did her justice, setting off her auburn hair and dark amber eyes.

From what Maggie had learned, the sweet girl had worked as a parlor maid for a family of financiers. When the son had shown too much interest in her, the matriarch insisted that she leave their employment. "Just as well" Sadie had said during their journey to Kansas. "I'd rather cook and clean for one man than an entire family of five." However, Maggie could see when Sadie wasn't looking, how sad she was. Maggie didn't know any man that was worth such melancholy.

Anna followed, a wide smile on her face as she stepped out into the hall and shut the door. Her brown eyes sparkled with merriment. "I mean to enjoy myself for as long as I can before I settle down to one beau. Working at the Bend in the Road Tavern did have its advantages."

Rebecca rolled her eyes. "And it's not hard to imagine what those might be."

"For your information, Miss Simpson, I learned to

dance. But I've never been the belle of the ball. I'm hoping that changes this evening for all of us. We are all belles tonight."

"Make sure you don't trip on your enthusiasm. A suitable match demands more than the man be a good dancer." With her nose hitched slightly higher in the air, Rebecca turned toward the stairs.

Maggie pressed her mouth tightly together to keep from retorting immediately. What made Rebecca so very different than the rest of them? They were all here for the same purpose. Well, except for herself. She turned to Anna and Sadie. "And this from a lady who needed our help to bake a pie this very morning!"

By the tightening of her frame, Rebecca had heard her, but she continued down the stairs as if their words didn't matter.

Sadie shook her head. She'd been an unwilling accomplice in the kitchen when they adapted the pie recipe particularly for Rebecca. Her protest had fallen on deaf ears.

Anna grinned. "Oh, don't be a spoilsport. We didn't hurt anything. Just had a little fun."

Sadie could use a little of that in her life, Maggie thought. "Come on, ladies. There's a party starting and I intend to eat my fill of desserts." Her smile widened as she linked arms with the two. "Just not Rebecca's."

Mr. Austin met them at the base of the stairs. He tucked Rebecca's gloved hand into the crook of his arm to walk her outside. The other three followed together. Maggie noticed, a bit piqued at the thought that they had all straightened to copy Rebecca's graceful air.

With the air warmer than yesterday and the sun shining down from a cloudless blue sky, Mr. Austin accompanied them away from the train tracks and to the opposite end of town, where the endless tall prairie grass waved under a hazy azure sky. Wide boards, suspended between upended barrels made several makeshift tables. Chairs had been carried from the restaurant and were set up around a fire pit. A few wagons had been pulled off to one side with men and two women unloading the dishes and pots to the tables.

Farther out in the meadow, several children played a game along with two barking dogs. Other men—several who had met them at the train station—played a noisy game of horseshoes, the dust flying high into the air and the shoes clanking loudly against the metal spike. Other people milled around, chatting and watching.

All in all, Maggie couldn't understand what made Rebecca, Sadie and Anna willing to stay in this uninspiring place. How could they marry and live here? How? Maggie had never missed the lush green hills and trees of eastern Ohio more than she did at that moment. Thank goodness that, unlike the others, she had a choice. Thank goodness Mary had a plan.

They stopped before a large square dance platform where a man bent over hammering the last few nails into place. Suspenders crisscrossed the center of his back and he wore a battered cap. Familiar—the shoulders, the back, the shirt. Buzzing started up in her belly, so much so that she put her hand there, holding tightly to herself.

"Ladies—" a man stepped forward and cleared his throat "—Mayor Melbourne was called away on business this morning and hasn't returned, so it falls to me to get this event started. I'm Theodore White, the owner of the *Oak Grove Gazette*—"

"Now, hold on, Teddy," Mayor Melbourne called out as he strode swiftly up to the gathering. His face was red with exertion. "I made it back. I'll take over."

There was a polite round of applause. Maggie glanced over her shoulder and realized the carpenter had straightened and now wiped his hands on a red rag. He scanned the crowd and met her gaze briefly, then he focused on the mayor as he stuffed the rag in his back pocket.

"I'd like to welcome you ladies and introduce you to the men who first brought you here. We formed the Oak Grove Betterment Committee because we believe in this town. With the stockyards and with the train, we are set to grow. But for that to happen we need men and women willing to put down roots, willing to do their part and contribute their talent to a growing community. May I be the first to thank you personally for responding to this call?"

It all sounded so grand, the way he put it, but his words didn't pertain to Mary or herself. They had sold Da's horse to pay their passage and didn't owe the committee a thing. It was only the matter of voiding the contract they had signed, which the sheriff in Bridgeport had assured them would be a simple fix.

"The terms of the contract are..." He paused for emphasis and looked over the gathered men and women. "Ladies...you have one month to get to know the men of this town and make your choice. At the end of that period, if you cannot decide on a suitable groom, a lottery will commence among the bachelors with one of their names to be drawn for the reluctant lady or ladies. Today, Friday, marks the official start of the contract period. Four weeks from tomorrow, we will all meet at the church for a wedding to beat anything you've ever seen before."

Maggie pressed her lips together. Four weeks. Such a short time. She understood that it was practical. The committee could only afford to house and feed them for so long. At least it would be nice to have free room and board without worrying where her next meal would come from. She and Mary would be sure to be long gone before the last week was fully upon them.

"Men?" the mayor continued. "You know who you are. Form a line. The ladies will stand on the platform and you can walk by and speak to each one for a moment. That'll keep everything cordial. We don't want to overwhelm the potential brides now, do we?"

There was a crude joke by someone—Maggie couldn't tell who—but then the men hustled across the grass toward the platform. A fair share of jostling, backslapping and one-line quips commenced as they found a place in the line. The show of camaraderie was most likely to cover up the embarrassment of the situation—or the excitement. She was relieved that she didn't see the outspoken cowboy who had pestered her yesterday.

The mayor took Sadie's arm and helped her up to the dance platform. Mr. Austin did the same with Rebecca. Then Mr. White tipped his hat and offered his arm to Anna.

"Miss?" Sheriff Baniff held out his arm.

She caught herself before she flinched away. Her escort *would* be the sheriff. "I thought you'd be out looking for my sister."

"She's safe. I'll explain after the introductions here."

She wasn't happy about waiting, but glancing at the eager line of men who watched, she also didn't want them all privy to her conversation with the sheriff. She took his arm and he helped her up to the platform.

The first man in line started with Sadie, giving her his name and occupation, then moving on to Rebecca and then Anna and then her. The first six men she kept straight, but after that, all the names and faces melded together in a hopeless muddle. She would never remember every detail.

"Brett Blackwell here is the last bachelor that contributed to the committee," Sheriff Baniff said.

"Vilcome to Oak Grove."

The large dark-haired man grabbed her hand enthusiastically and pumped it. Along with his size, his strong Swedish accent and deep voice set him apart from the rest of the men. She tried to extract her hand from his crushing grip, but he seemed oblivious to the fact that he still held on to her. The man didn't know his own strength. "And what is your occupation, Mr. Blackwell?"

"He owns the feed store along with serving as the town's blacksmith," Sheriff Baniff said.

Now she understood the strong grip.

"Your sister look yust like you!"

He finally let go of her, and as he did, his words registered. "You've seen Mary?"

"Ya. I give her ride yesterday to Circle P. She cook there now."

"Cook!" Relief washed through her. Mary had found a job! Saints be praised, she was so grateful for the news that she wanted to hug the big man. Instead, she bestowed on him her brightest smile. "That's wonderful!"

He cocked his big head. "You good cook too?"

At the question, several men drew closer to hear her answer.

"Not nearly as good as Mary. But yes, I can cook a little."

His eyes lit up.

"You'll find out soon enough, Brett," the sheriff said. "The women went all out and baked pies this morning for the picnic."

He escorted her off the platform and over to a smaller group of people standing nearby. She met several families—farmers, ranchers, the schoolteacher and a few children. A young girl toddled over to her, throwing her arms around Maggie's hips. Her throat constricted. It was a wholly different feeling than she had ever experienced before. Strange—and yet wonderful. These people welcomed her! They didn't know a thing about her, yet they were willing to open their lives to her.

It came to her then, that despite the plain look of the buildings and the fact that Oak Grove was a "cow town," perhaps she could like the people here. There was something steady about them. Something down-to-earth and friendly. They all had so much hope for their small town that she could fairly feel it in the wind.

It would be the perfect place to set up shop! She couldn't wait to tell Mary.

In the next breath she gathered in her enthusiasm. There were other towns that had turned on the McCarys. Some where they had been forced to leave quickly—in the middle of the night. She couldn't know what would happen here. Close-knit towns tended to take care of their own. Which meant she was the outsider. She would have to be cautious.

She surveyed the people milling about now. Why hadn't the carpenter been in the bachelor line? She had hoped to learn his name. Not, of course, that she cared all that much. She was just curious.

At the sound of a sudden loud cheer from out in the street, Jackson left off sanding the pew and stepped to the open doorway of his shop. Suddenly twelve riders raced down the center of the street, their mounts kicking up a cloud of dirt and dust which coated the boardwalk. It was something to see—all those men racing for a chance at a first dance with one of the brides. He imagined he'd be reading about this day in the *Oak Grove Gazette* before the week was out. The horses' hooves pounded the earth as they shot past, sounding like thunder and, like it or not, Jackson's heart sped up in kind. The reaction annoyed him enough that he turned away from the street and strode back to the kitchen.

He didn't want anything to do with the town's festivities. The only reason he had gone to the start of the welcome party was to finish assembling the dance floor. He'd been sniffing the savory scent of beef over an open spit and pounding in the last nail when he looked up and there stood Miss McCary.

He couldn't remember any of the other brides' names, but once he heard the sheriff address her last night at the hotel, her name had stuck. Margaret—but she went by Maggie. The name fit. He wouldn't be alive if he didn't admit to himself that there was something special about her. She sure didn't blend in. Not in her dress. Not in her manners. She didn't even try. He liked that about her. Whatever it was, grit or gumption, he figured whoever ended up marrying her might have a hard time with it.

Take for instance her attitude over her torn dress. The skirt was easy enough to mend given a needle and thread. Women! They could make a mountain out of a prairie dog hill.

It was interesting how she had acted when the sheriff showed up—last evening and then again today. Each time, Miss McCary had backed up so fast she'd nearly fallen. And if that wasn't a guilty expression plastered across her face for an instant before she hid it, he didn't know squat. Yep, Maggie McCary had definitely had a run-in with the law before. That was another thing a new husband would have to handle—assuming she confessed to it before tying the knot.

The yelling of the crowd died down and with it Jackson realized he'd been thinking a little too long on one Maggie McCary. He took a swallow of cider and walked back out to the front room to look through the window. The riders had disappeared down by the river among the few scrub cedars. As they reappeared and raced back toward town, the bulk of the men on horseback thinned out into a single line. A roar went up from the bystanders.

They rounded the corner of the livery, passed the blacksmith's and Blackwell's Feed Store, and then dashed right in front of him. Wayne Stevens was out in front and from the looks of it crossed the finish line down at the bank first, which meant he would get first pick of the brides for the starting dance. In a flash of inspiration, the mayor had decided that the men would be given a number depending on their order crossing the finish line and that would be their ticket to a dance partner. After the first round, the dancing would continue with different partners.

With there being four brides and fifteen bachelors, that was going to make for a lot of dancing for the ladies and a lot of watching for those sitting out. He was sure the men would want more than just one dance apiece. He almost felt sorry for the women. Almost. But he knew there were a few good picks among the men. Not all of them rode a fast horse. Between the shredded beef sandwiches, the salt cracker pies and the cider to wash it all down, he imagined the entire party would last past sundown. The women wouldn't get a chance to sit. And when they retired, he wouldn't be surprised if the other townsfolk kept the revelry going.

One thing he'd learned since moving here was that his neighbors liked to celebrate. They got few chances through the year since their farms and ranches demanded most of their attention. When the occasion for a party came up, they went all out. And this was the biggest occasion he'd heard tell of.

They were all friendly enough. And the ones he'd helped with the building of their homes could sometimes be overly friendly. But he didn't want to know his neighbors any better than he already did. Getting too close—learning their hopes and their dreams—was awkward. He'd expect things, and they would expect things of him. A man could get bogged down when that happened. A man could get hurt.

*Don't get involved*, he had told himself after his brother died. All he wanted was to tend to his carpentry business and finish this last addition to the church. With the pew anchored in place, his promise to his brother would be done. He glanced reluctantly at the crate he'd stashed in the corner. His jaw tightened, thinking of the bell that resided inside. Almost done.

And then, who knew? He could leave Oak Grove if he wished. He'd come at his brother's request. He could leave just as easily when he had fulfilled it. Nothing to hold him here. If he stayed, the church would be a daily reminder of his brother and all the dreams they'd had that had gone to waste.

Music struck up—a fiddle and a harmonica. It was enough to make him yearn for the quiet peacefulness of the river and an afternoon of fishing. Well, he would have no customers today with the party going on. That was a given fact.

He took his pole from the corner and stepped onto the boardwalk, listening to the sounds of the celebration. A woman began to sing. Whoever it was had a beauty of a voice and, if he wasn't mistaken, a bit of a lilt.

The image of flashing blue eyes and black riotous hair filled his thoughts.

He gripped his fishing pole tighter and turned away.

# Chapter Four

Maggie hid in the shadows behind the water barrel and leaned against the school building while she caught her breath. The last dance had been a fast-paced square dance that left her gasping. In the meadow, a long stone's throw from where she stood, the campfire blazed up for a second, and then settled back down as the cheerful sounds of the fiddle continued. Stars glittered in the immense sky overhead and the cattle confined to the stockyards to the east of town were lowing and settling in for the night. Unfortunately, the breeze that had swept away their strong scent was dying down too. *Ugh.*

But the people? They were lovely. She had never enjoyed herself more or felt so welcome. Otis Taylor had even enticed her to sing by playing an Irish ballad they both knew. She remembered most of the lines and those she didn't she simply made up. The children and even a few of the grown-ups had had a good laugh in the end, trying to make sense of her silly verses.

The families with small children were leaving now. Many of them spoke of cows to milk early and farm chores waiting for them.

Maggie wouldn't mind going back to the hotel herself.

Sadie had succumbed to weariness an hour ago. Anna, she could see on the dance floor with enough spring in her step that it was likely she was in no hurry to end the evening. Anna's wish had come true. With her infectious laughter and pleasant humor, men had lined up to dance with her.

Rebecca stood to the side of the dance platform flanked by Mr. Swift, the banker, and Mayor Melbourne. She had them eating out of her gloved hand—surely in no small part due to the tonic that Maggie had added to Rebecca's pie before they had baked it. Upon sampling it, several of the men had grown quite congenial—as had Rebecca. Maggie didn't feel even a small twinge of guilt for the trick. Rebecca thought she was perfect, and she thought it her duty to help everyone around her be perfect too. A little tonic eased that tendency.

Unfortunately, someone had added a splash of whiskey to the cider barrel an hour ago. Coupled with the effects of the pie, things had started to get rambunctious. Particularly for one cowboy. Throughout the evening Jess Rader had vied for her attention. When he had grabbed her hand to dance with her a third time, hinting that he had a secret to tell her, she had yanked herself free of him and escaped to her current hiding place. Secret indeed! As if she would fall for something so obvious. She wasn't Anna, for heaven's sake!

Footsteps sounded. She crouched down farther. Peeking over the barrel's edge, she found the sheriff standing not twenty feet from her. Light flared on his face as he struck a match and lit his rolled cigarette. Wonderful. Just wonderful. How long would he remain between her and the hotel's front door?

"You seen Miss McCary?"

Her heart sank to her stomach. Of all the luck! Mr. Rader

had joined the sheriff and now stood there, puffing on his own cigarette.

"Been a while," the sheriff answered, and then tipped the brim of his hat toward the street. "'Night ladies."

Maggie raised up just a little. Rebecca with her two escorts, and Anna with the newspaper man and his sister, ambled past. If only she could join them. It would be awkward, however, for her to come out from behind the water barrel. They headed into Mr. Austin's hotel.

"Fairy dust!" Maggie mumbled under her breath. A shiver coursed through her. The warm vapor from her lungs curled up in the cooling air. One thing was certain—she couldn't remain here much longer. Dampness had settled in.

"Maybe she's already back at the hotel," Sheriff Baniff said with a shrug. Then he looked toward the campfire. "Looks like people are packing up." He strode back to the partiers who loaded the wagons.

Mr. Rader watched him go.

*Please leave, please leave*, became her silent litany. She stayed as still as a mouse, barely breathing. Waiting, waiting…

Five minutes to eternity later, Mr. Rader abruptly dropped his cigarette stub and with the heel of his boot crushed it into the dirt. Then he strode down the middle of the street and planted himself on the front steps of the hotel.

Was she to have no peace from him? *Now* how was she supposed to get to her room? Surely the hotel would have a back entrance.

Silently, she slipped around the back of the school. The next building however, stopped her. It was the church, and to circle that meant she would have to walk through the small cemetery.

Oh. She couldn't do that.

She blew out a breath. The other way then.

Retracing her steps to the water barrel, she eyed the expanse of dirt and grass she would have to race across before the next building would hide her. Mr. Rader might see her but he might not. And she had no other recourse if she wanted to get back to the hotel.

All right then. Go!

She plunged across the edge of the meadow, and then kept going behind the buildings that lined the main street opposite the hotel. One, two—almost directly across from the hotel now. Just one more building to go.

"Someone there?" Rader called out.

She stopped and peered through the narrow opening between the buildings. Mr. Rader had risen from the steps and was crossing the street. No! Oh, no! He was coming toward her!

The flutter of small wings sounded. A bat swooped out from under an eave and careened in front of her. Gasping, she covered her eyes and moved back quickly, her foot sliding on a patch of mud.

*"Ech!"* Disgusting! It had to be from someone's slop bucket.

"Who's there?" Jess Rader called out, the sound of his voice closer.

Drat! He was coming this way! She was in a fine fix. Her heart pounded in her chest.

"Who is back here?"

She scrambled to her feet and glanced about for a place to hide. All the buildings were dark, save one directly opposite the hotel. A soft light glowed through the back window. There. It would have to be there. She raced up the back steps, threw open the door and stumbled inside.

The scent of fresh wood shavings assailed her, so sweet after the odor from the stockyards. The glow from a lamp illuminated a small plain room that held a cupboard in one corner and a cookstove in another. In the center of the room was a wooden table where a man hunched over a long rolled paper with pencil and ruler.

He looked up and locked his green gaze on hers.

She opened her mouth to explain, but the sound of a boot on the steps behind her made her heart race even more. She had to hide!

Jackson had just been thinking of the dark-haired slip of a woman. Her image had disturbed his concentration as he designed a coatrack for the hotel's entryway. And here she was—as if he'd conjured her.

"Frog hair and fairies!" she whispered. "I'd be eternally grateful if you didn't see me!"

And talking nonsense. Again.

She stood with her hands behind her, pressed against the door frame, her brow furrowed. Her hair was halfway down her back, the soft curls dancing wildly around her flushed face, her blue eyes sparkling. She was, in essence, a vision. An out-of-breath vision, he amended as he noticed her chest rising and falling quite becomingly.

She turned her head to the side, listening intently, and then bolted, racing past him and into the next room, her skirt flying.

He stood to follow when a knock sounded on the open door behind him. A cowboy from the Circle P stood there. Jackson had seen him a time or two heading into the saloon. "Shop is closed."

"Name's Rader. Thought I heard a noise back here. Just checking things out. You hear anything?"

"Just the sound of you banging on my door."

The cowboy leaned in to look around him and survey the room. "You didn't see anyone come this way?"

Jackson could smell liquor on Rader's breath. Miss Irish was smart to run. "Have you lost someone?"

Rader's gaze settled on him for a long moment. Finally, his shoulders lowered as he huffed out a breath. "Probably just kids. Those two Austin boys have been causing a ruckus at the party."

"They're not here."

Rader took his time looking over Jackson's shoulder. "Guess not. Sorry to bother you." He turned and headed slowly down the steps.

Jackson closed the door. Hopefully the girl had escaped through the front door and was safe and sound back in the hotel where she belonged. She was that—a girl—by the way she acted, and hardly old enough to be a bride.

He squatted to pick up the papers that had blown off the table when she rushed past.

Mud splattered the floor.

He sighed.

He put the papers back on the table and set the salt shaker on them to keep them there. Grabbing the broom from the corner behind the door, he swept up the half-dried clods of dirt, following the trail Miss McCary had left through the door to the front room. Like bread crumbs found by the birds, the trail stopped abruptly halfway through the room.

Had she darted in a different direction? No—no more bits of mud.

Then he saw it. A familiar bit of torn fabric dangled from the closed lid of a large trunk.

He drummed his fingers on the lid. "Miss? He's gone. You can come out now."

"No. He's relentless. He's been chasing me half the evening."

Her words were muffled, but he understood them well enough and didn't like what she said. Her first full day here and some randy cowboy had bothered her to such a degree. It grated on his conscience. "You can't stay in there."

"I believe I will."

"No, you will not."

There was a moment of silence before she replied. "You are not being very helpful."

She said it with such petulance that he could imagine her generous lips mashing together and turning down in a frustrated frown. The image almost made him smile. Almost. This was exactly what made talk in a small town where news traveled faster than lightning. Gossip wasn't something he ever worried about but if she was to be someone's bride she had better keep her reputation clear of any speculation. She had to get out of his shop. She had to leave.

"I don't like interruptions."

"Well, I don't like being chased like a poor rabbit before the dogs."

He tried another tack. "Aren't you worried what people will say with you being gone so long?"

"I'll make up a tale. I'm fairly good at it when necessary."

"So you'll lie?" What kind of woman had Mayor Melbourne acquired for the Betterment Committee?

"Not really. I'll simply 'bend the truth a little.' That's what my da would say."

Interesting. "A white lie, then."

"Mmm… Yes. I believe that is what it is called."

A shout from the street made him glance up. A wagon pulled by two mules and filled with children and adults headed out of town. The party was over and people were leaving. Miss McCary really had to get out of here. He didn't want to be wrapped up in one of her "bent truths" in any way. He wanted her out of his shop.

"Look, miss. That cowboy is long gone. Come out so we can talk face-to-face."

"No."

He ran a hand through his hair. Short of dragging her out of the trunk by brute force, he couldn't think of a way to make her leave. "Then you better stay. Make yourself comfortable in there."

"Comfortable!"

She sounded exasperated. Good. It couldn't be near the irritation he was feeling. Two entire days had been disturbed by the arrival of the brides and the party, and now this.

"In that case do you have a pillow I could use?"

The audacity of her request would have been amusing if he hadn't been so frustrated. "You can't stay, miss." He spotted the dolly stored in the corner. "Matter of fact, I think I'll move you, trunk and all, outside."

A muffled gasp sounded. "You wouldn't!"

In answer, he slipped the flat plane of the dolly under the trunk's edge and wheeled it slowly toward the door.

Suddenly the lid popped up and she appeared. "Stop! Stop this instant!"

He tilted the trunk back to the floor. She was prettier than he remembered. Bewitching in a way. In the dim light, her lips were set in a stubborn bow and her skin appeared translucent and pale as the moon. Her eyes looked larger and darker. And, he realized with a twinge of amusement, she had sawdust sprinkled in her dark hair.

With catlike grace, she slipped over the edge of the trunk. When she straightened, the entire room seemed to shrink as her presence filled it. Which was ridiculous, considering how tiny she was physically.

She looked about the room, her inquisitive gaze lighting

on the secretary in the corner and then the table and chairs by the front window. "What is this place?"

"My shop."

"You make furniture? Cabinets and such?"

He nodded. "Whatever is needed."

She ran her fingers over the edge of the trunk as if assessing its quality. Then she squared her shoulders and faced him, her chin high. "I suppose the situation calls for an introduction. I'm Maggie McCary."

"I heard. I'm Jackson Miller."

"Pleased to meet you, Mr. Miller. Thank you for not handing me over to that scallywag," she said, strolling over to a half-finished hutch nearby.

She moved gracefully, with a subtle swing to her hips that drew his gaze. He scowled when he realized it.

Slowly, she pulled out one of the small drawers as if testing the smoothness of the fit. She pushed the drawer back in and faced him. "Tell me—are all cowboys so brash?"

"No."

A pretty pout formed. "Obviously not you. You didn't even stay for the party."

She had noticed? For some reason that surprised him. "I'm not looking for a bride."

"Well that is a good thing. A sensible thing, I think. After tearing my dress, you didn't even think to apologize," she said flatly. "A woman could do better."

Was that a challenge in her voice? A subtle tease? The fact that she was the one who had pulled away and torn her own skirt seemed to have escaped her. If anyone should be sorry, it was her for interrupting two perfectly good, *quiet* evenings. "Well then, miss," he said with a hint of a smirk, "I apologize for attempting to assist you."

"Are you implying I should be thanking you?"

"I never imply anything. I mean exactly what I say. Always."

She put her hands on her hips and gave a small shrug with her shoulders. "Well, we will just leave it at that. We're even now."

Even? Not by his count. If she left now, immediately, he'd consider it, but she didn't seem in a hurry to go.

"Mr. Miller, don't you ever smile?"

He didn't think that deserved an answer.

Another wagon, this one pulled by two large shires, headed down the center of the road. "Farmers," he murmured, watching it slowly trundle by. The Perkins family and their passel of redheaded kids to be exact. He watched the wagon disappear into the gathering dusk before turning back to Miss McCary.

She was studying him intently with those large sky-blue eyes of hers. Then she repositioned her shawl across her shoulders. "I can see that I've interrupted your evening. I'll be going." The challenge, the teasing was gone from her voice.

"I'll walk you back." Why didn't he let her go on her own? Her problems weren't his.

She shook her head. "There is no need. I was assured several times at the party that this is a safe town for a woman to walk about without an escort."

"And yet you found yourself hiding in my trunk."

"I came here on my own two feet—I can get myself back."

He opened the door, stepped out on the boardwalk and checked the street. "Looks like the way is clear."

As she passed in front of him she paused and looked up into his eyes. "You thought I was being silly about my dress. I want you to know that I don't usually get worked up over a bit of material." Her voice was softer now. She bit her upper lip, contemplating him. Then she lifted her skirt slightly. "This was a present from my da. The last before he died."

Why was she confessing this? He didn't want to be weighted down with her confidence. Or, he thought with a frown, one of her "bent truths" if this was her way of manipulating him. But studying her pretty face now, he didn't think it was.

"If Rader troubles you again…" He should end with something gallant like *Hide out at my place anytime*, but those words that would have been easy three years ago, wouldn't come now. He was used to being on his own. He liked the quiet. Let a person close—like he had Christine—and it was an invitation to get hurt. "Let the sheriff know."

She blinked and her mouth dropped open. "I'll be sure to do that. Thank you, Mr. Miller. You've been kind. Good evening." And with a flounce of her skirt, she turned and marched across the street to the hotel.

## Chapter Five

The next morning, Maggie left Rebecca sleeping while she dressed, and then headed downstairs for breakfast.

Anna had chosen a table near the tall front windows of the hotel's restaurant for breakfast, and now sat with her chin resting on her palm and her fingers tapping her cheek. "And just where were you after the party last evening?"

Maggie slipped into the chair next to her. "I was here," she said with a quick lift of one shoulder. Then she busied herself adjusting her skirt, avoiding Anna's probing gaze. "I came back here."

"Not directly, you didn't."

Mr. Austin appeared from the kitchen with a tray of cups and steaming tea. The man looked flustered as he put the tray down and handed off the cups and saucers. "Usually no call for tea here. Just coffee."

"Good morning, Mr. Austin. I'm sure it will be fine."

"Boys made this. No tellin' how it'll taste."

"You can't ruin tea," she said gamely, and then took a sip. It was the most bitter tea she had ever had.

He watched her face carefully.

She splayed her hand across her neckline and forced the liquid down quickly. "How long did you steep this?"

Mr. Austin sighed. "By the look on your face, I'm thinking too long. Honey?"

She nodded.

Sadie pushed a jar toward her. "I used some too."

Maggie stirred a spoonful into her cup, and then licked her spoon. It had a different flavor than the honey back home. How would that work in the tonic? She would have to discuss it with Mary. She took another sip of tea. "Much better."

"I'll bring you a plate," Mr. Austin mumbled and disappeared back into the kitchen.

Sadie leaned close and whispered, "His cook couldn't come in today and since it is Saturday his boys are off from school. All told, he's in a bind."

Maggie studied her over the rim of the china teacup. "I recognize that look in your eyes. You're considering helping him."

Sadie stiffened. "I'm not doing anything special today."

"We're guests, remember? At least enjoy your freedom for a little while. Soon enough you'll be married off and will have to do all the cooking and dishes. If it's to Mr. Austin, there will be plenty of those."

"Unless she marries the banker," Anna said smugly. "Then she would have a cook and a housekeeper. However, if you want him, you will have to fight Rebecca."

"I won't fight anybody," Sadie said, shrinking back into her chair.

Anna raised her brows at that, and then turned her attention to Maggie. "What are your plans for the day?"

"For certain it won't be work! I'd like to take a walk and see what shops there are here in town."

Sadie made a sound close to a giggle. "That will take all of half an hour."

A flash of yellow caught Maggie's attention and she

looked over to see Rebecca coming down the stairs in a pretty butter-yellow dress, trimmed in black. She moved slowly, almost what Maggie would call regally, until she realized the only people in the restaurant were two ancient farmers and her three friends. Her grand entrance having gone virtually unnoticed, her shoulders relaxed and she walked over to the table.

"You're up," Maggie said. "I thought you would sleep another hour by the way you were snor—"

"A lady doesn't reveal things of such a private nature," Rebecca said, interrupting Maggie. "I'll make an allowance of course, considering your upbringing."

Maggie frowned. "My upbringing was just fine. Da and Mary used common sense." She looked pointedly at Rebecca's hat, which was covered in silk flowers. As pretty as it was, this one wouldn't protect her from the sun. It was an old argument between them—if a couple of days could be considered long enough to have an old argument.

"Come have a seat," Sadie said while she patted the empty chair next to her. "Mr. Austin is having a difficult time of it this morning and breakfast may be a while. Here. He brought out a cup for you." She proceeded to pour tea for Rebecca.

Rebecca sighed as she sank into the seat. "Thank you. I'm fairly parched. Did you notice how that cider took on a different taste toward the end of the evening? Not bad, mind you. As a matter of fact it was rather delicious."

Anna let out a snort.

With a sideways warning glance at her, Maggie said innocently. "Seemed fine to me. Are you sure?"

"You should tell her," Sadie said.

"Tell me what?" Rebecca asked, suspicious now.

"Somebody added hard liquor to the barrel after sundown," Maggie admitted.

The blonde's eyes grew wide. "No! Then I'm relieved that I stopped drinking it immediately."

"Thought you said you liked it." Maggie prodded her.

"Well…it's unseemly for a lady to imbibe. Our natures are much too delicate. At least, mine is." She repositioned the netting on her hat in order to see them better. "You came back to the room quite late—after I retired. Just what did you do after the party?"

Leave it to Rebecca to bring up that question again. "I had to evade Mr. Rader."

"Which one is he?" Sadie asked.

"A cowboy with more ambition than good sense," Maggie said.

"Ambition is good," Sadie said. "I'd hate to marry a man who didn't want to make things better."

Maggie wrinkled her nose. "He's straight off the ranch. Smells like it too." Then she paused and in her mind went over her words. Had she been too hasty? Could Mr. Rader be from the same ranch where her sister had found work? Perhaps she shouldn't have been so quick to run from him. He might have had news of Mary.

The thought of her sister didn't help. Maggie missed her terribly. And yet at the time she was still angry. Mary shouldn't have left her to fend for herself. Anything could happen with them separated. What if things didn't go well? What if one of them got hurt? They had never had an argument that ended up like this. One of them always gave in. Wasn't Mary worried about her too?

Maggie only half listened to the conversation between Anna and Sadie as she considered her situation. She was doing all right. She had friends, lodging. She might even be faring better than her sister, and wouldn't that make Mary jealous? But perhaps she could find transportation to the ranch today and see how her sister was doing.

Mr. Austin interrupted her thoughts, finally bringing bowls of porridge to the table. His two boys followed behind him with a small crock of butter and a pitcher of milk.

"By the way, Maggie," Rebecca said a few moments later when it was just the four of them again. "With all the excitement of our arrival, I am having trouble sleeping. Do you think your tonic would assist with that?"

"Some say it helps."

"Then I'll give it a try. Will you part with a bottle? I'll pay you."

Her first customer! "Certainly. I'll get it for you when we go back upstairs."

"Lovely." Rebecca continued talking about the other men that she had met at the dance, discussing who would make good husband material versus who would be impossible. Anna and Sadie appeared to soak up all of her advice.

Maggie listened for a while but soon lost interest. From the gist of things, it seemed that Jackson Miller was the only man who wanted to remain single in this town. She could just picture him as she'd first seen him last evening, bending over the table, a look of concentration on his face. It was an interesting face—a strong forehead, a thin straight line for his nose. She was not sure why he stuck in her mind so easily.

He was not winsome like James O'Mally down at the corner grocery in Bridgeport. James had laughing eyes and a ready saying behind every word, but he was as fickle as a rooster among hens. Everything about Mr. Miller was solemn and serious and rather disagreeable. Yet he hadn't given her away to Mr. Rader. That was commendable of him. And despite all the others that she'd danced with last night, he was the one her thoughts kept returning to.

She looked about the table at the others. It was a good thing Mr. Jackson had no intention of taking a bride because none of the women here would make a suitable match for him.

Rebecca would expect coddling and courting with flowers and sweet mints. She had spoken of evenings at the opera before she came upon her "unfortunate circumstances." Mr. Miller was definitely not the doting sort. If anything he was short-tempered and easily irritated—not at all suitable for Rebecca.

Then there was Sadie. As Maggie contemplated the quiet, serious red-haired girl, Sadie rose from her seat and carried her dirty dishes to the kitchen, stating she was going to see what she could do to help Mr. Austin. As much as Maggie liked her, she couldn't imagine Sadie standing up to Mr. Miller. She would bend over backward to be his helpmate and he would let her without the least concern for the girl's true feelings. The balance of personalities would be completely off-kilter.

Maggie shifted her gaze to Anna, who laughed at a remark made by Rebecca. She was pretty and, although too easy to trick, she learned quickly. That she was always willing to try something new made her fun to be around. She would be perfect for Mr. Miller. Anna might even bring a smile to him. Now there was a thought! Mr. Miller with a smile… She imagined it would make him rather dashing. Yet, for some reason she didn't like the idea of him bestowing a smile like that on Anna.

What was she worried about? He wasn't looking for a bride. He'd said as much. And with the little she did know about him, the thought of him smiling was preposterous.

When they were finished their breakfast, Maggie stepped out on the boardwalk with Anna and Rebecca. They made their way slowly down their side of the two-block main street, looking through the windows and when waved at, going inside to greet the owners. A few men passed by and tipped their hats.

Mrs. Taylor stepped from her husband's barbershop to let them know that she was the one seamstress in town should they require any sewing. Maggie asked her about repairing her torn skirt and agreed to bring it in later in the week. When the woman rubbed the knuckles of one hand and complained of her rheumatism, Maggie mentioned the tonic she had with her and promised to bring her a sample.

In a small town like this, she and Mary would need a different way of selling than her father had used. In Bridgeport, every Saturday morning Da had sold the tonic out of the boot of his carriage. Since she and Mary did not own a carriage—and since the town was only a few blocks— likely word of mouth would make more sense. From what she'd overheard between the sheriff in Bridgeport and the conductor, Oak Grove had rules about selling tonic and didn't allow women a permit. She would just have to do things a little differently.

At the end of the street they passed the church, which, with its tall white steeple, was in her estimation the prettiest and newest building in town. Then the school which was closed up tight. They started down the opposite side of the town. When they came to the *Oak Grove Gazette* office, Abigail White welcomed them. She was a tall, gangly woman who constantly adjusted her glasses on her nose.

Abigail surprised them all by saying, "Folks here will want to know all about you. If you are agreeable, I'd like to interview each of you for an article in the newspaper."

Maggie didn't want anyone here knowing that she had left Bridgeport to escape a spell in jail—not even Rebecca or Anna or Sadie.

"I can't imagine that this is very proper for a lady," Rebecca said slowly.

"Oh, come now. It is an opportunity to let the people here know what issues are important to you. For example, your position on women voting. Or the saloon opening on Sundays." She leaned forward, as if revealing a great secret. "There has been more and more talk of that since you ladies arrived."

"When you put it like that, it does sound sensible," Anna said.

"What do you think, Maggie?" Rebecca asked.

She was surprised Rebecca cared about her opinion. Anna obviously saw nothing wrong with baring her soul for the sake of a good match. But what, Maggie wondered, would Mary say?

"Perhaps it would be best if I did this individually?" Abigail said when they didn't answer immediately. "Why don't you talk it over among yourselves, and whoever decides to be first can come tomorrow morning." Her brown eyes lit up with excitement. "I know! I'll print only one interview a week. That will sell more newspapers."

They left the newspaper office with a promise to let Abigail know their decision. The morning was glorious, warm with a cool breeze, despite that they were in the middle of nowhere Kansas and the air carried the slight odor of cattle from the nearby stockyards.

"Are you ready to go back to the hotel?" Rebecca asked, squinting into the sunlight. She pulled the small brim of her hat down trying to shield herself. "My head aches. I'm going to lie down for a while."

Maggie shook her head. "I want to check on Mary. I'll walk down to the livery and see if I can find a rig."

"You don't even know the way."

"Someone will tell me."

"Maggie. Please," Anna said. "It isn't wise. Everything looks the same out here. You might get lost."

"I'll talk with the livery owner and find out how far it is to the Circle P. Maybe he will have a suggestion."

"But you won't go by yourself. Promise me?"

She didn't have the money to rent a buggy anyway. She would have to find someone who was traveling that way on the chance she could ride along.

Maggie left them and headed for the edge of town. The livery was near the train depot. When she got there, the building was deserted. A cool breeze swept through the large wooden structure where a buggy, a flatbed wagon and five horses rested, but there was no sign of the liveryman.

Now what? That blacksmith had given Mary a ride out to the ranch on the day they arrived. Perhaps he would be willing to do the same for her.

She walked next door and found Mr. Blackwell hunched over and struggling to nail an iron shoe on a buckskin horse's hoof. His face, from her angle, was reddened to the point it was almost purple. Just as she started through the open doorway to speak to him, a long string of frustrated words exploded from his mouth.

"I vill be getting this done, whether you help or not, you cantankerous, four-legged—"

She stopped. Perhaps now wasn't the best time to bother him. Quickly, she skirted the door and walked on.

She came to a stop before the carpenter's shop. Maybe Mr. Miller would oblige her. A ride in the country might be good for his disposition. Fresh air, sunshine.

She stepped inside.

With sunlight streaming through the two tall front windows, the shop had a more welcoming tone than the evening before and she noticed a few more pieces he'd made. Two rocking chairs sat in the corner—one adult-sized and the other matching and child-sized. It was a bit whimsical for such a serious man and she felt a smile tug at the corners of her mouth.

Footsteps sounded overhead on the second floor.

Ah. He was upstairs. She would wait.

It looked like he had been hard at work since last evening. A sandpaper block sat on a nearby church pew and sawdust littered the floor. Against the wall, an ornate box rested on two sawhorses. Last night she had assumed it was a table, covered as it had been by a dark gray cloth. The box was long and narrow, with fancy scrollwork along edges. As she neared, a growing realization of the purpose of the box formed. A coffin—a very fancy coffin. Mr. Miller was called on to do all sorts of work then.

Of course it would be empty, but curiosity got the better of her and she edged closer. She held her breath as she peered over the side. A stout body reposed there. It was an older man, perhaps in his seventies, with curling silver hair and ruddy cheeks. He wore a new black suit with a bow tie. A black top hat rested on his chest.

She made the sign of the cross over her. Dead then. What was he doing all alone? Where were the mourners? Where were the women to keen and carry on? A body shouldn't be left alone until it had a proper send-off. He looked so peaceful...

Wait.

Did his fingers just twitch? Her heart pounded. She looked back to his face.

His eyes popped open.

She screamed.

At the sound of a woman's scream, the hair on the back of Jackson's neck rose and his scalp prickled.

He took the narrow stairs two at a time.

In the main room, Angus O'Leary sat up from within

his coffin, a look of astonishment on his face. Through the door that led to the kitchen, Jackson caught the last swish of a deep purple skirt. "Ma'am? Miss?" he called out and ran after her. "Wait!"

Whoever it was had already fled through the back door, leaving it wide-open. He raced after her, recognizing the form and the shiny rich blackness of Miss McCary's curls. She was quick, but was already slowing as she reached Doc Graham's place—situated behind the cabinet shop. He caught up to her at the doc's side yard swing. She had stopped and seemed to be looking at it without quite seeing it.

"Miss McCary?" He touched her shoulder.

She turned toward him. The shock he'd expected to see in her eyes wasn't there. Instead, those blue eyes flashed daggers.

"What is a man doing in a coffin in the middle of your shop?" she demanded. "My heart's in my nose!"

"Just calm down."

She held up both hands. "Calm down! I should be lying dead on the floor!"

"No one dies from being surprised." Although he could see it brought a nice bit of color to her cheeks.

"Oh, no? I've heard tell of it. Scared to death. It happens."

"Well, you are not dead." As a matter of fact, he'd never met anyone more alive. Miss McCary seemed to jump from one exciting moment to the next.

She glared at him, and then marched toward his back door. "I'll just have a word with your corpse. The two of you should be ashamed of yourselves for planning such a row. Did you see me coming down the street? Is that what this was all about?"

He couldn't help it. The absurdity of her words struck him. A snicker escaped.

The sound only heightened her ire as she took hold of her skirt and climbed the two steps to his back stoop. She strode through his kitchen and into the front room in a swirl of righteous fury.

Angus stood in his coffin, apparently at odds as to how he could safely get himself back to the floor. He swept his top hat off his head and bowed low to Miss McCary in an elegant flowing movement for one so stout. "My apologies for having startled you, miss. Miller, help me down from this blasted thing."

Jackson strode to his side and offered his hand. When Angus teetered halfway between the coffin and the chair he was using as a step, Miss McCary let out a huff and hurried to his other side, taking hold of his arm to steady him.

Once safely on the floor, Angus again bowed to her. "Angus O'Leary at your service."

"This is Miss McCary, one of the women from the train."

Angus's crinkly eyes lit up. "McCary is it? From Dublin?"

"No. Bridgeport, Ohio. But my da said I have kin in Dublin."

"And you've come to be one of the brides."

"Yes…I mean no. I mean…I don't intend to marry."

Jackson had never heard the old codger speak so civilly. He had totally disarmed Miss McCary's ire. But this business about her not marrying—what was this all about? "Wait a minute. You came on the train."

She stiffened. "I won't be forced into something I don't want to do."

"What about the contract you signed?"

She waved her hand as if shooing away a fly. "A bit of paper. And the words can be changed. Don't worry, Mr.

Miller. It doesn't concern you anyway. If I remember, you said you preferred to remain a bachelor yourself."

Angus watched them with an overly interested eye.

Jackson scowled. "I know what I said. Guess I'd hate to see anyone marry against their will. That's all. Doesn't sound like a decent start to a life together." He felt a warm flush under his collar. There was more to it than that. A vow meant something. It wasn't just words spoken or written on paper. *Till death do us part.* A man couldn't take that back. It was a pledge of faith that no matter how rough things might get he would always be there as a helpmate for his bride. And the same held true for the woman. It was a matter of honoring each other, of honoring the feelings, the hopes and the dreams between a man and a woman. It was a matter of helping each other through the hard times too. Because hard times would come. They came despite all a person's preparations against them. The contract the mayor had cooked up for the women on the train had nothing compared to the vows a man said when he wed. Miss McCary's attitude bothered him. She seemed to have no problem going back on her word.

The woman under his consideration turned to Angus. "What were you doing in the coffin, Mr. O'Leary?"

Angus grinned. "Well, it's like this. I came upon a bit of extra money recently and thought I'd have a nice send-off when the time comes."

Her eyes widened. "Are you tempting fate?"

"No, lass. I just want to go out in style."

"Well, I'm glad to see that you are still very much in the here and now."

He grinned again. "That I am, but I had to make sure I could wear me new hat when the time came. To my great sorrow, the box is too short."

"Well, it's a lovely coffin. Mr. Miller seems to know what he's about."

A compliment? In the middle of talking about death and coffins? The entire conversation struck Jackson as at odds with what most people would consider normal.

"That he does," Angus said with a wink at her. "Whatever he sets his mind to, he does and does it well." Angus tugged the hem of his coat down and squared his shoulders. "I won't be needing his services today so I'll be on my way. Ever so nice to have made your acquaintance."

He stepped outside and closed the door. The sudden silence made Jackson realize how much he'd enjoyed listening to Miss McCary, with her clear, high bell of a voice. He dealt mostly with men, since that was the main population of Oak Grove. A woman's voice could be pleasant. What, he wondered, had brought her to his shop in the first place?

She bent to pick up her satchel. She must have dropped it in her fright.

Jackson slid the lid to the coffin into place, then draped the box with the dark gray swath of material he kept for such items.

"Mr. O'Leary reminds me of my da." She stepped closer and helped him straighten the edge of the cloth. "I need a favor, Mr. Miller."

"A lawyer?"

Her brows knit together. "No. Why would I need a lawyer?"

"How else do you plan to get out of the contract?"

"The cost of my train fare has already been paid. I only need to pay back Mr. Austin for staying at his hotel and perhaps pay a small bit to have the contract voided."

So she had some money put away. "You should know that Mayor Melbourne wrote that contract. He is also the town's only lawyer."

She pressed her lips together. "You are full of bright observations, aren't you? I cannot be bothered with that at the moment. I need to ride out to the Circle P and I have no idea how to get there. I want you to take me."

He noticed she hadn't actually *asked* if he would take her. If Angus's visit hadn't been enough this morning, here she was yet again, disrupting his routine. He had things to do. The pew needed more sanding and another coat of stain. Yet the prospect of another afternoon working with his wood and tools paled when compared to an afternoon with Miss McCary. As much as he yearned for solitude and quiet and routine, when she came around things happened, like a kaleidoscope constantly changing.

And she sparked his curiosity. Why was a trip to Putnam's ranch so important that she would approach him? He was practically a stranger.

She started to loosen her satchel. "I can pay…"

He scowled. What were folks like back where she had come from that a good turn left her expecting to pay him? "I don't want your money."

She let out a sigh. "That's a relief. Truth is…I don't have any money with me. I must have left it back at the hotel." She carefully cinched up her purse.

He had the distinct feeling that she really did not have the money to pay him. As such, he was aware that he had just been manipulated. The fact didn't bother him as much as it should. Perhaps he owed her—for the scare she'd just had. "The ranch is a fair way out. It will take the better part of the day to go there and back."

"I'm ready."

That's not what he meant. "Aren't you forgetting something?"

"I don't believe so."

"A chaperone?"

The light in her eyes dimmed. "I'm used to having my sister with me. That's why I want to go out to the ranch. I need to make sure that she is all right."

He could understand her worry. Once it had been the same between him and his brother.

She rubbed her forehead. "Perhaps Anna or Sadie will accompany us."

"I'll get a buggy from the livery, then pick you up in front of the hotel."

A quick smile flitted across her face. She spun around and slipped out the door.

Her smile dazzled him. *She* dazzled him.

And he wasn't sure what to make of that.

He headed to the kitchen to get his hat and rifle as he contemplated her mercurial moods—from screaming in fright to scolding a man three times her age to being worried about her sister. She felt and lived life to the fullest. She was beguiling and beautiful.

The woman would lead some young man on a merry chase.

Maybe, once she married—because he really didn't think she'd find a way out of that contract—he would finally get some peace and quiet.

The thought wasn't quite as enticing as it had been before he met her.

## Chapter Six

Maggie sought out Sadie first. Unfortunately, Sadie was up to her arms in soapsuds—literally—having offered to help Mr. Austin. When she checked on Rebecca the curtains were closed and her head still pounded. And so it was Anna who agreed to chaperone—a bit too wholeheartedly.

Mr. Miller pulled up before the hotel in a covered buggy drawn by one horse. And he wore a cowboy hat! It was a bit silly, but the fact that he owned one and had worn it pleased her immeasurably. When he tugged on the brim in greeting she couldn't help smiling. It reminded her of her first words to him the night they met. Apparently, by the quiet mirth in his eyes, he had not forgotten either.

Her pleasure was short-lived when Anna sidled up next to him on the buggy seat and started chattering about her interview for the *Gazette*.

They took the road south of town and then at the fork by the river turned north, traveling along the water's eastern bank. After ten minutes Mr. Miller only half listened to Anna, which relieved Maggie immensely. She refused to question herself about why it mattered if Anna and Mr. Miller became more than friends. All Maggie could think was that she had spoken to him first, and for some reason that made him her particular friend.

His hands on the reins were darkened by the sun, strong and yet gentle as he maneuvered the horse and buggy along the dirt road. They were also scarred with a white jagged slash across the heel of his left hand and a dark red wound on the side of his right hand. One nail was blackened. That had to have been painful. Was it because of his work?

Maggie memorized the way. With the river on her left she thought she would be able to make the trip again on her own if necessary. She was on pins and needles with excitement. How would she find her sister? Happy and well? Or miserable? Maybe she could talk her into coming back to town with her.

"Mr. Miller, can you tell me anything about this ranch we are going to?" she asked, interrupting Anna.

He took his time gathering up his answer. That seemed to be his way—no unnecessary chatter.

"It's large. Steve Putnam is the owner. His family has ranched here since he was a youngster, but he's all that's left of them. I know him to be a decent man. Fair."

She had hoped for more details. "That's it?"

"Isn't that enough?"

"For a man, perhaps."

The slight uptick at the corner of his mouth surprised her. He had nearly smiled! The reaction pleased her. "How much farther is it?"

"We're halfway there."

"Not so very far," she said, cheerily. She enjoyed the deep timbre of his voice. It was settling to her. "Were you raised in Oak Grove?"

He glanced at her, raising one brow.

She guessed it was the first real personal question she

had asked. It took him so long to answer that she wondered if he thought her too nosy.

"I came here three years ago from Virginia."

*What craziness had persuaded him to stay in such a desolate place?*

"And what...what made you decide to stay?"

"My brother had a small congregation here and needed someone to build a church. He wrote and asked me."

"Oh! Your brother is pastor of the church?"

"No. No...he's gone now. Died in an accident. But I'll finish what I started."

She wasn't sure what to say to that. She was curious to know what had happened, but she judged by his tone that he would not appreciate her prying.

Then, rising out of the sea of waist-high grass, she recognized the shape of buildings against the blue sky and clouds in the distance. "Is that it? Why, we could almost walk there!"

"That's it," he said. "But distances can fool you out here. Things look closer than they really are. Those outbuildings are another two miles yet."

He was right. It seemed to take forever to go those last few miles. They passed the stable first and then the corral where three ranch hands worked at breaking a young horse. When Jackson finally stopped the horse and buggy before the large white house, Mary was already coming down the front porch steps, wiping her hands on her apron. Mary in an apron? Goodness!

Jackson jumped out, and then helped Maggie from the buggy, his hands strong and firm on her waist. She felt the muscles in his shoulders bunch and relax beneath her fingers as he swung her effortlessly to the ground. Had all that sawing and sanding given him such strength?

He met her gaze, his own green and serious. "Looks

like Steve's over at the corral. I'll take a walk over and say hello…see how he's doing with that colt. That will give you a moment with your sister." Then he turned back to help Anna down.

His words, his actions, impressed on her his kindness. He could be quite agreeable when he chose to be. She turned and ran straightaway to Mary, flinging her arms around her. Tears burned in her eyes. "I'm sorry about the train."

Mary wrapped her arms around her and hugged her tight. "'Tis forgotten. We both have our tempers."

Her familiar shoulder felt like coming home. Oh, how Maggie had missed her! "I couldn't wait another day to make sure you were all right."

"It's good you came. I've been so worried about you."

She sniffed. "You smell of onions!" The words came out muffled against her sister's shoulder. "You really are working, aren't you?"

Mary chuckled, and then peered over Maggie's shoulder. "I see you brought Anna."

Maggie pulled back from her sister and looked across the expanse of dirt and long grass toward the stable. "She's making eyes at Mr. Miller. I don't know who was chaperoning who on our trip here."

Her sister took her hand and squeezed. "Looks like she's following him to the corral. Come inside and we will catch up."

Maggie followed her into the front parlor. Two tall windows let light into the room. An upright piano stood against the inner wall. An oval braided rug in shades of green and blue had seen better days, but still added a bit of cool color to the room.

"Would you care for something to drink?" Mary asked. "I have some fresh buttermilk."

Maggie giggled. "Goodness, you sound like I'm a guest rather than your sister."

"You are both. And someone I'm extremely happy to see."

Mary glanced out the window as she spoke and Maggie took the chance to study her. She looked well. Happy even. For the first time in three days, Maggie relaxed. "I had to make sure you were all right."

"I am," Mary said. "Jess tried to tell you that, but you kept disappearing on him."

"Jess Rader? You know him?"

"Yes. He works here. Steve had sent him to town last night to fetch Dr. Graham."

She lowered her shoulders on a long sigh. She had led him on a merry chase when all he had been trying to do was Mary's bidding. "I had no idea. I thought he was after me for another reason," she admitted.

"A dance mayhap? Or to join him in a song?"

"No." They had danced twice together and not once did Mr. Rader mention Mary's name. Part of the fault was his.

Mary had that look on her face. The one that said she was frustrated with the choices Maggie made. A sinking sensation filled her. She hated to be at odds with her sister.

"Come into the kitchen. I need to put the beef in the oven."

"So you really are cooking meals for people?" She'd never thought of Mary as a cook. She was just her sister.

"Yes, that's what a cook does, and what I've done for years. Cooking for ten isn't that much different than cooking for two or three."

Maggie had strong doubts about that as she followed Mary. It sounded awful. Like an indentured servant. "Ten?"

Her sister grinned. "Some of the men eat enough for

two, and unlike you and Da, they are all very appreciative of my skills."

Maggie stiffened. "Da and I were never unappreciative of your cooking. We both knew neither of us would have had anything to eat if not for you."

"I'm sorry. I was teasing you. I just wanted you to know I'm appreciated here, and well, enjoying it. However…" Her voice dropped to a whisper as she stopped in the hallway. Her eyes twinkled with suppressed excitement. "I have a plan. This is the perfect place to bottle up the tonic and to make a second batch. Steve has an entire crock of honey in the root cellar. By the time I'm done working here, we'll have more than enough money to leave town with enough tonic to sell in order to get us wherever we choose to go."

Jackson finished taking measurements for the storage cabinets Putnam had asked him to build and tucked the stub of his pencil and the paper with his figuring in his shirt pocket. He'd had an excellent cup of coffee and sampled Maggie's sister's amazing ginger cookies, and now he was well and truly ready to go. He'd have to round up Miss Anna Camp. After a polite suggestion from Putnam, she had wandered off with a couple of ranch hands set on showing her the sights of the ranch.

He walked from the barn and joined Putnam outside. The cool breeze of the morning had warmed considerably. With the sun just past its zenith, it would be a hot drive back to town once they started.

Maggie approached with her sister and he found himself searching both women for hints of a difference between them. They walked alike, talked alike, even laughed alike. If they were wearing the same clothes, would he be able to tell them apart? It would be a pleasant task. They were both very pretty. But, noting the sparkle in both their eyes, would that make them double the trouble?

Maggie chose that moment to look directly at him and smile. "Mr. Miller, I believe it's time for us to return to town."

She probably realized exactly what he'd been thinking. He got warm under the collar. People staring—it must happen to her all the time when she was with her sister. "Whenever you're ready."

At that moment, Miss Camp appeared from around the far corner of the barn. "I believe I've seen enough cows for a long, long time."

They walked toward the front of the house and the waiting buggy.

"You're welcome to visit anytime, Maggie," Putnam said.

"Thank you, Mr. Putnam. I will be back, and in the meantime I do expect you to take very good care of my sister."

The sweet smile she bestowed on the rancher, made something twist in Jackson's gut. A response he wasn't about to analyze.

They waited while the sisters said their goodbyes to each other, hugging and clinging like they might never see each other again. He tightened his jaw. They sure hugged a lot. He'd never been that way. It was his brother that would hug, his brother that had a heart for everyone and everything.

Putnam helped Miss Camp into the buggy.

Maggie released her sister, dabbed at her eyes, and then walked around the horse to him. It took him by surprise, but warmed him too, that she would prefer he helped her into the buggy. Her eyes glistened more than usual, but he tried not to notice. A woman's tears were a private thing. Suddenly Maggie seemed fragile and delicate, like his mother's fine china. He helped her up, slow and gentle-like. Then taking a deep breath, he climbed up and sat down next to her.

He unlatched the brake, nodded to Putnam and Mary, and then turned the horse toward the road.

At his side, Maggie held herself tight, her arms criss-crossed over her waist while she locked her gaze on her lap.

He studied the pale curve of Maggie's cheek and was at a loss for words to comfort her. "Giving you a ride out here ended up helping me too. Steve Putnam ordered new storage for his barn."

Her chin trembled. "I'm glad it worked out for you. It was a long way to come for someone you didn't know all that well."

"I didn't mind." And surprisingly, he meant it. "I liked those ginger cookies your sister offered us. That a family recipe?"

She looked up at him. "My granny showed us how to make them. She's gone now. Mary's cookies are better than mine. I…I'm not the cook that she is. Matter of fact, I'd rather have someone cook for me."

"Can't blame you there. I'm not much for cooking either…unless it's fish fresh from the river." For once, he wished to see the laughter—or even the anger—in her eyes that he'd witnessed over the past two days. Seeing her sad did something to him. Inside. He wanted to fix it the way he could fix a broken chair or table, but he didn't know what to do.

"Looks like your sister is getting on all right."

"Yes. I'm much relieved on that count. Thank you, Mr. Miller."

The heartfelt, grateful look she gave him had him swallowing hard. "Wouldn't mind if you called me Jackson."

The wisp of a dimple appeared, and then was gone. "And you are welcome to call me Maggie."

He met her gaze. "Maggie." Then he forced his focus back to the road. It was becoming entirely too easy to get lost in those shifting blue depths. "Suits you."

Miss Camp talked briefly about her tour of the ranch, but when Maggie didn't show any interest, Anna soon fell quiet. It was completely different from the trip to the ranch. He should have been happy for the quiet.

He wasn't.

The road skirted a bend of the river and they were about half an hour from the ranch when the back wheel dipped into a deep rut.

"Oh! My!" Maggie said, suddenly emerging from her thoughts and grabbing his forearm to steady herself. "If you are able, do try to avoid bumps. Mary gave me a few things to take back that I stored in the boot. They won't take kindly to sudden jolts."

"I'll do what I can." There was only so much he could realistically do to smooth out the ride. He removed his Stetson, wiped the sweat from his brow with his sleeve, and then resettled his hat. "Day's heating up some."

Miss Camp drew a handkerchief from her satchel and blotted her face. "May we stop by the river? The water looks so cool and inviting." She threw him an encouraging smile.

He stiffened. How had he gotten himself saddled with two of the brides when he didn't want any? He'd leave answering Miss Camp up to Maggie, but he'd sure like to get back. He glanced at Maggie.

"Not today," she said. "I need to get back to town."

The buggy jostled over another rough spot in the road. Maggie gripped her hat. "Please be careful!"

"Couldn't avoid that one," he mumbled.

A slow hiss sounded. A cougar? He glanced at the floorboards to make sure his rifle was within reach.

Maggie's eyes widened and fixed on him. "Stop! I need to—"

The hiss grew steadily louder—and no longer sounded like a big cat. It was from somewhere behind them.

The buggy jostled over another rut.

"You must stop! Now!"

Bang!

The horse jumped and pranced nervously.

"Whoa, girl!" Jackson rose to his feet, adding leverage to his steady pull on the reins. They had better stop and see what made that sound.

Bang! A second, much-louder noise ripped through the air.

The horse reared, and then bolted.

Jackson slammed back into his seat as the horse careened around the curve of the road. "Whoa!" He yanked back on the reins.

Miss Camp screamed. The high-pitched sound only frightened the horse more, increasing its frenzied dash.

"Whoa!" Jackson called out. He added a slow, steady pull on the reins. "Slow down there, Missy. Slow and easy."

The road curved further, following the river's bend, but the horse didn't, instead racing straight down the embankment and into the water before it finally stopped, halfway to the opposite side. Cold water flowed over the footboards and seeped into his boots. He grabbed his rifle. Wet powder would be worthless. The current shifted the buggy, carrying them sideways another five feet along the river.

He had to get them turned around. Now.

"You'll have to hold these," he said, shoving the rifle and the reins to Maggie. He jumped into the river—waist deep—and tried to ignore the rush of cold, wet water that immediately seeped through to his skin and robbed him of his breath. Holding on to the traces to steady himself, he made his way to the mare's head. All the while, he spoke in a low voice to the frightened creature. He grasped the bridle and carefully, slowly, slogged ahead, turning her into the current.

"I can help!" Maggie said, setting the rifle on the seat and holding out the reins to Anna.

Anna didn't look too sure that she wanted them.

"Stay there!" he called out, fearful that he couldn't watch out for her and the horse at the same time. "With that dress, you'll only go under."

She hesitated. "But the buggy is too heavy with both Anna and me."

The mare's ears flicked forward and back, listening to him and then Maggie. It was still nervous. Maggie might be right—the horse could move a lighter rig easier—but he wasn't about to let her get into the water. "The current is too deep and too strong. I'll take this slow and steady."

By the mutinous look on her face she wasn't pleased with the way he commandeered the situation. Too bad. "I'm not moving this horse another step until you sit down. And just so you know...my toes are already numb."

She glared at him, but finally she sat down. "Very well. I'll help from here."

Together they maneuvered the horse and buggy around and up the small embankment to dry, level land.

Jackson took the reins from Maggie and wrapped them around the brake handle. Anna clung to the side of the buggy, still nervous that the horse would bolt again. Maggie wouldn't look at him. As a matter of fact, she looked guilty. Those loud bangs had something to do with her.

"What have you got in the boot?"

"I told you to watch those bumps!"

He couldn't believe it. She was using the same tactic as when her dress tore. Fix the blame somewhere else instead of owning up to her part of it. "What have you got that's so all-fired temperamental? What's in the boot?"

She peered at him, her jaw set stubbornly. "It's none of your business."

He didn't even try to contain his temper. "Not my business? Not my business when any one of us, not to mention the horse, could have been badly hurt? Could have drowned?"

Maggie lifted her chin. "Well…we weren't hurt."

He started for the back of the carriage. "I'm not going anywhere until I know what's back here."

"Wait! No!" She scrambled down from the buggy and rushed after him. "You'll only make it—"

He threw back the tarp covering and found four bottles nestled in a tin milking pail that was now full of river water. A soggy old work shirt braced them from rattling and moving. Two bottles, their corks missing, had foam dripping from their openings. He pulled one out. "'M&M's Finest Recipe Tonic,'" he read out loud. He sniffed the lip. The strong scent curled his nose hairs. He took a small sip, swished it around in his mouth, and then couldn't spit it out fast enough. It tasted worse than it smelled. Tangy and tinny at the same time. He wiped his mouth with the back of his hand.

"What is this stuff?"

"Medicine."

"Are you sick?"

She glared at him and reached for the bottle. "Of course not! Why would I travel all the way to Kansas if I was sick? Give it back!"

He held it just beyond her grasp. Then he took another sniff of the open bottle. Now that he took the time to analyze the smell, it had the distinct odor of alcohol. Strong alcohol. Still-fermenting alcohol. No wonder the combination of heat and jiggling had caused two bottles to explode. No doubt the others would have popped their corks eventually had they not been doused in the cool river.

"Explain this."

"I'd rather not."

He couldn't believe she argued with him! Slowly he tilted the bottle and poured what was left of the contents onto the ground.

"What are you doing?" She tugged on his arm. "Stop!"

"It's no good."

"But I might be able to save some! Here. Give it to me!"

"It's full of river water." He picked up the second bottle and poured its contents onto the ground also, then handed the empty bottle back to her.

"I can do this all day." He reached for a full one—one that still had a cork.

"No!" She grabbed hold of his hand atop the bottle. "Please! I cannot afford to lose any more."

He glanced at her hand covering his—so small, so soft. The back of his hand tingled where she touched him. He met her gaze.

Quickly, she drew away. "If I explain, will you leave the rest alone?"

He was calmer now. They were all safe. The possibility of another exploding bottle was unlikely now that the last two bottles were half-submerged in cold water. He let go and waited for her explanation.

"It's for the treatment of ailments and nerves."

"You brought this on the train? Why so much?"

She glanced at Anna, who watched the entire exchange with interest. "It's not so much. And it's the last of my da's recipe. It's helpful…with nerves and such. Good to have on hand. I asked Mary for an extra bottle for Rebecca Simpson. She has trouble sleeping and often has headaches."

Miss Simpson's health wasn't any of his business. Neither was Maggie's but he had to ask. "Do you use it?"

"No."

"Why not?"

"I can't stand the taste. And…"

He waited.

"I don't feel poorly."

Something wasn't adding up. "But you keep it around to give away?"

"In a way."

If these were the only two bottles, he supposed it didn't matter all that much. It was obvious that she didn't want to talk to him about it. He pulled the tarp back over the boot and strapped it into place.

Her cool, wet fingers covered his again. "Thank you, Jackson."

Hearing his name in that soft voice of hers—something uncurled inside and relaxed. He snorted softly. "You are a lot of trouble, Maggie McCary."

A slow smile brought the dimples out on her pretty face. "I am at that."

# Chapter Seven

Sunday, the women were approached by four men from the Betterment Committee who wished to take them on a picnic. It was a pleasant afternoon, but Maggie found herself comparing each one of the men to Jackson. When the depot agent for the train asked if she would accompany him on a second outing, she declined his offer. She had to keep up the appearance of looking for a match for herself, but knowing that she would be leaving town with Mary, she didn't want any of the men to waste their time on her. Let them vie for Rebecca, Anna, or Sadie. Those women *wanted* to marry.

That evening the four women gathered in Maggie's room and discussed Abigail White's request for the interview. Rebecca was adamant that each woman share only their own story and no others, which suited Maggie fine. She certainly didn't want anyone talking about the tonic. Rebecca also pointed out that leaving a little mystery made for a more interesting courtship.

It made Maggie think of the secrets she had kept from Jackson even though their friendship was not a courtship. She liked Jackson. He had gone out of his way to take her out to the Circle P. He seemed to understand how hard it was for her to leave her sister. And he'd been kind.

She didn't like keeping secrets from him.

She would have never imagined how tough he was, but after seeing him handle the runaway horse there was no doubt in her mind of his strength. Recalling the way his muscles bulged with the effort to draw the frantic animal to a stop and the way he looked with his wet shirt plastered to his skin—the thought of it now had an alarming effect on her pulse.

Monday, two other men stopped by the hotel to take them on a ride. Sadie declined, saying she was giving the first interview. Maggie had been invited also, but she'd had enough of new faces the day before. Besides, she wanted to have her dress mended.

After Anna and Rebecca left, she carefully folded her skirt and slipped it into her carpetbag.

On her way down the stairs Jackson strode into the hotel lobby, toting a box of tools. He wore the same coarsely woven shirt he'd had on when she'd first seen him right here on the stairwell and the same brown pants. He had rolled his sleeves up to his elbows and looked for all purposes as if he intended to put in a hard day of work.

The dreary attitude that had dogged her since leaving Mary lifted. "Hello, Mr. Miller."

He nodded. "Miss McCary."

She descended the stairs to the last one and leaned against the banister. It put her eye to eye with him. She rather liked looking into his extraordinary green eyes. "What are you up to today?"

He set his tools down on the floor and removed his cap. "A few things Mr. Austin has ordered. I'll be in and out through the week."

That brought a warmth to her heart. "How pleasant."

"Pleasant? If you say so. Work is work."

"I mean it will be nice to see a friendly face about the place—one that isn't weighing whether I'll make a good wife."

"I imagine that can be trying," he said dryly.

"Sarcasm, Mr. Miller?"

"That *is* why you are here."

Was that jealousy she heard in his voice? Impossible.

His gaze narrowed on her. "So, what have you planned today?"

She hefted her bag. "Nothing as daring as a runaway horse." She stood there a moment, realizing she really didn't have to leave just yet. She liked talking to him. "You weren't in church yesterday."

His expression closed off. "I don't go to church."

"Oh." The sudden change in him startled her. She pulled back from the banister, unsure now of her welcome. A cool breeze blew from the direction of Jackson Miller.

"If you'll excuse me…" He crouched down and began searching through his tools.

She raised her chin. Fine. She would be about her business then.

## Chapter Eight

Maggie turned away from the hotel window. A full week had passed since her visit to the Circle P and she'd taken to peeking out to the street more and more often, actually toward the vicinity of Jackson's shop in the hopes she would see him come or go. Nosy is what she was.

The hotel room was coming to represent a gilded cage more and more, and out there was the freedom she desired. It would be lovely to see Mary, but her sister had warned her not to come again—that she would come to town when the tonic was ready. Although she tried to keep a cheerful attitude, as the days of the contract wore on she became more anxious for the tonic to be ready so that she could start selling it.

She had had her fill of men coming to call. They were all attentive during a stroll about the tiny town, but she felt as though she was wasting their time and hers. She avoided talking about herself and instead recounted the attributes of Anna, Sadie and Rebecca. Truly, the other girls were so much more agreeable than she.

Rebecca sprawled across her bed reading the newest edition of the *Oak Grove Gazette*.

"May I have a look?" Maggie asked, more to have some

noise in the room than anything else. She felt positively stifled. The afternoon was much too quiet for her taste.

"I'm nearly finished with it. Sadie's interview is not very long."

Maggie looked over Rebecca's shoulder. "Sadie isn't one to talk about herself. It must have been awkward for her."

Rebecca chuckled. "She spoke of the wonderful accommodations on the Pullman train, and then glossed over the horrible train we had to take from Kansas City."

"Leave it to Sadie to make the best of a situation."

A knock came at the door.

"Miss McCary?" The voice was high-pitched. "There's a man downstairs asking for you."

Maggie sighed. "Thank you, Kade. I'll be right down."

Amusement filled Rebecca's face. "You really should find one quickly before the best ones are snapped up."

"Easy for you to say. You've set your cap for the banker. You do know that he's not the brightest of the bachelors."

"I have good reason for my choice."

Maggie rolled her eyes. Although Micah Swift was pleasant enough in appearance, Rebecca was only looking at the size of his wallet.

"It's just…I want you to understand. I've known difficult times—very difficult. I can't let that happen again. You have a sister to help you. I don't."

Maggie hadn't thought of things that way. She was fortunate to be able to depend on Mary. "He's a nice man," Maggie finally allowed. "And with your intelligence, you'll be a good match."

"I hope so."

Maggie tied the yellow ribbons of her straw bonnet beneath her chin, and then checked her appearance in the mirror.

"Your blue dress would bring out the color in your eyes."

Maggie smoothed her light green skirt. It made no difference how she dressed. She wasn't trying to impress any
of the men who came to call. "Mrs. Taylor still has it for
mending." She slipped out the door.

To her surprise, the man waiting at the bottom of the
stairs was not a hopeful bachelor at all. Angus O'Leary
wore the same clothes that she'd seen him in at their first
meeting. He tipped his top hat as she approached. "Will
you have time for a walk on this fine day with the likes of
me, young lassie? I've had a shave and a haircut and I'd
hate it to go to waste."

"A walk sounds lovely!" Anything to get her out of the
hotel room, and she couldn't think of a more congenial
companion. She took the arm he offered. He was shorter
by five inches, his shoulders stooped with age, but she felt
an immediate closeness with him. "Are you off to a party?"

"The suit is wasting away in my closet."

They stepped outside and she took a moment to breathe
in the fresh air only to find the wind was blowing from the
direction of the stockyards. She wrinkled her nose. "Cattle."

"You'll get used to it," Angus said, patting her hand in
the crook of his arm. "And you'll find it means money for
this town."

They strolled along the boardwalk, taking their time and
looking in the windows of the different establishments. She
told him about Jackson taking her to visit with Mary and of
the men who'd called on her. The cabinet shop was closed
up and dark. Where was Jackson?

"Have you come to a decision on any of the men making a path to your door? I might be able to give you some
pointers."

"None that hold a candle to you, Mr. O'Leary," she
teased.

His gray eyes twinkled. "I'm afraid you'll have to set

your sights a bit lower, me girl. There's not a worthy Irishman in the lot except for me."

A laugh bubbled up. And suddenly the day was brighter.

They sat to rest on the bench outside the train depot, grateful for the shade of the overhanging roof.

Angus took out his handkerchief and dabbed at his brow. "Have you seen our fine friend, Mr. Miller lately?"

"Often. He is working on the lobby at the hotel." The fact that Jackson had barely nodded the last time she had passed by bothered her.

"And what do you think of him?"

"Well. I don't. I can't. He doesn't want to marry." She swallowed. "But a bride might be good for him. He's always alone." Why, why had it begun to plague her so? If he had given to the Betterment Committee, then he would be courting one of the brides—and she would hate that. It was ridiculous. Her thoughts were all jumbled since she'd met him.

"Ever wonder why that is? Why don't you ask him?"

"Oh, I couldn't. He's a very private person."

"That he is. But I imagine if the right lass comes along, he'll want to marry."

She took in a deep breath and pasted on a smile. "Well, it won't be me. I have other plans."

Angus studied her with his watery gray eyes. "I see that in your face. You've got your own rainbows to chase."

A wagon lumbered into town, pulled by two draft horses. Maggie watched the dust kicked up by the animals. Dusty, dirty, no trees, no green… She missed Bridgeport.

Angus stood. "Can ye walk a bit farther? I've a hankerin' to see the river."

They crossed the railroad tracks, and then followed a walking trail through the tall prairie grass. She began to worry that Angus would tire before they reached the water, when suddenly the Smoky Hill River opened up before her. Something very close to the feeling of freedom lifted her heart as she watched the water drift by.

"This…I could love about Kansas," she murmured.

"Aye. A little piece of heaven on earth." Angus sat on a rocky prominence along the bank. "I've seen her in all her seasons. Muddy when the cattle cross and spilling over her banks in the spring. She's never the same twice."

Maggie stared at the river. Watching the water move gently by in rolling swirls and small ripples gave her a sense of calm. It had been the same in Bridgeport on the banks of the Ohio.

After a few moments, Angus stood. "I thank you for humoring me with a stroll. No need for you to leave. I've walked this bank a sight of times." He rubbed his freshly shaven chin, and then pointed past her with a bob of his head. "If you continue on past that bend, you'll come to a sight not to be missed."

She glanced downriver. When she turned back, he'd already started through the tall grass toward town.

Jackson whipped the pole around his head and snapped his wrist, sending the angle far out into the river. The tension of the past week evaporated as the light breeze blew off the water. He planned to catch a few fish, fry them up and enjoy the peace and quiet.

Which meant he would stay away from the hotel. Maggie had stepped out with six different men over the past week. Six! Each time she grabbed another man's arm, his chest would tighten and fill up enough to choke him. He had to remind himself it wasn't any of his business. She was doing what she was supposed to according to the contract.

He still didn't have to like it. She was getting under his skin. Even when he focused on his carpentry thoughts of her disrupted him. He would be sanding a plane of wood, only to realize that he'd stopped in the middle of the task for ten minutes while his thoughts circled on her. He had thrown himself into his work to distance himself from her and all it accomplished was to make him want to see her more. He wondered what she was doing at all hours of the day.

On Wednesday, with Blackwell's help he had loaded the last pew on a flatbed wagon and taken it to the church. The new parson and Blackwell saw to securing it in place. All that was left for him to do now was to hang the bell. After that he might take a real break. Leave town. Go to Dodge City for a few days. Maybe then he would be able to wipe Maggie from his thoughts.

The tip of his rod dipped toward the water. A nibbler. Slowly he reeled in the silk line, stopping every few turns of the crank, just enough to tease the fish in hopes it would latch onto the hook good and hard.

"What are you do— *Oh!*—have you caught anything?"

The line went still. Great. The fish had heard Maggie and skedaddled.

Maggie skirted a small limestone formation and walked toward him. Her dress caught here and there on the grass and thistles but she didn't seem to notice or care. Perhaps she *had* been truthful about that one dress after all.

"Anyone ever tell you you'll scare the fish away?"

At his growl, she stopped. Then she set her jaw and stomped the rest of the way into the small clearing. "My da."

"Your father liked to fish?"

"Mostly when we needed to eat. He bid me sing to them."

He chose to ignore that idiotic statement.

"You don't believe me."

"No."

She walked over to the fire pit and looked over his things—a tin pitcher full of black coffee balanced on rocks over the small fire. "Why have you not spoken to me? Why are you ignoring me?"

"I've been busy." And frustrated—wanting to see her himself and yet hating when she talked with other men.

She glanced at the tin cup on the ground. "Digging worms?"

"Bait," he said, knowing he sounded grouchy as all get-out.

She frowned, flushing, one hand to her hip. "I'm trying to be pleasant here, Mr. *Jackson* Miller."

"You are scaring the fish away."

"Well, you would like to scare everyone away. Don't you like people?"

He looked at her sharply. What did she mean by that?

She pressed her lips into a pout and counted things off with the fingers of one hand. "You didn't come to the party. You don't go to church. You tuck yourself away in your shop. And you try to fish. All alone."

He raised his brow. He wasn't about to bare his soul to her after she had been stepping out with other men all week. "I *do* fish. Quite well when not interrupted."

"Well I don't see any."

He wound up the rest of his line, his movements jerky with pent-up irritation, and set his fishing pole aside. He wasn't angry. Only frustrated. The longer she stayed, the longer she pressed him, the more he felt his life was lacking...*life*.

"I thought we were becoming friends. Why are you pushing me away too?"

He couldn't tell her it was because he hated the thought that she had to choose a husband from the Betterment Committee. Every time that she'd gone up or down the stairs that week with him working there, he'd caught her sweet scent, heard her bell of a laugh and detested the man who had come to call on her. "It's easier."

That stopped her. "Easier? Than what? What do you mean?"

"Easier. That's all." He let out a long breath. He wasn't about to explain about Christine. "It's been two years since my brother died. Ever since it is just easier not to get too close to people."

"Because they let you down? You forget I lost my da. I had Mary to help me afterward, but you've had no one." She stepped close and put her hand on his arm. "You could use a friend."

He wanted to move away but her gentle touch held him as captive as an iron grip. His skin tingling beneath her fingers. It was all too... He pulled away. "Friends? According to you...you are leaving in three weeks. How does that make us friends? And if that doesn't happen, you are marrying. I don't think your husband will appreciate us being too *friendly*." He'd like to shake some sense into her. He'd like to...to...

He was shocked to find himself grasping her shoulders with the strong urge not to shake her, but to kiss her. Immediately he let go and stepped back, his chest tight, his heart pounding. "You should have considered things before you signed that contract."

"I had my reasons," she said, her brow furrowed with concern. "So did Mary."

At least he hadn't frightened her.

"We will figure it out. There is time yet."

"You don't have the money."

"I'll have it by then."

"How?"

"I can't say."

He turned away, angry with himself because he *did* care. She saw the world through rose-colored glasses. Sooner or later the real world would catch up with her and crush that part of her that was wild and free. He couldn't stand the thought of that.

"How about leaving me to my fishing?"

With a tilt of her head and a mysterious smile, she moved away from the fire pit and began searching through the grasses. She came back with a cricket pinched between her fingers. "Use this on your hook."

He had used crickets before. To humor her, he baited the angle with her cricket and whipped the line back out into the river. She moved away from him, sat down on a limestone rock and concentrated on the point where the line disappeared into the water.

Then she began to sing! Startled, he listened as her voice floated out over the river, sweet and clear. The current seemed to carry away her song and with it he drifted to another time, another place where mermaids and mermen protected sunken treasure and fish had the esteemed position of guards of the deep. The melancholy tune and the haunting words reached out and tethered his soul.

The pole arched to the water's surface.

"There!" She broke off from her song.

He gripped the rod tighter and let the line play out.

Maggie ran up beside him and grasped his upper arm almost as if she could help him in some way. "You've got one! You've got one!" She jumped up and down, and then ran to the water's edge. "Don't let it get away! You are supper now, Mr. Fish!"

Just then a trout leaped from the water, its wet scales shining silver and gray in the late afternoon sunlight before it fell back and slipped beneath the surface.

"You've got it! Oh… What can I do? What can I do to help?"

He felt a smile threaten. "Be still."

She couldn't. She danced down to the water and then back to him. Then over to the fire pit to throw a few small dried grasses on the embers to encourage the fire not to go out.

Slowly and carefully, he worked the crank, drawing in the line until the fish flopped up onto the bank, worn-out from its struggle.

"You've got yourself a fine-looking trout! What did I say?" She grinned. "They love my singing!"

He laughed out loud, caught himself, and then laughed again. When was the last time he'd heard that sound? "All right. That one's yours. Help me catch another and we'll cook them up."

She eyed him saucily, her blue eyes sparkling. "Cricket or worm?"

"Cricket."

"Very good, sir." She curtseyed.

It wasn't long before he caught another trout, cleaned and gutted the both of them and cooked them over the fire. He broke the largest fish apart with his knife to make sure it was cooked through, then he brought the frying pan over to the flat rock and set it between them.

"I wasn't expecting company. I only have the one fork," he said, handing it to her.

"Thank you." Her dimple showed.

Without letting go, he studied her, mesmerized by the two freckles on her nose and the gentle way a black curl blew across her cheek. With his other hand, he reached across the short distance and tucked it behind her ear.

Her eyes grew large, and then uncertain. She pulled back slightly.

His fingers tingled. It felt so natural to touch her. To him perhaps—not to her. He lowered his hand. "We should eat quickly, and then get you back to town. I'm sure you are missed."

"They think I'm strolling with Mr. O'Leary."

"A long stroll for the old codger." He grinned. "Still, it's time you started back."

"I suppose." She took a small bite. "Heavenly!" Twisting up a morsel on her fork she held it out. "I'll share."

He leaned forward, his gaze never leaving hers. She popped the fish into his mouth. It might as well have been potatoes as fish. He didn't even taste it. His entire body was thrumming. This wasn't exactly the way to be friends. "You go ahead," he said, his voice gruff. "I'll wait until you are done."

She finished, then handed the fork to him. Eating was the last thing on his mind. He couldn't stop staring at her lips and wondering if they were really as soft and smooth as they looked. He loved it when her mouth curved up in a winsome smile.

When they were both finished, she walked to the water's edge and rinsed out the pan along with his fork. The sun was behind her, just above the horizon, and streaking orange and pink paint across the sky overhead.

"I should go now," she said. Still, she didn't make a move to leave.

He took her hands. "Your singing worked."

She smiled. "See? I really can catch fish."

Among other things. He felt like he was being reeled in and she didn't even realize it.

With her finger, she traced the white scar on the heel of his hand. "How did this come about?"

At her touch, he found it difficult to answer, difficult to

breathe. "Climbing a tree. I was ten. I got caught on a nail that held the line for drying laundry."

The setting sun turned her skin to gold. He reached for that tendril of dark hair that danced gently in the evening breeze. This time she didn't flinch at his touch or back away when he tucked it behind her ear, but seemed to wait, suspended in the moment.

It wouldn't be right to kiss her when he couldn't court her, but that didn't seem to matter at the moment. He forked his fingers through her thick hair, and then touched her under her chin, raising her face to him. "You are a beauty, Maggie McCary."

Her eyes darkened. "Just what do you think you are doing?" Her voice came soft, breathy, washing over him.

He moved closer. "I'm kissing you."

"Oh," she said, her voice full of wonder. "Well then, perhaps you should be about it."

"Perhaps I should."

He bent down and gently touched his lips to hers. A tingling sensation thrummed between them. His heart raced. He slanted his mouth and pressed firmer against her. Her breath came in light even puffs against his cheek and mixed with the pounding of his heart. Warmth grew in the pit of his belly. Her lips were smooth and supple and sweet. He'd never be able to get the taste of her, the softness of her, out of his thoughts after this.

Never.

She parted her lips and slid her hand up his chest, her fingers curling around his neck to pull him closer. It would be much too easy to let this kiss go too far. Steeling himself, reluctantly, he pulled away.

Her gaze was unfocused, stunned.

He'd done that. He swallowed. Hard. "I better take you back now."

She didn't speak, only nodded.

They walked in silence back to town. Saturday evening, and a number of cowboys from nearby ranches were in town, already making use of their pay at the Whistle Stop. At least fourteen horses were tied in a line at the saloon's hitching post. He recognized a few of the brands—the Lazy R, the Circle P.

Three things he knew for sure when he said goodbye to her at the hotel door. One—Maggie McCary had never been kissed before—at least not more than a peck. Two—any idea about leaving town after he finished his brother's church had come to a grinding halt. And three—he wasn't about to let her go.

## Chapter Nine

"Are you sure about this?" Maggie asked Sadie Tuesday morning at breakfast. "It's only been a short while. You have time to consider other options."

"I truly think it will be a good match. Rollie needs the help. I like to be useful. And I do like his two boys."

The spoon dropped from Maggie's hand back into her cup, splashing tea onto the table. "You call him Rollie now? Not Mr. Austin?" That didn't bode well for Sadie considering other options.

The fact that the same thing had happened between Jackson and her didn't count. After all, Jackson wasn't interested in marriage. Which made that kiss very confusing. That kiss had weakened her knees and stolen her breath. A kiss like that meant something, didn't it? It was all she had thought about for the past three days. What would she say when she saw him again? It had to have been a mistake on both their parts. It just had to. And yet all she could think about was how she wanted to have him hold her in his strong arms and kiss her again.

It was the uncontrollable wanting that scared her. She would have to set him straight.

She was leaving just as soon as she got the money. They

could be friends, but nothing more. Something inside shriv-eled up at the thought. She wanted to be more than friends with him.

In the next breath, she wondered what Mary would think of that—think of *her*. Was she selfish for desiring both him and her freedom?

Across the table, Sadie shrugged. "I have two and a half weeks before the end of the contract. I'll be sure about Rol-lie by then."

Two and a half weeks! She certainly hoped Mary would hurry with the tonic. They would never get enough money if she didn't start selling it right away. If her sister didn't bring it soon, she would have to rent a buggy and go get it. She couldn't ask Jackson again. She didn't trust herself alone with him now. She was too confused about him.

"Miss McCary?" Jess Rader approached, removing his worn hat. "Ah…could I…ah…have a word with you?"

She had her interview over at the *Gazette* and stepping out with another suitor was not in the least appealing. "I'm afraid I have plans, Mr. Rader."

He shifted his weight. "Well. Your sister out at the Cir-cle P sent a message."

She stood immediately. "A note? She didn't come?"

"Feedin' all us men keeps her busier than a banty hen in…ah…never you mind. She's busy. If you'll take a stroll with me, I'll tell you all about it."

If he truly did have word from Mary, she had to know. "Very well."

Outside on the boardwalk, he offered her his arm. When she hesitated to take it he flapped his arm. "You want to find out about your sister, right?"

She grabbed onto him, disturbed that he goaded her.

He grinned so large she thought he might just trip on it. Then he started walking, dragging her along. "That sister of yours sure can cook a decent meal, Miss McCary. All the cowpokes are speculating if you can cook as good."

"Nothing like Mary."

"Guess that ain't no deal-breaker. A gal can always learn."

He led her down the boardwalk past the bank and barbershop, strutting like a rooster as he passed each window. They arrived at the far end of town and crossed to the other side of the street. "Sure wish we could spend the day getting to know each other."

"I can't think about courting when I'm worried about my sister," she said firmly. She wouldn't be holding out false hope to anyone. She would be leaving and that was that. Besides, Mr. Rader couldn't hold a candle when compared to Jackson Miller. No one in this dusty little town could. "What is it Mary had to say?"

He patted her hand that still rested in the crook of his elbow, but he didn't answer.

They passed the mayor's attorney building and then the *Gazette* office. Through the window, Maggie saw Abigail busy setting type. She glanced up, waved an ink-smudged hand, then went back to her work. The next storefront was Miller's Cabinet Shop. Maggie peered through the glass. No sign of Jackson. Disappointment swept through her.

Mr. Rader tightened his arm as he stepped down from the boardwalk and onto the dirt, bringing her with him. "It don't take no genius to see that you got your mind set on other things, Miss McCary. Guess I'll head down to the saloon so that the day ain't a complete waste of time."

"What about my sister's message?"

"She had me bring a box of that bottled stuff for you. The boss don't like her messing with it. It's a load off her mind to have it off the ranch."

She had a feeling Jackson wouldn't entirely approve of

her selling it either, considering the way he'd acted when he discovered it.

"I would have brought it sooner but I had to wait until the boss needed supplies." He stopped in front of the hotel. "Figured it was the only way you'd take a stroll with me. Can't blame a man for trying. Especially since I donated to the fund."

She smiled. "You know… Miss Camp would be delighted to step out with you. She enjoyed the tour you gave her of the ranch."

"Miss Camp?" He rubbed his chin.

"You could call on her before heading back out to the ranch."

"Might do that. Just might do that. Although, you are a sight prettier."

Just then, the hotel's front door opened and Jackson stepped out on the boardwalk. He carried his toolbox and was covered in a fine layer of sawdust, a sheen of sweat on his face. He stopped when he saw her and then looked from her to Mr. Rader, his mouth tightening at the corners. "Hello, Miss McCary."

She withdrew her hand from Mr. Rader's arm. Her heart thudded in her chest. Oh, how she would like to talk to Jackson, walk with him. Explain that he mustn't kiss her again while hoping secretly that maybe he would. What must he think of her walking with Mr. Rader after the kiss they had shared?

Beside her, Mr. Rader shifted his weight. "Miller."

Jackson narrowed his gaze. "Rader. You can tell your boss I'll have his cabinets ready in another week. I'll bring them out to the ranch. Miss McCary, if you want a ride out to see your sister then, I could take you." He nodded, and then headed across to his shop.

She hoped he understood about Rader. This was business. She stared after him, wishing she knew what was going through his mind. "Mr. Rader? About that tonic?"

"Your sister said to keep it out of the sun so I stored it in the hotel's storm cellar. I told Austin about it so he wouldn't throw it out."

"Thank you. You've thought of everything."

He touched the brim of his hat, and then sauntered down the boardwalk, whistling a tuneless melody.

Maggie headed to the back of the hotel to locate the storm cellar. She had never been in a cellar with dirt walls and bits of roots sticking through. It was dark and musty and large enough for ten men to stand in, and much cooler than above ground. Shelving lined the walls and several jars of fruits and vegetables canned last year were still stored there. It was the perfect place to store the tonic.

She found the box under a burlap sack. Twenty bottles nestled inside. She picked one up and examined it. M&M—their family's familiar label. Mary had perfected the artistic script years ago, with the two *M*s tilted slightly and intertwined. Holding the bottle made her feel closer to Mary—closer to Da.

She withdrew three bottles. No time like the present to start selling. First stop would be Mrs. Taylor. Maggie had purposely waited to return for her dress so that she could offer the woman a sample of the tonic to ease the swollen and sore joints in her hands. Then Mr. Austin's cook had complained of her neck bothering her. Both of those women might have suggestions for others who were ailing.

She had to sell by word of mouth. It was the only way around the need for a permit. As long as she explained that to her customers, she didn't think they would give her away. After all—the tonic would make them feel better.

She covered the box and climbed back up the steep ladder steps, closed the heavy door atop the cellar and latched it. Perhaps Rebecca or Anna would take her place for the interview with Abigail. She had too much to do now that the tonic was ready.

Mary had come through. She did her part in making and bottling the tonic. Now it was up to Maggie to finish even though her heart wasn't in it. Mary was depending on her. The sooner she sold all the tonic, the sooner she and Mary could leave Oak Grove. It was the same litany she had told herself ever since arriving in town, yet more and more it rang false to what she really wanted, which was more time with Jackson.

## Chapter Ten

Rollie Austin and Brett Blackwell each held the end of the massive coatrack that Jackson had just finished. All that was left was to secure it to the wall in the lobby entrance. "One. Two. Three," Jackson said. Together the three hefted it into place.

Immediately, Jackson screwed the back of the coat rack into place against the wall studs. "You can let go now."

He continued adding screws for support, wanting to get the job done that morning before he ran into Maggie. He was still sorting through the strong anger that had overtaken him when he had seen her with Rader. He had never considered himself the jealous type and he wasn't all that sure that he liked the feeling. He was drawn to her and would have to get a handle on that.

The lobby door opened and a fresh breeze blew through the foyer.

"Miss McCary!" Austin said. "You are up and about early this fine Friday morning."

Maggie stood there in her "favorite" blue dress and wearing her straw bonnet, looking good enough to eat and completely disrupting Jackson's concentration. Again. All he could think about was her with Rader. Why had she stepped out with a randy cowboy after that kiss they had shared? And what was she saying, standing so close to Blackwell now?

It was her business how she conducted herself. Not his. He turned back to his work. Five more screws to go. Every nerve ending tingled, knowing she was there. After Blackwell left, Maggie continued to stand there and watch him.

"What do you think of the new coatrack?" Austin stood back, surveying it critically.

A charming smile appeared as she looked directly at Jackson. "I've come to see that everything Mr. Miller does is absolutely lovely."

"Well now." Austin looked from one to the other. "Is that a fact?"

Jackson wasn't willing to play games. Not after that kiss. "Will you excuse us?" Jackson asked.

Austin raised his brows, but then he nodded politely to Maggie and walked away.

Jackson set down his screwdriver. He should keep his distance, but all he could think about while she was so close, was pulling her into his arms again for another taste of her. "Is there something you wanted, Maggie?"

"I've been thinking about our…fishing expedition the other day."

"Fishing expedition?" It was obvious she meant the kiss. "What about it?"

"Did it…I mean… It meant something to me. And I've been wondering if…maybe…you felt something too."

He stared at her upturned face. "I don't play games."

"Then…you are saying that it was special for you too." Her gaze searched his. She blew out a breath. "I've never been kissed that way. I didn't know kisses like that existed."

He had figured that out. "Then what was all that with Rader?"

"Rader?" She looked confused for a moment, and then her expression cleared and she stepped closer. "Oh, Jackson... Mr. Rader brought news of Mary. I wouldn't have walked with him otherwise."

He wanted to believe her.

"I thought I annoyed you." She gulped in a breath. "And I thought this week, when you didn't even talk to me, that you regretted kissing me."

How could she think that? He took her wrist, pulling her against him. "You do annoy me. So much I can't think straight."

Her eyes widened. "You don't look annoyed right now."

"I am." He brushed his lips across her forehead. She closed her eyes and turned her face up to his. Looking down at her mute appeal for more, the tightness in his chest eased. It was plain there was something special between them. Something too big to ignore. He took her mouth with his. Soft, generous and sweet.

A sigh escaped from her as she leaned into him with her soft body.

When he ended the kiss he looked deep into her eyes. "I don't regret anything that has happened between us from the moment you tore your dress on this staircase to right now. Especially that kiss."

The warm glow that came into her eyes answered any lingering doubts he had about her feelings toward him. Guess with what was happening between them he should see about contributing to the Bride Fund. Better late than never. It was a big step for him, but he didn't want to lose her.

Brett Blackwell strode back into the lobby. "I bring da mo—"

Maggie jumped back as if she'd been caught doing something she shouldn't. "Mr. Blackwell! I didn't expect you to return so quickly."

She was expecting him? "You have something for Miss McCary?" Jackson asked.

Blackwell frowned, looking from him back to Maggie, almost as if waiting for permission from her.

"It's all right," Maggie said.

"I bring you da money for—" He glanced again at Jackson.

"What's going on, Maggie?"

"He's here to pay for a bottle of tonic." She walked over to Brett and accepted the coins. "Thank you, Mr. Blackwell."

"Ya. It works good."

"I'm glad. Let me know if you need more."

Something inside Jackson jolted at her words.

With a parting look at him, Brett strode back out the door.

"More?" Jackson asked her now that they were alone again.

She met his gaze. "I didn't explain completely the other day. The tonic is…was my father's business. Mary and I helped him make it. And when he died, we kept on making it to support ourselves."

"This is what you did in Ohio?"

"Yes. It really does work—for aches and pains and nerves too. Mr. Blackwell probably needs more because he is larger than most men."

"Is this what Rader brought from the ranch? More tonic from your sister? Is that why you saw him?"

She nodded.

"And you are selling it?"

"To people who can benefit from its healing qualities." She glanced about. "Jackson. Please. I'd rather not let the entire population of Oak Grove know. I don't have a permit to sell it."

He'd been a fool not to realize there was more to her story after the way she had acted when she lost two of the bottles in at the river. "Maggie. People use this stuff instead of seeing a doctor. They believe it will help when all it does is cover up their problem. It doesn't heal anything." Then another thought struck him. "Is this how you are making the money to get out of the contract and leave town?"

She went still as stone, confirming his suspicion.

She had just kissed him and he'd considered contributing to the bride fund. For her. And yet she still planned to leave!

She crossed her arms over her chest. "I don't expect you to understand. Not everyone does."

He picked up his toolbox. He had to step away from this—from her. He had to think things through. "I understand that you just kissed me and yet you still plan to leave. That's what I understand."

He left her standing there in the lobby and walked out the door. If he stayed any longer he'd say something he would regret.

A heaviness took up residence in Maggie's chest as she ascended the staircase. Each step became harder to take as Jackson's parting words convicted her. How could she feel the way she did toward Jackson and still consider leaving town? It was impossible to fall in love with someone in only a few weeks' time, wasn't it? It just couldn't happen.

She entered her room and walked over to the window that looked out over the main road. Jackson stepped up on the boardwalk with that long stride of his and entered his shop. What had happened? Up until he'd learned about her selling the tonic, things had been going very well between them.

If only Mary were here. At least she could confide in her and figure out what was happening. Her sister would put an end to all these crazy thoughts and emotions running through her in her no-nonsense way.

Maggie stopped. She was only fooling herself. She didn't need Mary to help her or to fix her problem. She knew how her sister would react and that was what caused the jumble of doubts plaguing her. Mary would have a fit if she knew how Maggie really felt about Jackson. She was falling head over heels in love with the man. But was he truly tumbling with her? It was hard to tell what he felt sometimes.

There was no help for it. She had to continue with her sister's plan. Mary was depending on her. She must, even though her heart might break with the effort. Mary was the only family she had and family had to come first. That's all there was to it.

Family.

Came.

First.

## Chapter Eleven

Monday afternoon, Anna poked her head in the door of Maggie's room. "Did you forget? Martha invited all of us to her quilting bee. We are waiting downstairs."

"But I know nothing of quilting," Maggie said.

"Then it's high time you learned! Martha will supply the threads and material and the other women are bringing a few things for a light evening meal. It's all for a good cause."

"All right. I'll come." It might be a chance to sell a few more bottles of tonic. Already half of the supply was gone and customers were starting to ask for seconds. The thought didn't thrill her as much as it once had. Realizing that Jackson disapproved of her trade had bothered her from the moment he'd spoken of it. Now all she wanted was to hurry and finish the job once and for all so that her conscience could stop bothering her.

At the quilting bee set up in Martha Taylor's parlor, the afternoon rushed into evening as the four "brides" and the four other women worked on a quilt. She had been introduced to the women before, but now she really got to know them as they talked and laughed together.

The young schoolteacher was happy to teach them a few

different stitches and Martha talked about how nice it was to have more helping hands. The other two women from nearby farms chatted about their families. As before when Maggie had talked with them at the welcome celebration, she felt immediately drawn to them.

They all wanted to know which men Maggie, Sadie, Anna and Rebecca were interested in, promising to keep it within the circle. When Maggie refused to admit to anyone, Anna piped up.

"Maggie always has someone calling on her but the only one I've seen her talk to more than once is that carpenter, Mr. Miller, who took us out to the Circle P."

Leave it to Anna to say too much. "Only because I asked him to. I needed to check on Mary."

"I'm surprised he stopped working long enough to help you," Martha said. "That man is already married to his work. He's designed and helped build half the buildings in this town."

"He was just being a good neighbor," Maggie said quickly. *He doesn't always work*, she wanted to say in protest, knowing that he relaxed just fine when fishing. But she didn't say anything. She was pretty sure that he *would* prefer his privacy.

At the end of the evening, Maggie walked back to the hotel with the other three women under a canopy of twinkling stars. As the others started up the staircase to their rooms she heard a noise behind her.

"Maggie."

Her pulse quickened at the sound of Jackson's voice. He stood in the doorway to the dining area. "We need to talk."

A knowing look passed between Rebecca, Anna and Sadie. *Drat*. After her words at the quilting bee, she would hear of this again. "I'll be up in a minute," she said to Rebecca.

She turned back to Jackson and the darkened restaurant. "Here?"

He nodded.

The faint odor of onions from the evening meal lingered in the stillness of the room. Maggie brought a lantern and matches from the sidebar over to a table. She sat down as Jackson lit the wick and resettled the chimney, then moved the lamp to the side. The low glow illuminated his face and cast half of him in shadow. Not a hint of welcome resided in his dark, serious expression. The dark whiskers on his upper lip and chin had thickened since she had seen him two days ago. The urge to reach across the table and stroke his jaw came over her, but remembering the way he had walked away from her, she kept her hands tightly clasped in her lap. "What is it?" she whispered.

"I want you to stop selling your family tonic."

Her heart thudded to a stop. "Why?"

"I know you believe the tonic helps, and it probably does to a small amount. But people who are ailing need a doctor. They need healing. Not something that just makes them feel better for a while."

"I…can't stop. I'm sorry. Truly I am. But I have an agreement with my sister. She is counting on me to get it all sold." She hated that she couldn't do as he asked, but it couldn't be helped. She stood to go, her chest aching with the knowledge that she was upsetting him.

He blew out a breath. "Your loyalty is…commendable. But you see…the way you feel about Mary…I felt the same way about my brother."

"Your brother?" slowly she sank back into her chair. "The one who was pastor?"

He nodded.

"What happened?"

"Something I haven't told you is that I was engaged

once. Christine ran off with another man. I lost my best friend, Paul, and my fiancée in the same minute. After that I had to get away from Virginia and anything that reminded me of them.

"When Ben wrote and asked me to come here and build his church, I jumped at the chance. He was anxious for the building to be finished and often helped out with the work—nailing or hammering or sanding. The day I rode into Salina for the bell, Ben fell from the tower. He broke some ribs and his collarbone. Doc Graham wrapped him up.

"We thought he was getting better. His pain was less every day and he was coughing less. I thought he was in the clear, and then suddenly pneumonia set in and he was gone."

She sucked in her breath. "I'm so sorry." She couldn't imagine losing Mary. Just the thought of it was unbearable.

"I found out later that someone, meaning well, had given him an elixir so he could rest. Something homemade to stop him from coughing. But Ben needed to cough to get that fluid out of his lungs. Doc Graham said that medicine interfered with his healing. It probably ended up killing him."

The heaviness in her chest made it hard to breathe. She had nothing she could say. No wonder he hated her selling the tonic. No wonder...

"I understand how it is with your sister, but you have to stop selling that stuff. Now. For the sake of the people here."

She put her palm to her forehead and stared at the small dancing flame on the lantern's wick. "I don't think our tonic would cause something like that."

"Can you be sure?" Jackson scraped his chair back and stood. "I care about you, Maggie. A great deal. I don't want to see you leave Oak Grove, but if that's what you and your sister want, I'll give you the money to go. But for now, I can't abide what you are doing." He strode out the door.

His words echoed long after he'd left her. She sat in the dark a long time thinking over his words. He didn't want to see her leave! But she couldn't take his money. A McCary always paid their own way. And whether she stayed or left, it didn't change the fact that both she and Mary had to get out of the contract. That would take more money.

She had always thought the tonic was a good thing. Da had said so and she believed him. Yet now doubt crept in. What was she going to do? It all seemed so hopeless.

## Chapter Twelve

Jackson sat in his back room, the designs for a new house spread out before him on the table. He wasn't seeing them. A lie of omission sat hot on his lips. Sheriff Baniff had stopped by and mentioned that Doc Graham was up in arms about Maggie's tonic. Apparently the stuff wasn't illegal— there was even a slight medicinal quality to it—but people didn't realize they were buying mostly concentrated alcohol under the guise of medicine. Jackson had held his tongue. It was only a matter of time before Baniff found out Maggie was the culprit—if she didn't leave town first. Which was probably her plan—to get out before she was found out.

Three days had gone by since he'd last seen her and explained about his brother. The next step had to come from her. He wasn't about to dishonor Ben's memory or the people of this town by condoning her vocation.

Yet he missed her. He ached for her.

She had disrupted the careful life he'd built since his brother's death. She'd pulled him out of himself and made him care about things again—about people—about her. He loved her—but that only made what she was doing worse.

The door to his shop opened.

"I've come to have a word with you, Miller."

Angus? What was he doing here? Jackson started to rise when he heard a second softer voice—Maggie's.

"I don't think he's here, Mr. O'Leary. He's probably fishing."

"Now, lassie. You know the fish don't bite this time of day."

"I shouldn't have come. I'll…I'll tell him later. Maybe. Let's go."

Jackson walked through the doorway to the front room. "What will you tell me later?"

Maggie drew in a breath. "You *are* here," she said, obviously dismayed.

It must have been Angus's idea to come. Not hers. She looked pretty in her green dress and her straw bonnet. Then, she would look pretty in just about anything, even overalls.

"All right then." She put her hands on her hips. "I hope you are happy, Jackson Miller. You've ruined everything!"

He looked from her to Angus. "What are you talking about?"

She threw her hands up into the air. "I cannot sell one more bottle of McCary's Finest. Believe me. I have tried. Three times I have tried. But each time I stopped right in the middle of handing it over. *Each time!*"

His heart sped up. "That so?" he asked guardedly.

"Of course it's so! Right there I refused their good money and poured the tonic onto the dirt. I emptied three bottles! I don't know what I'm going to tell Mary."

"Why did you do it?"

"Well, because of what you said, of course!"

"You've ruined her enterprise," Angus said, grinning. "Told me so herself over breakfast."

She glared at Angus, but then turned back to Jackson. "It's an old, old family recipe, handed down for many generations. Years ago it was the only thing that helped with pain and nerves. Perhaps now there are better things…even cures and such."

"So you are going to stop selling it?"

"I already have. The people here have been good to me. I would never want the tonic to bring them harm."

He couldn't hold back his own grin. She had chosen. He scooped her up and spun her around. She might not realize it yet, but she had chosen.

Him.

She beat her fists against his shoulders—not very hard. "Put me down! This is serious! What am I going to tell Mary? You have to help me figure it out."

"I will," he said, putting her back on her feet. "I promise. But the first thing I'm going to do is see Mayor Melbourne about a way to get you out of that contract. If it takes money…I'll see to it."

Her eyes brightened. "You would do that?"

"I said I cared for you."

"Indeed you did," she said softly, and then smiled the purest, sweetest smile, just for him.

"As a matter of fact it's more than that," he said, his heart pounding, more nervous then he'd ever been before. "I love you."

Her lips parted as a stunned expression stole over her face. "Jackson!" she breathed.

"A letter from my brother brought me here. My promise to him kept me here. I've been buried in my work—shutting out the world. But then you showed up and I found myself…"

"Annoyed?"

He grinned. "A little. At first. But it's all changed now. For the first time in a long time I look forward to seeing what the next day will bring and…when I will see you again."

She sighed. "I feel the same way...about always hoping to see you."

He noticed that she hadn't admitted to loving him. He was willing to wait. He wanted her to be sure. "Angus? Turn your head. I'm gonna kiss this woman."

He heard Angus chuckle. "Go ahead. I won't stop you. I'd say it's about time."

# Chapter Thirteen

$M$aggie took what had become her regular seat in the hotel dining room with the other brides. The scent of bacon hovered in the air, making her stomach grumble.

While she waited for her breakfast to be served, she looked out at the storm clouds rolling in from the southwest and felt carried by a fog of happiness that had enveloped her since yesterday. Jackson's out-and-out declaration that he cared for her hadn't exactly taken her by surprise. After all, he had kissed her—twice. Yet for a man like him to talk about his feelings, to admit he loved her right there with Angus looking on—well, that was something.

His kiss had been nothing like the other two. His lips on hers were strong, decisive, intentional. He had claimed her. Stolen her breath and turned her bones to butter. And all she knew was that she wanted more of him—more holding, more kissing, more talking and teasing. More time.

She didn't want to have to leave Oak Grove.

They'd gone to the mayor's office about the contract, but the place was locked up tight. Jackson would try again this morning. He promised. She could hardly wait to see him and hear what transpired. She had always prided herself in being independent. She was new at this—having a man help her, having a man care. Mary once said a man was the last thing they needed and Maggie remembered agreeing. She didn't *need* Jackson, but she certainly wanted him.

"You could wait until she is done with her breakfast. She just sat down."

At Rollie Austin's sputtering, Maggie glanced toward the door. The sheriff and Mayor Melbourne brushed past him and strode to her table.

"Miss McCary," the sheriff said. "We need a word with you."

Her heart sped up. Had Jackson already said something to them? Was this about the contract? Before she had a chance to ask he slapped the new edition of the *Oak Grove Gazette* on the table and pointed to it. Front and center was Anna's interview and a small picture beside it—a sketched image of one of Maggie's bottles.

Maggie looked across the table at her friend. "What did you say?"

"Nothing! I talked about me."

A sinking sensation hit the pit of her stomach. What had Abigail written?

"The hotel's office will afford us privacy," said the mayor. "Or we can discuss things here."

She swallowed. This had all happened in Pennsylvania with her father. They had let him go after seeing his permit. She, however, did not have a permit. She followed the mayor into the small office.

"A strong substance…an elixir…is being dispensed throughout town." He set a bottle of McCary tonic on the office desk.

The label stared back at her. M&M.

"Is it yours?"

"Not anymore. I sold that one."

"Where did it come from?"

She repeated what she'd often heard her father say over the years. "McCary's Finest Recipe Tonic has a long and established history of helping folks with their ailments. It's a family recipe and my da, before he departed this earth, ran the business."

The mayor lifted a brow. "You make it, bottle it and sell it?"

"Yes."

"Then I take it that you have more? Where?"

She lifted her chin. "Unless I have committed a crime, I don't see that that is any of your business."

"You can't sell it here without a permit," said Mayor Melbourne. "And I don't give permits to women. I have to confiscate the rest of your supply."

"You mean steal it!"

"I mean nothing of the sort. It won't do you any good. I'm not sure who you've set your cap at for a husband, but unless it is Dan or Chris Sanders at the saloon, no man in Oak Grove is going to be agreeable about this family trade of yours."

Jackson must not have spoken to him yet. She wanted to ask about the contract, but now, considering his mood, it wasn't the best time.

"Where is the rest?" the sheriff said, cutting right to the point.

Pressing her lips together, she stomped outside to the cellar and showed them what remained of her supply— five bottles.

"How many originally?" asked the sheriff.

"Twenty."

"All sold here in town?"

"No. Three, I poured out."

He gave her a sharp look. "Was it tainted?"

She backed off at the insinuation of poor quality tonic.

Not her family! "Of course not! I decided to stop selling it. I realized that people might depend on it rather than seeking the advice of a doctor."

Mayor Melbourne grunted. "Well what do you think, Baniff? What should we do with our wayward young bride?"

Sheriff Baniff considered her. "Miss McCary doesn't appear to have acted out of malice."

House arrest—or rather hotel arrest—for the time being was their answer. Sheriff Baniff and the mayor made her give her word that she wouldn't leave the hotel until they hashed things out.

While Maggie walked slowly up the stairs to her room, they explained things to Mr. Austin and her friends. The sheriff, quite politely she thought, requested that they keep what was going on between only those who were present. Immediately, she thought of Jackson. And then Mary. In that order.

Oh, dear. Just what did that say about her?

She had really messed things up. She would have to figure things out on her own. It was her problem and she'd brought it on herself. It was up to her to get herself out of it.

Jackson finished his breakfast of bread and cheese and a glass of cider. Today he'd hunt down the mayor before the man had a chance to slip away on business again. Jackson was either getting Maggie out of that blasted contract so that she could be free to choose her own destiny—which he hoped would include him—or he would donate to the bride fund and convince her to marry him.

He'd never met a woman so alive, so fascinating, and he wasn't going to let her get away. There had to be some way to get her to stay, but he didn't want it to be because of any contract. He wanted her to stay because her heart was here in Oak Grove, because she loved the town and the people, and most of all, because she loved him.

Which was a tall expectation for a woman who loved her independence. A woman like that wouldn't give up her freedom easily.

He guessed he would have to charm her.

He wasn't much good in that area. It was Ben who had the easygoing charm. The women had flocked to him.

He, on the other hand, had preferred being at arm's length, at least he had since Christine. The easiest way to avoid getting hurt again was not to care in the first place. Ben had gotten after him about it more than once, saying that when Jackson finally fell, he would fall hard and for life. Looked like his brother had been right. No woman had caught his attention like Maggie, not even Christine.

He squeezed his fist. He had always finished what he started, always figured out a way to make things work out. This was no different. He shoved the plate aside and took the stairs up to his room two at a time. He rummaged in the bottom of a box he kept for his savings, counted out five silver dollars, and then sweetened it with a ten-dollar bill for insurance in case the mayor seemed reluctant to accept his plan. Stuffing the money in his shirt pocket, he headed to the office.

He hammered on the thick oak door twice. No response. He backed off the boardwalk into the street and studied the mayor's living quarters above his law office. The window was open and a dark green curtain fluttered in the light breeze.

"Melbourne!" he called. "Open up."

"Hold your horses."

At the sound from behind him, he turned and saw both the mayor and the sheriff striding up.

Mayor Melbourne unlocked his door, and then stepped

back and let Jackson enter first. "Now what's this about, Miller?" he asked, following him into his office.

"I'd like to take a look at that bride contract you drafted."

"You didn't donate to the fund, Miller. Afraid I can't let you see the contract. It doesn't concern you."

"What if I say that I want in now? Could I see the contract then?"

The mayor hiked his hip onto his desk. "Are you interested in one of the women?"

Jackson swallowed. "Yes. Maggie McCary."

"Well. This is a change. You—considering marriage."

"Only if she'll have me. I'm more interested in getting her out of her contract. What she does after that is her choice."

Mayor Melbourne snorted. "Sounds like she's got you hornswoggled. Look, Miller. We were supposed to get twelve brides and only got five. If you think the original men who donated to the fund are going to tolerate you jumping in at the last minute and stealing a bride away from them, you are crazy. It's not going to happen."

A cold knot formed in his gut. "If I could just see the contract. I'll pay double…triple."

The mayor shook his head. "You are entirely within your rights to get a bride out of the next batch that comes. I've already contacted my brother in Bridgeport. He's rounding up more."

Jackson stiffened. He didn't want the next batch. He wanted Maggie. "You make it sound like they are cattle."

Mayor Melbourne grunted. "Guess it does sound that way. Just a turn of phrase. Those McCary girls definitely are not cattle. Prettiest of the lot in my opinion, but they are also the most troublesome." The mayor picked up the newspaper on his desk and shoved it at Jackson. He jabbed his finger at an article in the middle of the page. "What do you know about this?"

Jackson scanned the article, his hope sinking with each typeset word. Anna probably didn't even know that she'd as good as sealed Maggie's future by revealing her as the one flooding the town with tonic. Now the mayor would never let her out of the contract. "She is done selling it. She has quit."

"So you knew about it." The mayor flung the paper back on his desk and stood, squaring off with him. "Listen, Jackson. I like you. I liked your brother too. I'm sorry you got dragged into this woman's scheme, but Maggie McCary has got you hoodwinked. She can't wiggle out of her contract. She has to stick to the original deal and marry by next Saturday. If she doesn't pick a husband from the bachelors, then there will be a lottery for her. You might as well let go of any thoughts of her."

Jackson wasn't about to admit defeat. "We'll see about that," he said with a scowl. He strode out the door.

He had to see Maggie. Although he hated to tell her that he'd failed about the contract, maybe they could come up with another solution.

He entered the hotel lobby and took the stairs two at a time. Miss Simpson answered his knock, peering through a cracked open door.

"I need to speak to Mag—Miss McCary."

Miss Simpson glanced over her shoulder quickly. "She isn't seeing visitors just now."

It was obvious Maggie was in the room. "What's going on? Is she all right?" He grabbed the door handle.

"She's not feeling well at the moment." Miss Camp blocked the small opening behind Miss Simpson.

"She's ill?"

"Just a headache."

He didn't for one minute believe Miss Camp, but barging into the room might not endear him to Maggie if she wanted to be alone. "Would you let her know I'll stop by later?"

A wrinkle puckered Miss Simpson's brow. "Certainly."

## Chapter Fourteen

Maggie paced the length of her room for the umpteenth time and stopped at the window overlooking Main Street. The dirt road was a dark void in the predawn light. No sound of footsteps on the boardwalk, no clatter of dishes in the kitchen below. Everyone still slept. At the Whistle Stop, she could barely make out the silhouettes of two horses at the railing, stomping their hooves and swishing their tails as they waited for their owners, who were probably asleep sprawled across a table.

Jackson had come and gone four times over the past three days. Each time she had refused to speak with him. He finally stopped trying. Now each time he left his shop and turned away from the hotel it ripped out a tiny part of her. But her feelings for him could no longer matter. She couldn't look to him for help to get out of the contract. The mayor had made a point of saying that when he went over the papers with her word for word, and then pointed out her signature at the bottom.

She was on her own.

Ever since Mayor Melbourne's visit the walls of her hotel room were closing in on her. It seemed like everything was converging to ruin her life. The mayor had confiscated the few remaining bottles of tonic, but she knew she wouldn't go back to selling it ever again. Not after learning of what had happened to Jackson's brother.

She couldn't get Jackson off her mind even though she had done her best to purge her memories of his kiss. And thinking about Jackson only confused her. The best thing for her was to keep her distance. She had herself to think about. Herself and Mary. Mary would always be there for her. She couldn't count on anyone else.

She must talk to her sister, but there was no way to get a message to her and she had been cooped up long enough! It looked like Mary would get something even better than a message… Her.

She had waited for just this moment while Rebecca still slept, while the entire town slept. She grabbed her carpet-bag and slipped out the door, silently making her way down the stairs to the lobby. Tiptoeing through the kitchen, she let herself out of the hotel's back door. Then, hefting the carpetbag up into both arms, she raced behind the row of buildings, passed the saloon and made her way to the livery.

She was not a horse thief. She was only borrowing the beast she quickly saddled. Once she collected Mary, they would leave the horse in Bexler at the train depot. She placed the note of explanation she had written and her money on a bale of hay and topped it with a horseshoe to keep it from blowing away.

As she left the town on horseback and followed the river north, the road was still shrouded in gray light. Crickets were giving up on their night chorus and the breeze was picking up, causing a rustling sound in the tall grass. How had she ever thought of Kansas as ugly? It carried its own beauty—its own sweet scent of the wildflowers. The prairie, the river—they whispered to her entreating her to stay.

What would Mary think if she found out that Maggie

had allowed—even enjoyed—Jackson's kisses. The thought of his strong arms enveloping her left her weak in the knees. And yes, she yearned for him to hold her again, yearned for the touch of his lips to hers. If there were any way that she could stay and not be made to marry another, she would gladly stay. It was a completely selfish thought. Mary would chastise her into next year for messing things up so badly.

And Sadie? Rebecca? Anna? They'd become good friends, proving their loyalty even more so over the past three days while she had had to stay at the hotel. All right, Anna had made life in Oak Grove tricky for her with the article, but she was too gullible for her own good and no match for Abigail White's questions. Maggie knew she'd never meant to harm her.

How could she leave these girls now and never learn how they fared?

But more than anything, how could she leave Jackson? It was breaking her heart.

Her chest weighed heavy with the ache of it, her muscles too lethargic to rein the horse properly. The horse slowed, and then stopped. Maggie stared at the long gray road ahead. At the Circle P, Mary would probably be rising about now and milking the cow, completely unaware of all that had happened in town.

Perhaps this separation had been good for them. A test of sorts. They had survived. Maggie had learned a lot— about friendship, about what mattered in life, about caring more for others than herself. She still couldn't get over the look in Jackson's eyes when she had told him that she could no longer sell the tonic. It felt good—that look. He had been proud. Of her. She could die happy remembering that, even if she never saw it again in her life.

He was such a good man and he had shut himself off for so long—because of Christine—because of his brother.

Would he return to that place once she was gone? The thought troubled her. She had brought him joy for a time. She was sure of it. And she wanted to be the one to make him happy every morning, to wake up excited for the day ahead and all its possibilities. To see his smile, hear his laugh. She wanted to share the rainbow and the sunset. With him.

If she left, that would never happen.

The road blurred before her. She swiped her face. Her cheeks were wet. She was crying.

She couldn't go on. She loved him. She loved him with a fierceness that she'd never known before, a fierceness that wouldn't burn out. Something deep inside told her so. The love she felt would endure. She would hold on to it and make it endure no matter what.

It was time to choose and she chose him, come what may.

She squared her shoulders. She had to go back.

Reining the horse around, she started toward town. From this distance she could see the dusky lightening of the sky behind the church spire. A new day was coming and she would face it. It wouldn't be easy. She did not care. She wasn't marrying anyone but Jackson. Mary would have a fit, but they weren't twins for nothing and she would count on that bond. In the end Mary would understand.

"Aren't you going the wrong way, Miss McCary?"

She inhaled swiftly and pulled back on the reins, stopping her mount on the small rise of the road. Just beyond it, leaning heavily on his saddle horn, sat the sheriff.

"You can't leave her in there," Rebecca railed at the sheriff. She stood before his desk, brandishing her parasol like a sword. "I'll have my fiancé see about this. He's a very important man. Likely he pays your salary."

"Likely he does, Miss Simpson." the sheriff said, looking up from his bowl of soup.

At the beleaguered expression on his face, Maggie almost felt sorry for him. He was tired—and getting little help from the mayor now that most of the people in town had taken sides about the fact that they both were holding a woman in the jail like a common criminal.

The news had spread through Oak Grove like a flash of lightning and nearly everyone in town had come to call to make their opinion known. Yesterday upon hearing the news and again just now, Sadie had marched across the street with the sheriff's dinner, plunked it down in front of the man and berated him for keeping Maggie behind bars. Little timid Sadie! The soup was probably cold after her and now Rebecca's tirades—a fact that gave Maggie a small degree of satisfaction.

It seemed the women were incensed about her being in jail in the first place and the men wanted her out—particularly Brett Blackwell—so that they could court her. Even Abigail had stopped by to get her final interview right there at the jail! Never in Maggie's life had she felt such support and camaraderie from others. She was grateful for it, and humbled.

Sheriff Baniff glared at Rebecca. "Now you are the fourth woman in here this morning. I'd like to eat my dinner in peace if you don't mind."

Rebecca ignored him and walked over to the cell.

"Doc Graham jumped at the chance to take word to Mary about you being in here. He's been keeping an eye on one of the injured cowboys there. By his actions, I think he also has been keeping an eye on your sister. He left an hour ago for the Circle P."

Maggie breathed a sigh of relief. "Thank you. I can't stand the thought of leaving without saying goodbye to her."

Rebecca drew her brows together. "Why are they sending you all the way back to Bridgeport to serve out your sentence? It makes no sense."

"I'm to be a cautionary example."

"Well, it is ridiculous. All that for selling tonic without a permit?"

"No. There is more to it than that. I refuse to honor the marriage contract."

"Oh. I see." Rebecca's eyes clouded over. "Is it because of that carpenter?"

Maggie closed her eyes as the image of Jackson invaded her senses. He hadn't come to see her. She had been here since yesterday and half the town had come—but not him. He must be embarrassed by her—or furious. She hadn't allowed his help before and so now he'd quit offering it. She had no one to blame but herself.

"Jackson knows where I am if he wants to see me." She pressed her palm to her brow, irritable and aching all in one miserable heap. "I'm facing things, aren't I? I will serve out my sentence. I will make it right."

Rebecca's gaze softened. "You do care about him, don't you?"

"It hardly matters." Her heart was numb. Jackson wouldn't want a criminal as a wife. He was all that was good in the world. And she was not.

"You don't belong in here," Rebecca stated flatly. "A fine would suffice. And perhaps an apology."

She recognized the understanding in her friend's eyes. Rebecca was her friend the same as Sadie and Anna. They had come a long way in the past few weeks. Each had been by to see her and tell her they were on her side. "Thank you," she murmured, and reached through the bars for Rebecca's hand, squeezing her fingers.

Rebecca turned back to the sheriff. "Enjoy your soup.

You'll be hearing from my fiancé as soon as he can break from his business at the bank." She threw an encouraging wink at Maggie before sweeping through the open door of the jail.

Maggie pushed away from the bars and sat back down on her cot. She hadn't anticipated that the mayor would send her back to Bridgeport. She hadn't thought out anything, except that she loved Jackson and couldn't leave him. Yet it had all came to naught. They would send her away. And after all that had happened, Jackson would forget all about her.

"Are you going to keep moping around this here mortuary or are you gonna head on over to the jail and let that lassie know you care for her?" Angus held on to the bowl of his pipe and poked the stem at Jackson's chest.

"I figured I'd go fishing," Jackson said irritably. He'd been pestered enough—by the other brides and now by Angus. Things were getting downright out of control. It was plain as could be that Maggie had decided on her own to run. She had given her word that she would abide by the terms that the sheriff and mayor had stated, and then she'd turned right around and gone back on it and run off. If the sheriff hadn't arrested her, she and Mary would be over the state line by now.

He returned to his task, applying the walnut stain sparingly over the top of the table with a wadded-up rag and trying, unsuccessfully, to rid his mind of the image of Maggie sitting in the jail.

"I walked over to the hotel four times, prepared to do what I could to help her," he mumbled. "Four times! And she wouldn't open the door to me. Guess that says things loud and clear."

Angus took a draw on his pipe. "She's refusing to marry.

Said she'd pay the penalty. The sheriff and mayor are fixing to put her on the train back to Bridgeport come morning."

He straightened. He hadn't heard that before. "What for?"

"What for? To serve out her original sentence and to make an example of her. That's what for. They don't want the same thing to happen with any of the other brides that decide to come this way."

"They aren't forcing her to marry one of the men who donated?"

Angus's eyes twinkled. "Well, now. She hasn't exactly endeared herself to any of them when they've called on her at the jail."

His mouth twitched as he thought what that might entail. "She does like to have her own way."

"That she does."

The fact that Maggie was in jail had eaten at him ever since he'd learned of it. Maggie, who found beauty in everything, who sang to the river, who loved her freedom. What would being locked in a cell do to someone like her? Ruin her? Destroy the part in her that was innocent?

It wasn't right. She had tried to do the honorable thing when she quit selling the tonic. Maybe being cooped up in that hotel room had gotten to her. If that were the case— being in that cell would be worse. The more he thought about it, the more worried he got and the more he knew that he couldn't let her go without seeing her one last time.

Angus watched him closely.

Jackson dropped the rag into a bucket and wiped his hands. "I'll go. If for nothing more than to say goodbye."

## Chapter Fifteen

The hot, muggy air weighed her down as she sat on the cot, her back supported against the cool iron of the bars. Sweat trickled down her neck and into the valley between her breasts. The sound of birds twittering and whistling in the meadow floated through the open doorway.

Being trapped in the cell was starting to inconvenience her in the worst way. At first she had focused on what she would tell Jackson, how she would explain. That had kept her mind occupied. Then, when he didn't arrive, she tried to concentrate on her sister. To counter the feeling of panic that slowly grew inside her chest at being confined, she paced the length of her cell, trying to remember all the songs she knew and sing them softly. Then she tried to sing them backward.

Her scalp at the nape of her neck tingled.

"You've got company, Miss McCary."

She glanced over to the doorway. Jackson stood there, his cap in his hands, watching her.

He looked worn, tired and very, very dear. He hadn't shaved or combed his hair. Like always, his shirtsleeves were rolled up to his elbows.

He nodded. "Miss McCary."

So they were back to that, were they? "Mr. Miller." She heard the tremor in her voice, the hesitation.

He walked up to the cell. "How are you?"

Those beautiful green eyes held her captive, as always saying more than his words. She had to make him understand how she felt, but he seemed so distant, so polite. "I'm well," she answered cautiously.

He stepped closer and gripped the bars, squaring off at her. "You ran," he said, his voice low and accusing. "You didn't believe in me. In us. You just ran."

Honesty came with a price, she realized. It was hard. Sometimes brutal. But she couldn't ask for his love if she wasn't honest. She had to admit it, even though she was sure he would leave. "Yes. I did."

Disappointment filled his face.

She rose and went to the bars. "I was scared. Frightened. I needed to see Mary."

"It was more than that. You were packed. Leaving for good." His gaze dipped to the carpetbag shoved against the wall. "Without a goodbye."

"I… It's what I've always done. What my family has always done. We leave."

"Well, you did a poor job of it this time. You got caught."

She was desperate for him to understand. "We were never in one place very long. Sometimes it was because Da didn't get a permit to sell the tonic. Sometimes it was because a doctor didn't like the competition and brought the law down on us. Whenever there was the least sign of trouble, Da would simply pack us into the wagon and we'd move to another town. That's why Mary and I left Bridgeport. There was a bit of trouble. So we signed the contract and got on the train."

"You were running?"

She nodded. "With the sheriff pushing us. But it was

different yesterday. I couldn't go through with it. I came back. I'm ready to accept my punishment."

"Maggie," he said flatly. "You came back only because the sheriff here dragged you back."

"No! That's not so. I couldn't leave you. I...I had to come back."

Distrust filled his eyes. "And you expect me to believe that?"

She shook her head. Her heart was breaking, but she would see this through. "No. I know how this all looks. I understand...even if you won't. It is too hard for you to accept after Christine and Paul betrayed you." She held one of his hands with hers and felt his muscles tense. Afraid that he might bolt, she reached up and tenderly cupped his jaw. "But I love you, Jackson. I couldn't leave. Please believe me."

Jackson stared down at the blue-eyed beauty before him. Her hand on his cheek was a hot brand, burning her deeper into his being. His skin tingled and for a moment he leaned into her caress, unwilling to draw away.

Then he bolstered his resolve. Maggie had refused to see him for the three days she'd been at the hotel, and then she ran, as though his feelings didn't matter. It had been like a fist to his gut when he'd heard. He both loved and hated her in the same breath. She made him ache. She made him hurt. And she made him feel more alive than he'd ever felt before.

"Please forgive me," she said softly. "They are taking me back to Bridgeport tomorrow, but if it were my choice I'd stay here. I'd never run again. I'd only go if you told me to. If...if you wanted me to."

It was no use. He let out a shuddering breath, his resolve to keep his distance crumbling. "That will never happen."

The wary hope that sprang in her eyes warmed him, and with it the last vestiges of his anger and hurt slid away.

He snaked his arm through the bars and pulled her close, kissing her forehead. "You are a lot of trouble, Maggie McCary."

She smiled—a forlorn, regretful smile. Tears pooled in her eyes. "I know."

"Will you marry me anyway?"

"Of course I will!"

He kissed her then. Sealing their words with his promise. "I'll get the preacher."

The sheriff scraped back his chair and stood. "Now hold on, Miller. I can't let you do that."

"Try and stop me. We're getting married, right here, right now. If you want to prevent it, you will have to lock me up." He tensed, and curled his fingers.

The sheriff glanced down at Jackson's fist and then looked back at his face. Then his gaze slid over to Maggie. "You are serious? Both of you?"

"Dead serious."

A slow, speculative look crossed over his face. "That might take care of this entire mess."

Jackson relaxed his hand. "What are you talking about?"

The sheriff grabbed his keys and unlocked the cell door. Before Maggie could step out, he took hold of Jackson's shoulder and shoved him inside. Taken off guard, Jackson stumbled backward a few steps before regaining his footing. In that time, the cell door clanged shut. Baniff turned the key in the lock and a slow smile formed on his face. "That should do it."

Immediately, Maggie pitched into Jackson's arms. Soft, desperate, sweet Maggie.

He kissed her long and hard, right in front of Sheriff Baniff. He couldn't care less that the man watched. He needed to hold her, to touch her and reassure her. Whatever came, they'd face it together. "I love you Maggie McCary," he murmured against her ear.

She drew back and looked deep into his eyes. "And I you."

"*That* is what you needed to tell me *before* getting jailed," he said with a slight growl to his voice. He glanced over at the sheriff. "I don't know what you are up to, but I appreciate this."

Jackson settled his arm around Maggie and sat with her on the cot. He wasn't letting her go.

An hour later, Mayor Melbourne strode into the office. He stopped when he realized there was not one, but two prisoners.

"Are you daft?" he yelled at the sheriff. "No man is going to offer for her if she's locked up with Miller."

Jackson straightened. His chest was tight with what might happen in the next few minutes. The sheriff hadn't said much since forcing him into the cell so Jackson had no idea what to expect. They both had been waiting on the appearance of Mayor Melbourne.

"You said she is headed back to Ohio," Sheriff Baniff said, a bit of a challenge in his voice. "What can it hurt?"

The mayor frowned. "That is only as a last resort."

"Oh. Then you were trying to force her hand?"

"She needs to keep to the terms of her agreement," the mayor said stubbornly. "Sending her back will cost us more money." He reached into his inner vest pocket and withdrew what looked to be her contract and waved it in the air. "I have it right here."

"I think you are missing what's important here. The entire principle of the Betterment Committee is to make Oak Grove a decent community for families. That means bringing new blood and business here. At the welcome picnic you said as much…and that you wanted the town to grow."

"Now hold on, Baniff. This isn't your call…"

"Maybe not. I agree that Miss McCary's tonic business needs to stop, but she's already complied with that. And she's willing to marry—maybe not the man you would choose for her, but she's figured out who she wants and it seems he's willing to put up with her. In my presence, he's just offered for her hand." He drummed his fingers on his desk, letting his words sink in.

"The way I see it, we can't afford to lose Miller's business. He has built half the town. Are we really going to repay one of our own this way? We need to do what we can to keep him here."

Jackson stood and gripped the bars. "My brother's church is done. There is nothing holding me here. If Miss McCary marries another or goes back to Ohio, you can be sure that I'll leave."

"And I'll not marry another," Maggie said, coming to his side.

The mayor, his face set in a horrible frown, looked from the sheriff to Jackson, and then to Maggie.

It seemed Maggie's entire future, along with his own, waited on the mayor's next words. When the official's shoulders slumped, Jackson felt the first give in the tight band that had cinched his chest.

The mayor held up the contract and slowly ripped the paper into pieces. "I expect to see you dressed and ready for a wedding on Saturday, Miss McCary. Let them out, Baniff." The mayor strode from the office.

The wide-eyed astonishment on Maggie's face was a thing to remember—always. Jackson squeezed her hand as they waited for the sheriff to open the cell.

The keys jangled as the sheriff did just that.

When Jackson stood beside Maggie on the other side of the bars, he faced the sheriff and offered his hand. "Thank you."

Sheriff Baniff shook his hand. "I meant what I said. This town can't afford to lose you."

At his side, Maggie took his arm. His chest swelled, his heart full of relief and joy.

"Right after the mayor learned about Miss McCary's part with the tonic, you showed up to pay into the fund. If you haven't noticed, our mayor likes control. He was hard-nosed about it. It probably had something to do with the fact that Steve Putnam put up a whopping amount of cash to keep another McCary on as cook for his men."

"Then I guess my amount didn't add up much compared to his."

Sheriff Baniff grinned. "Seemed to me if Melbourne accepted Steve's money, he couldn't pick and choose and not accept yours."

"You mean you *did* try to donate to the bride fund?" Maggie asked. Her tone held wonder.

"I told you I'd try. I didn't want you to go," Jackson admitted.

She looked at him as if he were some sort of hero.

The sheriff cleared his throat. "There's something you should know, Miller. Miss McCary might have sneaked away to see her sister, but she never got there. She had turned around and was heading back to town when I caught up to her out at the crossroads."

It was Jackson's turn to be surprised. He had made up his mind it didn't matter, but knowing she'd chosen to come back, chosen to face whatever waited for her, meant a heck of a lot to him. He couldn't seem to wipe the smile off his face. He'd been right. She had definitely chosen him.

"Guess I don't have to worry about the two of you skipping town?" the sheriff asked.

"No, sir," they both said in unison, and then smiled at each other.

"And I'll see you on Saturday, two p.m. sharp for your wedding?" the sheriff asked as he walked them to the door.

Jackson took Maggie's hand. "Yes."

They stepped outside.

"Maggie! Maggie!"

Was that Mary? Mary! Maggie broke away from Jackson and rushed to the edge of the boardwalk. In a thunder of hooves that matched Maggie's heartbeat, Mary galloped her mount down the main street of Oak Grove and reined to a stop in front of the sheriff's office. Steve Putnam was right behind her on a larger horse.

"Mary!" she cried. "You came!"

Jackson helped Mary down from her horse. Immediately she ran to Maggie and threw her arms around her, hugging her tight.

"When I learned you were in jail, I had to come. Tell me it isn't true! The mayor cannot send you back to Ohio!" Tears ran down her cheeks as she stepped back, yet still held Maggie's hands, squeezing them tightly. "I won't let him send you away."

Steve Putnam came up behind her and put his hands on Mary's shoulders. "*We* won't let him send you away," he said fiercely.

Maggie pulled away from her sister's grasp, looking from one to the other. What was going on? Something was there between them. "I'm not going anywhere. Mayor Melbourne dropped the charges, thanks to my friends here in town and—" she glanced at Jackson "—Mr. Miller here."

Mr. Putnam stepped up on the boardwalk and shook Jackson's hand. "Good work. How did you do it?"

"Guess that's for Maggie to say."

Her chest swelled with a mix of emotions. Loving him. Loving Mary. She was grateful that Jackson hadn't just blurted out their engagement. He knew this would be hard for her. He understood that she hated to disappoint her sister but it was on her to give Mary the news that she would be staying in Oak Grove.

The steady, patient love shining in Jackson's beautiful green eyes infused her with courage. She reached for his hand, grasped it, and then turned back to her sister. "Mary? Mr. Putnam? I'd like you to be the first to know—after the sheriff and Mayor, that is—Jackson and I are going to be married."

Mary gasped. "Why? Did they make you do this? Are they forcing you?" Then she focused on Maggie's hand holding Jackson's. "Or…"

Maggie smiled softly. "I love him. I want to stay. I don't want to run ever again. I'm…" Her eyes burned with tears. "I'm sorry if that isn't what you wanted to hear. I have the money from the tonic for you. I don't want it. I'm through selling it. And I'm through with leaving."

Mary moved forward again and wrapped her arms around her for a quick hug. "Oh, Maggie! I am through with the tonic also. Steve doesn't want it around, and…since I'm going to be staying out at the ranch I want to abide by his wishes. I never want to run again either."

Maggie was confused. "You're staying? But I thought that—"

Mary struggled to contain her smile and then completely gave up. "I'm getting married too."

Maggie stopped breathing. She looked from Mary to Mr. Putnam, who wore a similar grin. Then her tears truly did spill over as her throat clogged up with emotion. Mary—a married woman! Relief and happiness bubbled up inside. She reached for her sister and hugged her tight.

"I was so worried about being separated from you. And now I find that I haven't lost you at all. I've gained a husband and a brother!"

Mary giggled. "Me too."

Maggie sighed when Jackson gripped her hand firmly. "We will be together," she said. "We will all be together!"

Mary grinned impishly, her blue eyes shining with love for the man at her side. "Well—close enough to visit. Often."

The four of them enjoyed a celebratory meal at Austin's restaurant and a visit to Mayor Melbourne. He took the news that Steve and Mary would also be wed at the church on Saturday by throwing up his hands, muttering a questionable expletive and ordering them out of his office.

Maggie watched as Mary and Steve rode out of town, disappearing around the corner of the livery. She supposed she should go back to the hotel. Word had spread rapidly among the other brides when she and her sister showed up at the restaurant. They were all waiting to hear what had happened.

Beside her, Jackson squeezed her hand. "I haven't had a moment alone with you. Will you go to the river with me?"

She breathed a sigh of relief and nodded. She didn't want to leave him, even though it was just for a little while, just until Saturday.

The river was perfect. It's where everything had changed. They didn't speak as they walked. She was content simply to be near him, to feel the strength of his presence at her side. A warm glow filled her. He would always be at her side. Husband and wife. She could barely contain her happiness.

When they arrived at their spot he spun her into his arms. "This is where I fell in love with you, Maggie Mc-Cary."

She still found it hard to believe. "How could you? I was such a nuisance."

"A beautiful nuisance. I didn't realize I was lonely until you came into my life. I didn't realize there was more than my work. But then you showed up and completely upended everything."

She had to be sure he held no regrets. "And that was a good thing?"

"More than you know." His dark brow furrowed. "I know that you are used to being on the move, being with your sister, moving to a different home every few months. I don't expect this will be an easy adjustment for you."

She raised his hand and held it against her chest, making her pledge. "I love it here. I love the people. I love the other brides. I love the wide-open prairie."

"And the river? Don't forget the river."

She smiled and for a moment watched the dandelion seeds float through the air and land on the shimmering surface of the water. "That too. It's the river that brought us together. But more than any of those things, I love you. Wherever you are, is my home." She stood on her tiptoes and pressed her lips gently to his, sealing her pledge.

He slid his hand behind her neck, nuzzling, and then kissing her beneath her ear. "Ah, Maggie. It's going to be hard to wait until Saturday."

"For me, as well," she murmured, as tingles raced down to her fingertips.

He sighed against her skin. "You are a lot of trouble, Maggie McCary."

She smiled, her heart overflowing with joy. "Indeed."

# *Epilogue*

*OAK GROVE GAZETTE*
*Special Edition*

The first wedding by the Oak Grove Betterment Committee commenced on Saturday, June 15th, 1878, at the Oak Grove Community Church.

The ceremony was officiated by the new preacher in town, Conner Flaherty, and began with the ringing of the new bell for the first time in the bell tower, compliments of one of the grooms, Jackson Miller.

Five brides, their young faces glowing, marched one at a time down the aisle toward their respective grooms, who stood at the front of the church looking peacock-proud in their Sunday best.

Sadie Greenberg looked sweet in a light blue dress trimmed with crocheted white flowers as she stood beside Rollie Austin and his two young boys. Anna Camp wore a pale yellow dress with ribbons in her hair and couldn't take her eyes off Wayne Stevens, the depot agent. Miss Rebecca Simpson wore white taffeta with layers of lace and carried a matching fan as she said her vows to banker Micah Swift.

It was the McCarys, Mary and Maggie, who captivated the entire assemblage, wearing identical white dresses with white eyelet trim and deep blue piping. To the concern of the mayor, they both arrived stylishly late, with the excuse that they had to gather wildflowers for all the brides.

Their respective grooms, Steve Putnam and Jackson Miller, did not seem upset at the twenty-minute delay in the ceremony, allowing that both women tended to be a bit headstrong in their pursuits.

After the ceremony a reception was held in the meadow. Mrs. Putnam and Mrs. Miller delighted their guests—particularly one Angus O'Leary—with a lusty rendition of "The Star of the County Down."

A good time was had by all.

\* \* \* \* \*

*If you enjoyed this story you won't want to miss these great full-length reads from Kathryn Albright*

HOMETOWN HEARTS ♥

**YES!** Please send me **The Hometown Hearts Collection** in Larger Print. This collection begins with 3 FREE books and 2 FREE gifts in the first shipment. Along with my 3 free books, I'll also get the next 4 books from the Hometown Hearts Collection, in LARGER PRINT, which I may either return and owe nothing, or keep for the low price of $4.99 U.S./ $5.89 CDN each plus $2.99 for shipping and handling per shipment*. If I decide to continue, about once a month for 8 months I will get 6 or 7 more books, but will only need to pay for 4. That means 2 or 3 books in every shipment will be FREE! If I decide to keep the entire collection, I'll have paid for only 32 books because 19 books are FREE! I understand that accepting the 3 free books and gifts places me under no obligation to buy anything. I can always return a shipment and cancel at any time. My free books and gifts are mine to keep no matter what I decide.

262 HCN 3432 462 HCN 3432

| Name | (PLEASE PRINT) | |
|---|---|---|
| Address | | Apt. # |
| City | State/Prov. | Zip/Postal Code |

Signature (if under 18, a parent or guardian must sign)

### Mail to the **Reader Service:**

**IN U.S.A.:** P.O. Box 1867, Buffalo, NY. 14240-1867
**IN CANADA:** P.O. Box 609, Fort Erie, Ontario L2A 5X3

\* Terms and prices subject to change without notice. Prices do not include applicable taxes. Sales tax applicable in NY. Canadian residents will be charged applicable taxes. This offer is limited to one order per household. All orders subject to approval. Credit or debit balances in a customer's account(s) may be offset by any other outstanding balance owed by or to the customer. Please allow 4 to 6 weeks for delivery. Offer available while quantities last. Offer not available to Quebec residents.

> **Your Privacy**—The Reader Service is committed to protecting your privacy. Our Privacy Policy is available online at www.ReaderService.com or upon request from the Reader Service.
>
> We make a portion of our mailing list available to reputable third parties that offer products we believe may interest you. If you prefer that we not exchange your name with third parties, or if you wish to clarify or modify your communication preferences, please visit us at www.ReaderService.com/consumerschoice or write to us at Reader Service Preference Service, P.O. Box 9062, Buffalo, NY. 14240-9062. Include your complete name and address.

HHBPA17